Chasing the Wind

Rose Cushing

Cushing Publishing
www.cushingpublishing.com

Dedicated with love to Rodney Cushing, my children, grandchildren, and family, thank you for your patience and guidance.

Chapter One

I will never forget receiving the call that no one ever wants to get. "Miss Kent, this is Scott Bradshaw, Anne Wynn's attorney. I'm sorry to have to tell you Annie passed away this afternoon. I am deeply sorry for your loss. Annie wanted me to let you know that she left something specifically for you in her will. When you come for the funeral, please make it a point to come to our office. I will send you, our address."

Just like that, Annie was gone. How could this be? I walked to the kitchen and got a glass of ice and a Diet Coke. I sat on the porch swing to absorb all of this call and began crying. How could Annie be gone? She was only thirty-two.

Annie was my best friend growing up. She was my cousin on my mother's side. Annie was tall and slender with jet-black hair and piercing blue eyes. Annie's mother Bethany and her father Will lived in a single-wide trailer across the street from the Marina. Will, a big, burly man with kind blue eyes and black hair, worked at the Cherry Point Naval Base in aircraft, and Bethany was a stay-at-home mom. I remember that they caught rainwater in a cistern because their water from the ground ran through an artesian spring laced with sulfur. While highly healthy, it smelled like rotten eggs. The taste was phenomenal, but the smell was obnoxious. Her family was full of fun, loved music.

Annie's family was full of fun, and they loved music. Will sang. They lived in Hobucken, North Carolina, on the Intercoastal Waterway. It was always stirring to go to Annie's house. The Atlantic Intercoastal Waterway at that point looked like a glorified creek, but the water was deep. Watching the boats that sailed by on a lazy summer day was always exciting. There were all kinds of craft, from those belonging to the U.S. military to fishing boats, shrimp trawlers, and yachts.

Yes, yachts! Great big ones filled with beautiful people going to exotic places and travels of a lifetime. Yes, it was a genuinely great place to dream.

And dream we did. I remember when Annie and I were about seven or eight, we would run to Tripp's Marina to get Cokes. The rich folks from the big yachts would be inside, and I guess they felt sorry for us poor little ragged children because they would buy us Cokes and candy to make us smile. It was a wonderful time in my life!

When the shrimp trawlers came in with their catch they would tie up at the dock. Once they offloaded their catch, workers at the pier would sort through it and separate big and small shrimp, letting the ones they deemed too little wash down the sluice and back out into the waterway. Annie and I, the enterprising young ladies that we were, ran to her house for her mom's colander. Back at the dock, we hid at the end of the sluice box. When the shrimp they were trashing came past we would catch them in the colander. It didn't take long to get us a big mess of shrimp for supper.

Down the road from the dock was a crab house that took all the crabs offloaded from the shrimp boats and put them in big steamers. Once steamed, they were put in containers and shipped to fancy restaurants all over the country! The workers at the crab house enjoyed our visits I think they were amused by our curiosity. When we had to go home they would give us a few crabs to take for dinner.

The marina was just past the Goose Creek Game Refuge and the Hobucken Coast Guard Station. On a rare day, boats were in the harbor, normally they would be out fishing. We would roam through the marshes through the marsh and the grass was almost as tall as we were. While we were in the marsh it felt like we were in another world. We would dream, and make plans for worldwide trips. Annie once asked me, "If you could do anything in the world when you grow up, what would you like to do?"

I told her I would love to sail around the world on one of those yachts and visit all the beautiful places and faraway lands.

Aunt Bethany and Uncle Will died when Annie, their only child, was in college. Annie's husband Raymond had passed away about a year before Annie and they had never had children, Now, Annie, too, was gone, and I was the only family she had left.

I hadn't seen her in several years. She had grown up, gone to college, and become a well-known investment banking consultant. Annie had married very well and was set for life financially. I always wondered if she was really happy. I hope she was.

I, too, had grown up and gone to college, and I had a career. Nothing in comparison to Annie's career, but I felt I had had a measure of success. I sat looking through old photos, reminiscing about that earlier time. There was a photo of Annie and me riding horses in the field. Annie wasn't a fan of horses so much, but I loved them, so she came along for the ride. Those were good memories; freedom running through the fields.

Sleep came late that night, and I dreamed of all the fun we had as children, the dreams and secrets we had shared.

Chapter Two

The following day I followed my usual routines—my morning meditation ritual that today included memories of Annie, gratitude journaling, and getting my thoughts into perspective. I received an email from Annie's attorney listing his address, and details of Annie's funeral, and stating that a ticket would be waiting for me at the airport. Annie had houses all over, but her services would be held in Boca Raton. So, I guess I was headed to Florida; a trip I never expected to make.

As a freelance writer and photographer working with a regional magazine, I had no trouble getting time off. The following day, I arrived at the airport and collected my ticket - First Class! I had never flown first class. Thanks, Annie.

A car was waiting for me at the Ft. Lauder-dale International Airport, ready to take me the twenty miles to Boca Raton. The driver, who said he would be available throughout my stay, took me to my hotel— The Breakers Hotel!

Right out of our childhood fantasies! When we were little, Aunt Ella Mae, whom I loved dearly, worked as a seasonal maid at the Breakers Hotel. She used to tell us about the movie stars who stayed there. She gave me a comb that had been given to her by Loretta Young, a movie star famous in the fifties. I remember how special that made me feel. Now, here I was at the Breakers as a guest. WOW! I could never have imagined this. Again, Thanks, Annie!

The Breakers Hotel was grand in every aspect. My suite had an ocean view a balcony, and every luxury you could imagine. The maid brought me a shot of whiskey and a piece of chocolate right before bed.

Despite all the luxury, my heart was heavy. I missed my cousin, and I wished I could have shared all this with her. I could not imagine why the attorney needed to meet with me, and I was pretty nervous. I arranged for the car to pick me up in the morning and prepared to go to bed.

I could hear the sound of the surf, so I stepped out onto the balcony. What a magnificent view. The moon was shining on the waves as they broke on the shore. My heart was heavy.

I sat on the balcony in the morning, meditated, and cleared my mind of my emptiness, allowing happy thoughts and memories to fill the void. I prayed for all my family and friends as I realized that life was too short. I made my journal entries and got dressed.

Today's motivation was "Trust Yourself," and I hoped it was a good idea. I ate breakfast in my room, and since I hadn't placed a breakfast request, room service sent up a cart with a sampling of about everything, including gourmet pancakes, crepes, fresh fruit, an omelet, and toast. They served coffee, orange juice, and water. I guess they hadn't guessed that I drink Diet Coke like ordinary people drink coffee. Oh well. All this service was a lot of spoiling, and I wasn't sure I would enjoy having it every day. I was too used to taking care of myself.

Promptly at nine, the driver arrived, and I went down to meet him and ride over to the attorney's office. The office was in a very posh modern complex on the ocean, a high-rise building beautiful and gleaming in the morning sun.

Of course, his office was on the top floor, yep, the 37th. I'm not too fond of heights and I hoped there wouldn't be an exterior glass elevator, but here we go. Upon arrival, a secretary with a British accent greeted me and escorted me to a conference room. She offered me coffee, water, or soda, which I declined, and she informed me that Mr. Bradshaw would be with me shortly. There was a fantastic view of the cityscape right down to the ocean from the conference room. You could see for miles. I had to admire the view from the center of the room, however, because the glass windows ran from floor to ceiling, and I couldn't bring myself to get any closer.

After what seemed like an hour, Mr. Bradshaw appeared. He was a distinguished-looking man in his late fifties. He explained that he had been Annie's attorney for about ten years and had helped her set up her corporations and her worldwide businesses, and to buy her numerous homes.

He began with small talk about me, and then I asked him. "Mr. Bradshaw, why am I here"? He told me to call him Scott and asked when I last saw my cousin. I told him it was about a year ago when her husband passed away. Scott looked sad when I said that. He and Annie's husband Raymond had been childhood friends. Raymond had been very successful with his businesses and investments, and that was how he'd met Annie. Scott told me that Raymond had left everything he had built to Annie. His estate was worth $400 million. I knew she was well off, but I had no idea how well off. Wow! But that wasn't all. Annie had been very successful in her own right, and her estate was worth $600 million! Since I was Annie's only living relative, Scott explained, I had inherited the entire estate.

I almost fainted.

Scott went on to tell me that this was the cash value of their businesses. Their estates also included real estate holdings all over the world valued at an additional $150 million. All in all, I inherited $1.15 billion!

I didn't know what to say. I had never imagined Annie had been so successful. I knew she traveled and lived a perfect life, but I had no idea!

Scott replied that he knew it was a lot to absorb, and that it would take some time to get everything sorted out and transferred to my name.

I think as a tactic to let me catch my breath and stop my mind from reeling, Scott said, "I trust your accommodations at the Breakers were sufficient last night."

"They were terrific! Please thank whoever had made the arrangements," I replied, still too stunned to be more coherent.

"Great," Scott responded. "You now have a house here in Boca that was Annie's and Raymond's. It has a beautiful ocean view, and I would like to have your things moved there. I hope you can remain here in Boca for a couple of weeks while we get the paperwork sorted out and transferred."

"Of course, that will be fine," was all I could say.

Scott had one more thing for me, a letter from Annie which he handed to me. "I advise you to read the letter tonight after you have had some time to rest and digest all of this," he said. "There is a full staff at the house, including an excellent chef. We can talk some more tomorrow. Here is my card and if you have any questions or need anything, please don't hesitate to call me."

The letter was in a sealed envelope with my name handwritten on the envelope outside. The stationery looked expensive and was a pretty shade of blue, like Annie's eyes. It smelled like her, clean and fresh with a slight floral touch. I slipped it into my purse and left Scott's office.

The driver was waiting for me. He was friendly and explained that Mr. Bradshaw had sent someone to transfer my stuff from the hotel to the house.

"Have you ever been to Boca Raton before?" he asked.

"No," I said and explained that I had never traveled much outside North Carolina.

"Would you like the grand tour before I drop you off?" he asked.

"Yes, it would be good to get my bearings," I told him. He laughed and said that I would not need to know directions in the future. I had "people" to do that for me.

I thought, "Oh my goodness, people to do that for me?" I wasn't sure I liked that idea.

Chapter Three

Boca Raton is situated on the Florida coast just north of Fort Lauderdale. The city has all the opulence that South Florida has to offer. Million-dollar homes are everywhere, and so are million-dollar yachts! After a brief tour that boggled my mind, my driver turned up a drive that led to Annie's, or now, my house. The house was extremely modern, all-white, and multi-story. The ocean was within walking distance, and there was a fabulous infinity pool. At the end of the drive, down by the water, was a dock large enough for a huge boat.

The driver stopped at the entrance to the house, got out, and opened my door. He smiled and said, "Welcome home, Ma'am!" I didn't know what to say.

I was exhausted and relieved to be settled somewhere for a few days. Suzi, the house manager, met me at the door.

"Hello," she said, "I am Suzi Boggs, and I am so sorry for your loss. Annie was an extraordinary woman and will truly be missed." Suzi, dressed in a very nice soft turquoise business suit, was about 5'1", with platinum blonde hair and brown eyes. She escorted me into the house and offered to introduce the staff.

"Not right now," I told her, "I am drained and overwhelmed. Can you show me to my room?"

The house was enormous, and the décor was all white like pictures in magazine ads. At the back side of the house were almost all windows facing the ocean to capture that million-dollar view. It seemed more like a museum than a home. I assumed that Annie didn't live here; it was just a rest stop when she was in town. "The house is 12,000 square feet with six bedrooms. I took the liberty of having the staff prepare the room next to Annie's for you," Suzi said.

The room was beautiful, luxurious, and opulent. Of course, the walls were white, the floors were white marble, and the windows were open and airy, facing the ocean. The bathroom was huge, and the focus was an enormous shower that could easily have held six people. There were four showerheads and strips of spa-like heads going down the walls. In the center of the room was a beautiful deep soaker tub with jacuzzi jets.

Everything was designer-inspired and I wondered if Annie had done the decorating or hired someone.

My suitcase was waiting in the room for me, and my clothes were hanging in the closet. There was a sitting room with a comfy chair and television and a balcony overlooking the ocean.

"Will you be at the estate for dinner?" Suzi asked.

Dinner? I hadn't even had lunch. "I plan to, yes," I told her. Suzi indicated the telephone on a nearby table and explained that if I needed anything, I should dial two for her or zero for the maid.

"I will leave you to get some rest, but I will send up some choices for lunch and dinner on the house system. It is a kind of text message system so we can all communicate easily." Suzi told me.

At last, I was alone. I slid out of my shoes and into a comfortable pair of pajamas. climbed into that great big bed and those luxurious sheets. I took a nap; the morning had been overwhelming. I wasn't sure how long I slept, but sleep was a gift I needed. When I opened my eyes, it hardly seemed possible that suddenly, I was in Boca Raton, Florida, in my luxurious million-dollar mansion on the ocean! I should be happy, but none of this would bring Annie back.

I had a million questions and was anxious to read Annie's letter but at the same time, I dreaded reading the final chapter of her life. I remembered my mantra for today: Trust yourself, so I knew I had to read it.

The light was blinking on the messaging system, so I assumed I had a message. I hit the touchscreen, and my announcement came up. Was I hungry? Well, yes, so I casually typed that on the keyboard. The quick response offered anything I wished, so I asked for a chef 's salad with ranch dressing or a club sandwich. The prompt reply read okay, give me about fifteen minutes. Would you like to eat down here, or have it sent up to your room?

I will come down, I replied.

I combed my hair, straightened my clothes, and stepped out onto the ocean balcony. Yes, this was beautiful and peaceful. However, it still felt empty and lonely.

I unpacked my clothes and headed downstairs. Suzi was waiting for me in the dining room with the house chef. His presentation of the salad and sandwich I had requested was as elegant as you would expect, and they tasted wonderful.

"This is delicious and beautiful, thank you, Sir," I said.

The Chef shook my hand and, said "not yet, hopefully, just call me

Chip."

Chip, in his mid-thirties, was very hand-some with platinum blonde hair, and eyes deep pools of blue. He was tall, slender, and very tan.

The chef excused himself and Suzi sat down with me to talk about the house and the staff.

"How often did Annie and her husband stay here?" I asked.

"About once a year when they came to see Mr. Bradshaw," she said.

"Did they keep the house, the staff, and all of this up year-round?" I asked, waving a hand to encompass the house in general.

"Yes," Suzi replied, "Boca is all about appearances. Would you like to meet the staff now?"

"Sure," I said. "Just let me finish this great food."

After I ate, Suzi called each staff person individually. Arturo, the gardener, had a kind demeanor and face. Connie, the maid, was a lovely "mom" type. Chip the Chef and Suzi herself filled out the roster.

I greeted each one, and they all told me how sorry they were for my loss, adding if I needed anything during my stay, to please let me know.

"Suzi, is there a car that I can drive out to town?" I asked.

"No," Suzi replied, "they didn't keep a personal car. They always used the driver, Jim."

After my talk with Suzi, I went for a walk down the beach. I took Annie's letter with me to read by the ocean—just Annie and me. Was I ready? I wasn't sure, but it had to be done, so there was no need to keep putting it off.

My Dearest Stacy,

If you are reading this, then my time has run out. Please do not be sad for me; I had a good run and a great life. I did not tell you about my sickness because I did not want to worry you. I was diagnosed with cancer last year; unfortunately, it was an aggressive type. After Raymond's death, life seemed pointless, and, in many ways, I looked forward to the end. The good thing is that it gave me time to remember little things in my life. I remember how we were children roaming free all over the marshes and marinas in Hobucken. I remember the shared secrets, dreams, and desires. They were good times!

When we were kids, you told me when you grew up you wanted to own one of those big fancy sailboats, not a yacht, but a sailboat. I remember you talking for hours about living like Robinson Crusoe on an island, and you could write all about your adventure and sell the book!

You have worked hard to become a writer and filmmaker and you are good at it. You deserve this opportunity, and I know you will take it higher than we ever imagined when we were kids.

I have been very blessed with finances, and I am leaving my entire fortune to you on one condition. Scott has the title of a boat that I bought for you. It is a 1934 Custom Staysail Schooner. It was initially built for a famous screenwriter/director and was primarily used to entertain Hollywood's elite during the '30s and '40s. An actor from a famous movie skippered this schooner in the 1936 Transpac race to Hawaii. She was pressed into service during the Second World War, reportedly becoming part of the Hooligan Fleet, patrolling the West Coast for submarines. After the war, the boat was returned to Sturges, who sold her to a billionaire. He secretly married an actress on board and their marriage certificate was still aboard years later. In 1961, another very famous actor chartered her, sailing from San Carlos, Mexico, to Hawaii and San Juan Island. Her next owners commissioned Port Townsend Shipwrights Co-op to do a complete ($1.2 million) restoration!

I bought it just for you. Her name is Wind Dancer, and she is perfect, just like the one we saw once at the Marina. It is so you! Now, I know you, and you can find one million reasons not to do this. I am asking that you find one to do it for me. I want you to sail worldwide and write stories about your travels, just like you dreamed! I also want you to document your adventures and trips on film. You will find state-of-the-art equipment, names, and phone numbers for a crew standing by to meet you anywhere in the world at a moment's notice to help you film. You were always the smart one.

I lived my life to work, thinking I would have plenty of time to live it. Fate didn't allow that, so please do this for me, live, really live, and enjoy everything this life can offer you. I have accumulated a small fortune, leaving every dollar to you to do with as you please. Have fun, have adventures, and be charitable. If you are going to work, then have fun while working. Take chances and see what type of mark you can leave in this old world. Fall in love, have fat babies, and enjoy your life. I pray it is a long and happy one. Trust Scott: He will never betray you. When I think about my life, my dear Stacy, you were one of the best parts. I loved you then, and I always will. Remember our dreams and fly baby, fly!

Annie

Reading this, hearing her voice in my head I understood why she asked this of me. But how could I toss away the life I had built and pick up where her life left off? I mean, no question, her life was grander, but was it me? I had spent significant energy and time learning to live, live in the moment, and seek happiness. Yes, a fortune would buy some happiness, but maybe not the kind I was seeking. Again, today's affirmation of Trust in Yourself came into my mind.

Chapter Four

I had worked extremely hard learning how to be a reporter, a writer, a photographer, and a documentary filmmaker. Annie had not known I had won a small award for one of my films. I had success in the publishing world with over a hundred articles and hundreds of photos published.

I had a small house just outside New Bern, near where I grew up. I drove to Raleigh weekly to get assignments, attend meetings, and shop.

I had dreamed about owning a magazine and media company one day, but that dream would never materialize without big cash to back me. Could this be the break that I needed? Annie could have done many different and good things with her wealth but the fact that she gave it to me to fulfill my dreams was deeply touching.

I took a long walk on the beach, picked up seashells, and thought about Annie and her life. She had worked so hard. We were taught to work hard to make our dreams come true and we both had big dreams and goals. Annie had a gift for making money. She was the best at it that I had ever seen.

Annie just knew what a good investment was and what wasn't, almost like magic. She also had a great personality, so people trusted her right off the bat, and she never had a shortage of clients. Her husband Raymond was hit and killed by a drunk driver on his way to a business meeting. It was so sad. Thirty-two is too young to go, but Raymond is gone. Annie was barely thirty when she was diagnosed with cancer and died before her thirty-second birthday. Life is short and sometimes cruel. I will turn thirty-one in October. I can't help but wonder now how much time I have left. Maybe this came at a good time for me. Perhaps I'll give it a try and see, but maybe not.

Today's meditation and prayer would be about seeking the right path. The ocean in the background with its waves lapping the shore, the sounds of seagulls squawking, people jogging by, and the distant sounds of boats in the harbor were relaxing. I tried to rid myself of all worries and negative thoughts and focus on the here and now. Oddly enough, today's affirmation was "Live your dream," okay, and I get it.

When I returned to the house, I found Scott had left a message for me to call him. Suzi showed me the office where I could talk privately. Scott wanted to meet for dinner to go over some more information.

"I will tell your driver where we will be dining. Do you like seafood?" Scott said.

I laughed out loud, "What do you think?"

We agreed to meet at 7 p.m. Then it hit me, I didn't bring anything suitable for a fancy dinner. I had only three days' worth of clothes, and two outfits were ultra-casual beachwear. The other one was what I brought for the funeral. I messaged Suzi.

When she came to the office I explained my dilemma, and she, of course, knew just where to send me. She called for Jim and gave him directions to the shop.

Now we are talking Boca here, the streets are lined with stores, boutiques, clubs, and restaurants. Palm trees line the streets and everyone you see is glamorous. There aren't any stores like this back home. In the first boutique, a dress caught my eye, and it fit me very nicely, but the price tag read $599. I did not pay that much for my refrigerator! This lifestyle was going to take some adjustment. So, I kept looking. At the next stop, I found a dressy pants suit in a soft blue, and it was on sale for $350, so I purchased it and a delicate floral tank top to match.

I asked Jim to take me on a second tour of the area since I had most of the day to kill. He drove me down to Miami, which is a vast city. The drive was beautiful, with homes and estates you would expect to see in a tropical setting, palm trees, flowers, and loads of people! We went through Wellington, which is the horse mecca for the area. The farms and barns stretched for miles. "This is a wonderful area and I thank you for hauling me around and for your incredible patience with me," I said.

Jim replied, "You are no trouble, Ma'am. I am here to take you anywhere you want to go."

When we returned to the house in Boca, I looked at my watch and remarked, "Oh no! It's already 5:30! Jim, what time do we need to leave to meet Scott at 7:00?"

"We need to leave by 6:45; the restaurant is here in town, Ma'am," he said.

One hour was plenty of time to get ready. The sun was setting low over the ocean behind the house, and I could not help but step out on the deck to pay homage to God's beautiful work. Funny, no matter rich or poor, you still need to admire the beauty surrounding you.

Jim arrived promptly at 6:45. I was both curious and nervous about what this meeting with Scott would entail. Annie's holdings were broad, and I was sure there were a million legal intricacies with which to deal. I was delighted that she told me to trust Scott. That was a huge comfort.

The restaurant, Buena Comida, was a typical white tablecloth establishment. The ratings were superior, and I looked forward to their menu. Having grown up in coastal North Carolina. I had a deep-rooted love for seafood, so I could not wait to taste the local fare.

Scott met me at the door and escorted me inside to "his" table. After we ordered wine, Scott explained that the owners were long-time clients and friends. He also explained that Buena Comida means good food in Spanish.

To begin our dining experience, the manager sent us out a complimentary seafood tower of oysters, clams, shrimp, lobster, and clams. conch, Oysters Rockefeller, and crab-stuffed mushrooms. All my favorites. As we ate and chatted, I learned that Scott was married with kids in college. Instead of opening additional offices in nearby towns, he spent all his time in Boca Raton. Then we were served the best clam chowder ever!

"My office has been working on filing the paperwork for Annie's properties and accounts to be transferred to you. Scott said. "Over the next few days, you and I will go over all the properties and business information, and meet the people who keep it all running," he added.

The main course was boiled Maine lobsters with a delicious butter sauce. Mine was served with hand-cut fries and lobster mac and cheese. It was more food than I could ever eat, but I gave it my best shot. I began thinking about how long it had been since I had had fresh-off-the-boat seafood. Too long. My mind wandered back to Annie as a little girl running through the marsh grass carefree and full of dreams. How sad to have accomplished so much only to have her life cut short by cancer.

Scott was very considerate of how overwhelming all of this was right then and would continue to be for me. I decided to ask him about the boat; after all, today's focus was "Live your dream."

"The boat," he laughed and said, "Well, yes, I know all about the boat." He told me that Annie wanted to do something special for me, something I would never do on my own, so she searched high and low to find the right one. "She thought since you made documentary films, you would appreciate a boat designed for a filmmaker," Scott said. "1934 was an era filled with drama, glamour, and change. Think about it, Bonnie and Clyde were on the ten most wanted list, John Dillinger escaped prison, Capra's movie It Happened One Night with Clark Gable and Claudette Colbert hit the big screen. Franklin Roosevelt was president, and songs like I Get a Kick Out of You, I'm Gonna Sit Right Down and Write Myself a Letter and Blue Moon were floating on the airwaves. Yes, what a time in history it was!"

Scott explained the glamour of that era. "The boat is outstanding, and it was in perfect shape considering it was built in 1934. The history of the boat did not stop with the year it was built, and you will learn more about that when we give her a tour.

"Well, I probably wouldn't have ever bought a sailboat, that's for sure," I laughingly told him. "Does the boat have a crew?" I asked.

Scott laughed and said, "Yes, Annie thought of everything. She hired a crew to be on standby for your every whim."

That is Annie—so perfectly planned, I thought.

"Have you ever been on a sailboat?" Scott asked.

"When I was a little girl, my father had a sailboat. He used to take me out a couple of times a week," I replied. "We lived near Oriental, the sailing capital of North Carolina, so you almost had to have a sailboat."

I could remember the feel of the salt spray on my face, the sounds of the gulls as we were leaving the harbor, and the way the water changed from blue to emerald green when we got out a little deeper. Yes, I had been on a sailboat. It had been a bucket list item for a long time to own one.

When it came time for dessert, there was no way I could hold any more food, but Scott took the liberty of having them pack me a slice of seven-layer chocolate cake for the road. While sipping our after-dinner coffee, we finally got down to business. Scott began, "As I told you, the estate's total worth is about $1.5 billion. If you would like me to continue to handle your account as I have for Annie for several years, I will be glad to do so."

I quickly said, "Yes!" Then I asked Scott, "Where did Annie have other properties? I am curious."

"Well, let me see, you have a lodge in Jackson Hole, Wyoming; an apartment in Los Angeles, and one in London. There is a house in the Hamptons and the Boca property," Scott replied.

"Oh my! Well, it will be interesting to visit all those places," I said. As we sat in this beautiful restaurant sipping coffee Scott explained the ins and outs of Annie's estate. On Tuesday, we will fly to New York City to meet with the general manager of Annie's investment banking business, Ann Wynn Investments. While there, we would meet with Raymond's business manager and visit Wynn Management Group, a hedge fund corporation.

It was by now about ten-thirty, and Jim was waiting out front to take me home. It felt funny to be driven everywhere. I love to drive and I love my independence, so I expected this indulgence to be short-lived. On the ride back to the house, I was deep in memories and thoughts. There was so much to think about, and it was overwhelming. I didn't know anything about investments or hedge funds. How would I ever be able to handle it all? Maybe I wouldn't have to, and perhaps I would be just a figurehead.

Back at the house, I put my cake in the refrigerator. I was much too full to eat anything else. I went upstairs and out onto the balcony. The ocean was calm, and the moon shone beautifully on the water as the tide rolled back out to sea—such a beautiful place. I crawled into bed and fell instantly asleep.

I began to dream about the Wind Dancer, sailing around the world, and filming. That was such a big dream of mine. I could hardly believe that it was going to happen. It is one of those big dreams, and you don't dare speak it because you are scared that if you do, it will go away.

The sun was rising, and I could hear the seagulls and pelicans busy by the dock.

Living on the ocean was so different than living in the country. I was used to waking up to robins and blue jays' songs, the rooster crowing, and the horses telling me they were ready to eat. Could I be getting a little homesick? I did miss the soft whinnies from the barn when they heard me coming. The warm nuzzles in my hair while feeding, yes, I missed them.

Well, time for my morning ritual. My journal was filled with gratitude this morning. I was grateful that Annie had loved me enough to make me the sole benefactor of her estate, had thought about it enough to secure my future, but had left space for me to fulfill my dreams and provided proper guidance for me. The mentorship I would need to survive was given through Scott. I prayed about all these things and asked for advice along the way. My cup runneth over. Today's affirmation would be all about positivity.

Chip sent me a text about breakfast, and Suzi had sent a message that she was here and on the job. The maid, Connie, seemed to do a good job, but I had yet to see her. I slowly crawled out of bed and tried to begin waking up. The weather was already hot. I guess it was perpetual summer this far south.

The ocean was rolling in, and I could see dolphins in the distance playing in the waves. Eventually, I slipped on jeans and a T-shirt and headed downstairs for breakfast.

Suzi was in her tiny office paying the monthly bills and preparing the payroll.

When I walked into the kitchen, Chip was working on his grocery order and greeted me with, "Good morning."

"Good morning," I returned.

"Coffee?" he asked, holding out a cup.

"Thanks, but I'm not a coffee drinker, sorry."

"What's your poison then?" he asked. I began to explain my addiction to diet drinks. His face wrinkled, reminding me how bad they were for me.

"My one vice," I replied.

He laughed and opened the refrigerator he had stocked with diet and regular soda.

"That is awesome!" I exclaimed, grabbing a Diet Coke and some ice.

"So, what is your pleasure for breakfast this morning?"

"I think I'll just have some toast and bacon if that's not too much trouble."

"So, how long will you stay with us here in Boca?" Chip asked as he busied himself at the stove.

"Well, I'm not sure how long it will take to get all the legal stuff taken care of," I answered.

Suzi came in, saving me from more questions. "Good morning, Stacy," she said.

Chip had my breakfast ready, so I picked up the plate and my Diet Coke and headed to the dining room, where Suzi joined me.

"I was wondering if you plan to make any changes to the house or staff," she said.

"Gosh, I hadn't even had time to think about anything like that," I answered.

"How long will you be staying with us?" Suzi asked.

"You are the second person to ask me that today. I think I'll take a walk on the beach," I said, getting up.

Walking on the beach was an excellent opportunity to think. It was a beautiful morning; the seagulls were talking to each other, looking for food, and busy with their daily chores. I realized that I had to start making some actual plans for my life.

The staff seemed happy to ride the payroll and hoped that the owner (me) would seldom be around. What do they do when no one is around, I wondered? They didn't seem very necessary. Indeed, you didn't need a fulltime house manager, chef, driver, or maid if you would be at the house only a few weeks a year! I could see the need for a gardener to keep up the grounds, but the rest seemed like a waste to me.

It was something to talk about with Scott. I also needed to confirm when we were going to New York and why. I hoped the house in the Hamptons would not have a staff. Visiting my newly acquired property would be better without someone looking over my shoulder every minute. After the New York trip, I thought I would take a few days to go home and connect with reality.

When I returned to the house, I called Scott to find out when we were going to New York. "We will leave the day after tomorrow," he said.

The funeral was tomorrow, just a private event at the graveside in Boca, as Annie had wanted. I dreaded it, but I knew it had to be done for closure for everyone who knew her.

The following day, I prepared myself for the funeral. Jim picked me up promptly at ten a.m. The funeral was a sad occasion but made easier when Scott read a beautiful letter from Annie. In speaking to us through Scott, Annie reassured us that she was in a better place. Her cancer had been painful, her heart was broken by Robert's death, and she was ready to go. She urged us not to cry or be sad but to remember her often, send her love, and move on with our lives to make her proud.

Afterward, I returned to the Boca house and went for another walk.

Once again, the beach was my solace. I took a very long walk thinking about Annie's last words and her bravery at the end. She was a tremendous force here on earth, and she had left me the means to develop myself into a force that would make her proud. And I intended to do just that!

I was beginning to be hungry, so I hiked back up to the house and called Jim. He was there in five minutes. "I need to get some air and some lunch," I told him.

"I know just the place," he replied, and we were at the docks in minutes. Jim had taken the liberty of chartering a small sailboat to give me a trip around the bay and a picnic lunch. "I hope you don't mind, but I booked you something special that always makes me feel better."

There was a 32-foot sailing boat and a smiling captain waiting to greet me.

"Good afternoon, Ma'am, welcome aboard," he said, and I climbed aboard with a big smile.

Jim said, "I'll be back to pick you up when the charter is done, have fun!"

The water was beautiful, there was just a light breeze and a few waves as the captain skillfully piloted the boat out of the bay into the ocean. I relished the freedom as we cut through the water, the wind in my hair, the sun, and the smell of salt air. I knew why Annie wanted me to have the boat, to sail away, and to have an adventure, and I couldn't wait! The skipper pointed out dolphins and sea turtles swimming alongside us. It was a great way to honor Annie's wishes.

Chapter Five

I realized I hadn't spoken to Paula Perkins, my editor in Raleigh, to let her know about my extended stay in Florida, so I called her. "Good morning, Sunshine," I said.

"Good morning, long time no hear," was her quick response.

I told her that I was the executrix of my cousin's estate and that I would be detained a bit longer than planned but that I didn't have much choice.

"Have you thought about the next issue and what type of stories we should look for?" I asked.

The magazine was called Zest, a lifestyle publication for North Carolina. The next issue would be in November because you always work a couple of months ahead in a magazine. Paula told me she needed something about Thanksgiving traditions in North Carolina. "You know, something that hasn't been written about much," Paula said. She was a tremendous force in the media industry and moved to Raleigh in 2007 following a successful publishing career in New York City. She recognized a need for a publication that spoke to the soul of the South. Her goal was to craft a magazine that would appeal to men and women interested in outdoor sports, adventurous travel, and good food and drink. For over a decade, Zest has consistently been recognized as an industry leader. Award highlights included a second Hottest Launch of 2007 among more than seven hundred magazines; 2012 and 2016 included National Magazine Awards in General Excellence and many more. I felt honored to work with her.

One of my newest goals had been to own a magazine and build a publication as successful as Zest. In the meantime, being a featured writer and photographer in this widely-known publication was great.

"November traditions in North Carolina, okay, I'll research it and see what I can find. It is a great idea," I said. Good thing November is a few months away I will have time to really dig in and find something, she thought.

We caught up with some small talk; I told her I would have a couple of rough ideas for her in a few days.

Even though I was about to be mega-rich, I couldn't see myself giving up something I enjoyed doing. I decided to spend the afternoon researching. First question: Where do you find the most incredible ideas for November rituals or traditions specific to North Carolina? You ask an older relative or friend. I called Jessica Smith, my friend and early mentor. Jessica, an acclaimed author, and publisher was born in Eastern North Carolina at a time rich in tradition and history. I was sure she could put me on to a couple of really cool "secrets" about which to write.

I gave Jessica a call and greeted her with, "How are you doing this beautiful morning?"

With a half-laugh, Jessica replied, "Uh. Oh, this sounds like trouble this morning. How are you?"

"Now, Jessica, you know I never cause trouble," I countered.

"Where are you? The last time we talked, you were headed to a funeral."

"Well, it's a very long and crazy story and I'll fill you in when I get back home. In the meantime, Paula gave me an assignment that I need your help with."

"Okay, lay it on me, and let's see what I can offer," Jessica said.

I told her about Paula's idea and with so much already written about Thanksgiving traditions, I needed ideas about something a little unusual. I needed to avoid everyday traditions associated with November and giving Thanks but not explicitly thought of in that manner. Of course, Jessica never disappoints me. She said, "Oyster roast and oysters for breakfast!"

"Oysters?" I asked.

Jessica told me about growing up near the coast, and oysters were always "a special occasion" dish. I knew it was an excellent idea for the story. I could write about all the different parts of North Carolina and how they celebrate oysters.

"As always, my friend, I knew I could count on you," I told her as we hung up.

Oysters. Yes! A perfect idea! Oysters are only harvested in months that have an R in them, so they are coveted when they are available. The Carolina oyster roast is a time-honored tradition celebrated with family members for generations. Each family has twists on the recipes for dipping sauces for the oyster once it is roasted. Some like melted butter, ketchup, and vinegar, while others prefer a prepared sauce or just plain oysters.

Oyster roasts are a tradition that brings family and friends together and stirs many cherished memories like Dad enjoying a cold six-pack of Schlitz beer.

Old stories of Uncle Alfred's house on the Pamlico Sound, with fishing trips and dozens of oysters, broiled on the half shell at Christmas. Some people would think of late November parties in Raleigh after NC State beat rival teams. I remember backyard fires to cut the chill, drifting autumn leaves, and a long ride in the woods with my horse. Night falling and the smell of the fire, the saltiness of the oysters, and, of course, good Bourbon.

I sat down and banged out the story in a couple of hours. Yes, positivity was the critical thought for the day. I loved to write, especially when it was something that I was excited about. The story came in at the appropriate word count, so I sent it to Paula and hoped for a positive reaction. I didn't have any oyster roast photos, but we could always stage some when I returned to North Carolina.

Now to go shopping. I seriously hated not having my car. I was reasonably sure this particular issue wouldn't happen again. I am independent and prefer to be self-sufficient. So, a vehicle for each property, except Manhattan, would be necessary! But for now, I called Jim.

He was at the front gate in less than 15 minutes, glad I was dressed and ready to go. "Hello, Ma'am, where would you like to go?" he asked.

"Well, I need something for the fall as I will travel to New York tomorrow. I didn't bring anything suitable for the trip, so how about that boutique where I bought the pants suit," I said.

The streets were busy with traffic, it was late afternoon, and people were going about their daily routines. I liked the hustle and bustle of a city as long as I could retreat to myself in the less populated areas.

The boutique's fall fashions had arrived. I bought a couple of pairs of pants, lightweight sweaters, a jacket, and a pair of shoes that would work. Then I saw the most beautiful handbag. I have always had a weakness for shoes and pocketbooks. Dare I price it? It was one of a kind with a $5,000 price tag. That was more than I could pay, but it was a knockout.

Back at the estate, I checked to see if Paula had read my story. I put my clothes in my room and then sat down with my laptop. Yes, there was an email. Paula loved the story and suggested just a few tweaks, and it would be a go.

It was a beautiful evening. I decided to take a long walk on the beach. I would fly to New York in the morning, and who knows where after that. I was getting excited to see the other properties and, of course, the boat.

The beach stretched out for a few miles with just a few estates on this strip, making for a lovely and very private beachfront. The water was a beautiful turquoise blue at this time of day, and the sunset was insane.

I had always heard of how beautiful sunsets were in this world but had never had the opportunity to see them. In all honesty, it is worth the drive to sit on the beach and wait for this beautiful light show of God's creation. The morning-to-nightfall cycle here is impressive. You can feel close to Mother Nature and the earth's rhythm without the typical beach distractions. I have never been much of a beach girl, but this is something that anyone could appreciate. I could see why Annie chose this place. She was raised beside the Inland Waterway; saltwater was in her veins. I can see her jogging on this secluded beach, swimming, and even having a bonfire and a clambake.

At that moment, the total weight of Annie's death hit me. She was gone. Death is final, and you don't realize the full impact until you lose someone. Suddenly, the world that they'd lived in is still turning, but they are just gone. The emptiness and sadness consumed me. I crumpled on the sand into a pile of tears. I was so glad it was secluded; no one could see or hear me in my sorrow. I sincerely regretted not spending more time with her, knowing her as an adult and a friend. I made a promise to myself that despite money, situations, or life, I would never let myself drift so far away from family and friends again. Every moment is precious and cannot be gotten back.

After a long cry, a long walk, and deep soul-searching, I returned to the estate, exhausted. The crisp cool sheets felt good against my skin as I drifted off to sleep.

Chapter Six

At five a.m., the alarm was ringing. I rolled over, wanting to go back to sleep. Then it hit me. I was flying to New York in two hours. I jumped out of bed. I had to pack, shower, wash my hair, grab breakfast, and be at the airport in an hour. Well, nothing like flying by the seat of your pants and never being prepared. The time ticked by quickly, but somehow, I made it with a breakfast sandwich and Diet Coke in my hand while getting into the car. I postponed my usual morning ritual until tonight because there just wasn't time this morning. After all, positivity would take you a long way in this world, and today that seemed like the correct phrase to keep in mind. I made the airport check-in just in time—to sit and wait. Of course, with the airlines, nothing is ever on time. But this morning, that was okay with me.

Scott arrived moments later. He was a brilliant and kind man. Annie trusted him completely, so I felt that I could. too. He greeted me with a quick hug and "Hello."

The gate agent announced that it was time to board. I had one suitcase, a carry-on, and my laptop, so nothing had to be checked. Scott had one bag. After boarding we settled into the first-class section. The flight attendant stowed my carry-on and laptop for me. She showed us our seats and immediately offered us a beverage. Now, this certainly was an upgrade from my previous flying experiences.

The seats reclined, were big and roomy, with only one seat beside it. There was plenty of room to set up my laptop should I wish to. The flight would be about three hours long, precisely right for a movie and a nap. As we buckled in for take-off.

Scott said, "I hope you don't mind if we talk a little business during the flight. There are some things I would like to go over with you before we arrive."

"Of course," I replied, thinking, well, there goes the movie—and the nap.

Scott explained a little about the business that we were going to see and gave me some background on the management team, the overall mission of the company, and their profit and loss statements for the current year. The business seemed to be running smoothly, professionally managed, and in profit mode. "This was Annie's gift. She had a brilliant mind for finance," he said.

"I agree one hundred percent," I told him.

We talked a little about the Hamptons house and he gave me the key.

"This property does not have a full-time staff. Annie never felt it was needed," he explained.

"Good," I replied, relieved.

"Was there a problem in Boca?" Scott asked.

"No, not a problem. The staff was curious as to what my plans were for them moving forward. I told them that I didn't have any plans yet. But I don't see any sense in having a full-time staff since I won't be living there full time.

"However, I don't want to make any changes to the things that are working until I have time to assess how life will change and move forward for me," I said.

"I agree with you about the staff. They are a holdover from Raymond's family who felt one needed staff as a status symbol," he explained.

"Raymond's family?" I asked.

Scott explained that Raymond Wynn was the son of the Nevada silver mining magnate Jack Wynn. Jack Wynn became a turquoise mine owner at an early age and had a stake in several additional gem mines. The family was worth about $3 billion. They were old-school money earned the hard way, not given to them on a silver platter. When they achieved status, they wanted everyone to know it. So, they built enormous homes, drove exotic cars, and lived a big life. Raymond was a rebel, never wanting to be the spoiled little rich boy. He worked hard, got a good education, and amassed his fortune in his own right. He never took anything from his family. I could see why Annie fell in love with him.

"After Raymond and Annie were engaged, Annie always impressed him with her drive and work ethic. They were a perfect match. How tragic that both their lives ended at such a young age," Scott said. Scott told me that Annie talked about me a lot and he felt he already knew me through her.

"I hope I live up to all that. I am a very different person in many ways than Annie," I said.

"But you too are smart, and you certainly handle pressure well," Scott said.

The flight attendant came by to offer us a beverage and a snack and the relief from the conversation was welcome. I was in Diet Coke withdrawal.

Scott explained that the documents for the transfer of funds were complete and when we returned to Boca, I could sign everything and take ownership. I let out a deep sigh, and he smiled.

"That makes all of this very real," I said.

Scott gave me an American Express card and explained that he thought I might need it since I hadn't planned on quite so long a stay. "It doesn't have a limit, so use it however you wish. It is your money now," he said.

Now, isn't it every person's dream to be in Manhattan with an unlimited credit card? Somehow, I felt very guilty accepting it and wasn't sure I could spend any of it. My budget certainly wouldn't support living in this world.

Chapter Seven

As the plane was preparing to land Scott told me we had a limousine waiting at the curb. We retrieved our things and at the exit found a driver holding a sign saying, Scott Bradshaw. He realized we were his fare and promptly made his way to us and took my bags. He placed our things in his trunk and opened the door for us.

I had never ridden in a limo. This trip sure had a lot of firsts for this simple country girl! At Scott's hotel in downtown Manhattan, the driver got out and opened our doors. Scott explained that a chopper was waiting on the hotel roof to take me to the Hampton property.

Holy smokes! I thought: a helicopter that was just for me! Oh my gosh, this is crazy! Scott had arranged for a rental car for me at the heliport, with a map and tips about local places to shop, eat, and see.

The limo driver took my luggage to the lobby elevator, and I was off to the top of the 68-story hotel.

The view of the city from the roof was incredible, and there it was, my helicopter.

The pilot climbed out to retrieve my luggage and we exchanged "Good mornings."

"Have you ever been to the Hamptons?" he asked.

"The first trip," I responded as I climbed into the passenger seat.

"Great! I'll give you the $5 tour."

I buckled my seat belt, took a deep breath, and replied, "That would be awesome. I have heard so much about it."

We took off and I could see for miles.

There was the Statue of Liberty!

The chopper took a left, and we headed up the coastline with the pilot pointing out different areas. On our right was the blue of the Atlantic Ocean and there was Fire Island and Long Island.

You could see across the island to the other side, which bordered the Long Island Sound. The beach stretched out for miles from Long Island to the Hamptons. In the distance, I could see the tip of the island, Montauk Point, with its lighthouse. Mansions dotted the shoreline; this area was money.

The heliport in the Hamptons is near Sag Harbor. After we landed the pilot got my luggage out of the back and escorted me to the waiting area where a lady showed me to my rental car. The map and info were on the seat, just as Scott had promised. I was on my own for the rest of the day. Now to find the house, unpack, and absorb what had happened. Honestly, this was a pretty great place to chill.

I had seen the Hamptons on a Million Dollar Mansions episode, buying and renovation shows: the markets, famous people, the food, the horse barns, a lifestyle that was all its own. I realized it was about lunchtime, so before I started, I asked the receptionist to suggest a good spot to eat. She directed me to Highway 41, then Lilly Pond Lane which was about ten minutes away. She assured me there would be many places to eat all along the way then smiled and said, "This is the Hamptons; there are no bad restaurants."

It felt amazing to be driving myself again. I was so relieved there would be no staff at this house. I could explore it at my own pace and stock my refrigerator. Oh, stock the fridge. Scott had probably already stocked it, but just in case, I guessed I better stop at a grocery store and pick up a few things. The Red Horse Market looked like a place I would want to visit; homey and quaint, but clean and inviting.

Every table and shelf in the market held some type of delight: homemade chicken salad, crab salad, lobster cakes, fresh-cut meat in the butcher shop, and every kind of bread, cake, cookie, or pie I could imagine. They even had fresh local eggs and milk; it was heaven. It felt good to mingle with ordinary people, some dressed in riding clothes, some in casual wear. I made my choices and checked out. New York prices are significantly higher than those in North Carolina and even higher than in Boca. I took a minute to recover from the sticker shock and was glad for the American Express card Scott had given me.

As I drove down Highway 41, it turned into Ocean Highway. There were beautiful homes on both sides of the road with glimpses of the ocean now and then. When I got to Lilly Pond Lane, my heart was pounding. This area was so beautiful. How could I possibly have inherited such a fantastic place? I was honored to visit; I could hardly imagine living here. I knew Martha Stewart had a house on Lilly Pond Lane. I thought, wouldn't it be something if she were my neighbor? I was lost, daydreaming about cooking and gardening with Martha as I drove along.

Chapter Eight

Suddenly 711 Lilly Pond Lane was in sight; 711 was incredible. Only Annie would pick lucky numbers. Of course, there was a gated entrance. Scott gave me the code, 072056. My heart stopped. That was Annie's birthday, July 20, 1956. My eyes filled with tears as I drove up the drive.

There it stood; a massive, elegant 1920s-style beach house complete with cedar shake shingles. The lot was huge and beautifully landscaped. I stopped in front of the house and got my purse and paperwork. I couldn't wait to go in and explore.

To my surprise, inside the house was ultra-modern, wholly remodeled in warm wood and glass. The walls were white and there were some subtle punches of color with a throw or pillow, but it was minimalist and modern. The views were outstanding, and the house boasted tons of windows! A baby grand piano was in the den, and I wondered if Annie or Robert played when they were here.

The kitchen was built for a chef with every dreamy item imaginable right there, just waiting for the master's touch. The dining room showcased the view of the ocean. The house was enormous, with nine bedrooms and eleven bathrooms.

Holy cow, who cleans all of this? Maybe this house does need staff.

The master bedroom was enormous with another breathtaking view of the ocean. Glass doors opened to a terrace to embrace the salty smell in the air and the sounds of the ocean and seagulls fishing. I could imagine all the boats and ships passing in the distance and wondered if you could see them from here. I could imagine Annie standing here, soaking in these beautiful surroundings. It reminded me so much of where we grew up; this was on a much grander scale, but the salt air, the sound of the gulls, and an occasional boat passing? Yes, this would have felt like home to Annie.

The master bath was more significant than my entire house in New Bern and was done in shades of tan and gray with stone and marble. The shower could easily hold several people and had about a dozen jets with rain shower heads. It even had a heated towel rack. Off to one side was a giant Jacuzzi, big enough for at least two full-grown adults.

The master closet stopped me in my tracks. It was multiple rooms with built-in drawers, hanging space, a jewelry box with slide-out drawers, full-length mirrors, racks for handbags, and shoe storage that rotated at the touch of a button.

"Oh my gosh, this is heaven!" I exclaimed.

Oddly, there was nothing personal here. I saw an occasional photo of Annie and Robert, but nothing sentimental, no clothes, no memories, not anything to suggest that Annie had lived here.

I went back downstairs and out the back door. There was a jaw-dropping infinity-edge pool in the side yard with a statue of a beautiful young woman sitting and bowing her head, maybe in prayer. The guest house at the end of the pool was two stories high and decorated similarly to the main house, very modern and plush. Anyone I knew would have been happy calling it home. The large backyard was perfectly manicured with beautiful trees, flowers, and furniture. There was a pathway across the yard to a staircase that seemed to call to me: Come on, come down here. The steps led down to the private beach, the Atlantic Ocean, and beyond. I walked down to the beach and the water.

As I walked along the sand, listening to the sound of the waves lapping at the beach, I thought how relaxing it was. No people, no traffic, just me, the beach, the ocean, and the world! It was low tide, so I could walk out pretty far and explore the sand beneath the sea.

Down here by the water would be a perfect spot for me to meditate. Today had been such a whirlwind and so filled with changes I needed to quiet my soul and take it all in. My gratitude journal today had an entry about this house. There was something special about it, something I felt said 'home' to me. Thank you, Annie, this is amazing!

I was as excited as a young child, looking for shells, sea glass, starfish, and whatever I might find. Of course, I returned to the house with all the loot I could carry. I hadn't been beach exploring in a very lo ng time. It felt perfect.

I am a country girl in the Hamptons, I thought. I am all by myself. The world is my oyster, so what do I do now? Well, that was the question, wasn't it? What do I do now?

I slowly walked back towards the house. My mind was racing, and I could only imagine the writing I could get done in a place like this. I had wondered why Annie bought a house this far from the financial district, and now I completely understood why. Once you come here, you don't ever want to leave. I wasn't even a beach person per se, and I didn't want to leave.

I returned to the kitchen, and sure enough, the house was well stocked with food, wine, and just about everything I could imagine. I got the groceries I had picked up from the car and brought them inside. I was starving. I had been so occupied with sightseeing I hadn't eaten any lunch. I was looking forward to some of that homemade crab salad, which did not disappoint me.

My phone was ringing. I ran to find where I had put my bag. Scott was probably calling to see if I found the house okay. "Hi," I answered.

"Hi, did you have any trouble?" he asked.

"No, it was easy to find. What an amazing place," I said.

Scott agreed the house was a special place. He told me that Annie got a steal on the property at $52 million! Homes like that hardly ever come on the market.

"When she saw it, she knew it was the one," he told me. "Robert never told her no, so they made an offer, and it was theirs,

"So, Stacy, I thought I would leave you to explore on your own the rest of the day. Are you fixed for dinner tonight?" he asked.

"Yes, thank you for stocking the house," I replied. I told him about the Red Horse Market, and he knew it well. I could only imagine his family and Annie's family up here enjoying their successes on the shore of the Atlantic. I hoped there were many, many happy memories made here for them.

Scott told me to report to the heliport at 10 a.m. to fly back to Manhattan to meet him.

"Okay, I'll be there," I said. "When is our flight back to Boca? Should I bring my stuff?"

Scott asked, "This is your first trip to the city, isn't it?"

"Yes, I have never been to New York before."

"Well then, why don't we stay a couple of days, and I can show you around? It is quite a place."

"That would be awesome!"

"So, take the rest of the day, rest, explore, or whatever your heart desires, and I'll see you in the morning," Scott said.

As much as I wanted to tour the area, I was tired. All of it was so overwhelming. I thought I might go out for dinner later but for the time being, I wanted to veg out on the couch, watch some television, and be a regular person for a while.

Chapter Nine

I found The Last Holiday, one of my favorite movies, on television so I curled up on the oversized couch and enjoyed two hours with an amazing love story. Then I decided the day was too pretty not to take a drive. After all, it was September, the leaves were turning, there was a crispness in the air, and I was in the Hamptons. So, I headed out.

After reviewing the map, I could see that the area was laid out in a big circle so I really couldn't get lost. I took a right out of the driveway and headed back up the island to look at the opposite side. Over there I could see the Sound. It was equally beautiful, quite different terrain, but just as pretty as the ocean side of the island. This part of the Hamptons was filled with horse farm after horse farm, fields of hay, some freshly cut and some already dried and stacked. I could see young girls riding beautiful big horses over a jump course. It reminded me of my childhood, the love of horses and riding. There was a time when I could have given you a run for your money on that big Oldenburg!

I found Dune Road, which led me to loads of antique shops in Sag Harbor. I took some time to browse and enjoy stepping back in time. In one of the shops, I found some pieces of Depression Glass patterns, Iris, and Her-ringbone, that my grandmother had when I was a little girl. I had to purchase a couple of pieces. After all, the house needed at least a little of me in it. After the clerk carefully wrapped my pieces, she encouraged me to come back again. I visited a winery, tried a couple of sips of their pride and joy, and purchased a wine called Summertime in a Bottle.

Sag Harbor was a peaceful, relaxing place. It was like an entirely different country filled with artisans, farmers, and visionaries. The people who lived there, not the ultra-rich but the actual people, were lovely and down-to-earth. They were all hard-working people who farmed and raised livestock, had shops and stores selling local products and managed wineries. They are proud of their products and seemed like folks who would help one another any way they could if the chips were down. I liked this area. It felt like home.

I decided to drive up to Montauk Point and see the lighthouse. I was so glad I did. It was only about 30 minutes away and such a beautiful drive.

The only road in and out, Highway 27, was dotted along the route with shops, hotels, and places to visit. When I reached the end of Montauk Island and the lighthouse, I learned it is just seventy miles to Martha's Vineyard, seven hours by ferry. Nantucket Island lies just past Martha's Vineyard.

I had heard of all these magical places but had never had the opportunity to see them. At one of the shops, I picked up a map for sailing the area. I had never thought of sailing north, but there are many exciting places to see and things to do without being far from home. I thought that would be a great way to get my sea legs.

It was a big day with loads of new sights and ideas; I was getting tired, so after watching an incredible sunset over the ocean, I headed back to the Hamptons where I looked for a seafood place to have dinner. There are so many to choose from, it was a hard decision. I chose Jack's Chowder House which sounded incredible. There was a slight chill in the air, so it was the perfect night for chowder.

The restaurant was simple, clean, and boasted of delicious food. From the looks of the customers' faces, I thought that boast was probably a bit modest. The place smelled heavenly. I ordered a bowl of lobster bisque and a crab cake. The waitress asked if I wanted a local craft beer with my order.

"Sure, that sounds great; what do you suggest?" I asked.

"We have Montauk Craft Beer that all the locals love,".

"Well, the locals can't be wrong," I said.

The restaurant had an ocean view, was family-oriented, and had reasonable prices. The food was fresh and delicious. I didn't think I'd ever have a better beer or lobster bisque. The crab cake was incredible and came with a house sauce for dipping. The flavors were hugely different from the coastal fare of Carolina but equally delicious. I was stuffed by the time I finished eating and would recommend Jack's Chowder House to everyone I know.

Once in the car and headed home, I began thinking about everything that had happened to me over the past couple of weeks. Here I was driving on Montauk Island to the Hamptons, some of the richest in monetary value, history, tradition, and lifestyle. I had always wanted to visit, but now, by a twist of fate, I own a house here. That "home," on Lily Pond Lane was a 10,000-square-foot mansion. Two weeks ago, I was putting gas in my Altima, and today I took a private helicopter to my million-dollar estate. That is a lot for a person to absorb. "Wow!" I said out loud.

I worried about what tomorrow would bring, learning about the financial side of Annie's businesses. I certainly was not a candidate to run that part of the estate. I could hardly balance my check book. Scott was a great trusted resource, and I was sure he would know how to handle that part of everything moving forward. Inheritance is an awful responsibility to have all at once. Money, real money, is much more of a burden than people think. It is a luxury, sure, but it is also hard to decide what to do, and how to keep making, investing, and spending all that wealth. There are a lot of things to consider surviving in this world.

After about forty-five minutes I was back to seeing the familiar sites of East Hampton and Lilly Pond Road. I was glad to return to the house and kick my shoes off. I rambled around a little and found a great bottle of wine. A bottle of Moscato and a fire in the fireplace were just what I needed. I watched an episode of Song Land, my favorite show while enjoying the wine. Then I headed upstairs, set the alarm, and crawled into bed.

I decided I had better check in with Amelia on my horses. I have loved horses for as long as I can remember. I got the opportunity to ride for the first time on my neighbor's pony. I was in heaven. The little golden boy had a white mane and tail. His name was Lightning. He would patiently let each of us take a turn on him going as fast or as slow as we wished. I was hooked.

My parents, after long weeks of pleading, finally got me a pony of my own. A very handsome smoky black with a lot of spirit. We would ride with the kids next door for hours.

Eventually, I outgrew the pony and got a horse. Her name was Ruby. She was a sorrel quarter horse with one white leg. My friends were involved in ranching and had a lot of acreage. Ruby and I rode the pastures, checked fence lines, and watched the cattle every day.

I loved plugging along on her checking fences. When it came time to move the cattle, she demonstrated that she had a very powerful motor and she loved to work the cows. She was good at it, and I hung on. We competed in all types of ranching classes at shows and won a few ribbons.

Of course, I had pointed Ruby over some low trail course jumps and she did as I asked. I was always excited about jumping. It felt as if you were flying. What a magical feeling. Soon I met a woman who was going off to college. She had a big English horse for sale. He was a striking bay gelding with black points that stood 16.2 hands. He could easily do stadium jumping.

I remember watching him work and it was like poetry in motion. Smart, precise, and athletic. I was due a nice paycheck for my writing, so

I made arrangements to buy him. His name was Winston, a registered Westphalian. Westphalians aren't very common these days, so I felt special by owning one.

I rode Winston over the beginner course, and he was a great babysitter. Slow, easy, and sure-footed, but I knew I would want more.

I took him over the next course, jumps were 3' to 3'6". Again, we floated easily over these. An instructor that was watching approached us when we were done. She said, "you two look pretty good out there."

"Thanks" I replied. I rode towards this woman and stopped. "I haven't had him very long and we are learning from each other," I said as I climbed down. Then I recognized the woman, oh my gosh it was Kate Langford, the Olympic champion!

I introduced myself and she extended her hand and replied, "You two look really good out there, what level are you?" she asked. "I am just a beginner," I told her.

"You don't look like a beginner to me," she replied.

"I have ridden all my life, but I just got into jumping," I told her. "Then Winston came along, and a good horse can make anyone look good," I added. I remember it like it was yesterday. She gave me her card and told me to bring Winston over to her place. She wanted to see how we looked on a more professional course. I was on Cloud 9.

My long-time friend Amelia boarded my horses at her farm out in the country. I needed to let her know what was going on and how much longer I might be.

Luckily, she was up and texted me right back. She said "the horses are good, they miss you, of course, but no worries they are fine. Now I could go to sleep without worry. Tomorrow will be a big day.

Chapter Ten

Bright and early, I got up, showered, and dressed. I would make time this morning for my ritual. I try to stay focused on living in the moment and not running out the door with my hair on fire to the next big thing. It is essential to live in the moment, take it in, enjoy it, and be thankful for it. I did a quick five-minute meditation to quiet my mind and prepare for the day. Today's affirmation word was resilience. I need to remember that word as I meet all these successful, influential people.

All too soon, it was time to head to the heliport. The helicopter was landing as I drove up. The attendant parked my car while I boarded the bird.

"Good morning. How are you enjoying the area?" the pilot asked.

"Well, everywhere I look, it is beautiful!" I replied.

We flew over Long Island, Queens, and Manhattan. I could see the heliport on top of the hotel. How could you even soak up such a view, such a lifestyle? When we landed the attendant ran over to get to my door and help me out. The pilot told me to call him whenever I needed a lift and gave me his card, which I tucked safely into my bag. The attendant escorted me to the hotel lobby, where Scott was waiting.

We exchanged greetings and Scott said, "I hope you are excited about meeting your staff this morning.

"Well, let's say 'apprehensive,' I am way out of my comfort zone in this arena," I said.

"You'll be fabulous, and I'll be right here, so don't worry," Scott reassured me.

The limo driver was right on time. I thought to myself, at least we would arrive in high style, and I would look like a financial mogul even if I was not. We turned onto Wall Street, and I saw the building with Wynn Management Group written outside.

New York City is an experience all in itself. The streets are full of people, all hurrying to get wherever they are going. Men dressed in business suits, ladies in designer outfits with high heels or tennis shoes depending on how far they are walking; all hustling to get to jobs, homes, power lunches, or wherever. They all seemed to be hypnotized, some talking away on their cell phones, some utterly oblivious to everyone else on the street with them. No one smiles or makes casual conversation; they are all like marching ants.

The driver dropped us at the front door of the typical brick high rise, pleasant and well kept, but ordinary. The lobby was impressive with marble flooring and high-end furnishings. The receptionist recognizes Scott. greeted us and with a British accent said, "The management team is waiting for you in the Bradshaw conference room."

The elevator whisked us up to the 63rd floor. Again, with my terrible fear of heights, I was thankful it wasn't glass. It would have been embarrassing to cling to the wall like a madwoman.

Once we were seated at the massive table, Scott introduced me. The management team consisted of Roy Wilson, CEO; Jack Griffin, CFO; Sonya Miller, CMO, and a dozen more whose names I didn't get. They were polite and reserved.

Roy Wilson immediately took control of the meeting, thanking me for my visit and expressing condolences for the loss of Annie.

"Please know that everyone here will greatly miss Annie's warm smile and brilliant conversation," he stated.

Then they began giving me financial reports, their goals, and how they would achieve them. They sounded like they knew what they were doing. Scott had a few questions as the meeting progressed. Of course, I sat there like a dummy. I didn't know enough to even ask any questions.

"In closing, I want to assure Ms. Kent that Ann Wynn Investments are in capable hands, and we are continuing the traditions and practices set forth by Ann," Roy Wilson said, then adjourned the meeting.

Roy Wilson and Scott briefly spoke between themselves while I took in the view overlooking the city. Looking from building to building on just one street, I tried to imagine the number of money transactions that changed hands on any given day: so much money and power.

Scott came over and asked if I had any questions, and I replied, "Not at this time; I need to study the situation." I honestly believe that when you are the "new kid" on the block, you must observe and learn for a period before knowing enough to have an opinion.

From there, we went back to the elevator and went up to the 97th floor. From the elevator, we entered an elaborate lobby area with a fashionable receptionist to greet us. She seemed to know Scott quite well and greeted us with a warm smile. "Edward is waiting for you in his office," she told us.

Edward Perlman was the man in charge of the Wynn Management

Group. His smaller, more intimate office was a nice setting for our first meeting. Perlman was a well-dressed, relatively tall man. His olive skin and dark hair were quite handsome. He greeted Scott with a friendly handshake and shook my hand as Scott introduced us. He told me how sorry he was to hear about Annie's passing away.

Edward and Annie's husband had been college roommates, and their families had many great memories. I could tell by the tone of his voice that he was sincere, and I liked Edward instantly. "Ms. Kent, I thought I would give you a personal rundown on what we do here and where we are headed. I have copies of the financials for you to take home and review at your leisure," he said.

"Well, that sounds good," I replied.

Edward began by explaining the ins and outs of the companies. It was an impressive list, including Raymond's father's holdings worldwide. Some of the biggest names in the business were among the clientele. The financials were outstanding, and as he built a rapport with me, I was sure he had a true gift for this line of work, just as Annie had. Yes, this company was in good hands. "So now that I have bored you to death, would you like to go to lunch?" He asked.

"I made reservations at Briganti, but we would love for you to join us," Scott told him.

"Great, I am starving," Edward replied.

We headed down the elevator and onto the street just like that. New York is a walking town so we would walk the twelve blocks to the restaurant. As we started, we came upon a bicycle wagon thing that transported passengers.

Edward looked down at my feet and said, "You know what? I haven't ridden one of these things in years. Stacy, would you like to take this to the restaurant?"

"That would be fun," I quickly answered, "I'm not exactly wearing walking shoes."

Scott said, "I am so sorry; I didn't even think about that."

"This is called a cycle rickshaw," Edward told me. Whatever it was called, it was a relief because my feet were already complaining.

With this mode of transportation, reaching the restaurant didn't take very long, and we could smell the fragrance of good Italian food wafting in the air.

"You can't come to New York and not have Italian," Scott said.

The hostess seated us by the window and handed us menus. Edward told us, "The pizza here is amazing, but then again, I haven't had anything here that wasn't."

We all ordered pizza and drinks. Sitting by the window was enjoyable. I listened to everyone around us talking and planning for their afternoon and evenings. City people live a different lifestyle than rural people. In the city, their whole world is within a few blocks of where they live, work, shop, and play. I guess with so many people the time difference isn't much, just the distances traveled. Rural people don't think anything of driving 30 miles to town or a little further to a bigger town. It was just the way it was, and no one questioned it.

Lunch was enjoyable; Edward was funny and animated, warm, and sincere all at the same time. When lunch was over, Scott called and had our driver pick us all up at the restaurant. On the ride back to the high rise, Edward gave me his card and said, "Call me whenever you are in town. I would love for you to meet my family and let us show you some big-city hospitality."

"That would be fantastic," I replied.

The limo driver dropped Edward at his door and returned us to the hotel.

"Well," Scott said, "let's find a quiet place and sit down to talk about today's meeting and findings, shall we?" I followed him as he inquired at the desk, and we were escorted to a small conference room that would be all ours for the afternoon.

"What do you think about the financial operations," Scott asked.

"I like Edward, I think he is amazing. From his demeanor, I am sure his clients all love and trust him," I said.

"What about Annie's group?" Scott asked.

"I am so much a duck out of water regarding investments. Before this, I hardly had a savings account," I answered. "I don't know if I can have a valuable opinion."

Scott and I looked over the reports, and everything seemed good. Profits were holding steady in both organizations at about 25% overall.

"Scott, what responsibilities will I have going forward with these two businesses?" I asked.

Scott explained that I was the board chairman and would need to attend quarterly board meetings. "I am the counsel for both groups, so I will attend all the board meetings on your behalf and advise you if we need to do anything specific if that is agreeable to you," he said.

"Of course. It is a relief that you will over-see this," I said.

The pilot for the chopper called to let me know he would be arriving to pick me up in about ten minutes.

"Chopper is on its way," I told Scott.

"Well, back to the Hamptons for you tonight," Scott said.

"When are we returning to Boca to do the paperwork?" I asked. "I am anxious to get it all done so I can make some arrangements in my old life."

"We can fly back tomorrow if you like. I'll make the arrangements," said Scott.

I boarded the chopper once more, and away we went. I was beginning to like having a helicopter at my disposal; it sure beats traffic jams, and the view was amazing.

Chapter Eleven

We landed at the heliport, and I bid the pilot goodbye. It felt good to get in my rental car and hit the road. I was ready for a break from all of this. As I drove back to the estate, my mind was overrun with doubts and thoughts about this new lifestyle. I was not sure I was cut out to be a billionaire. I wanted to get home and air my head out to figure out how to merge these two vastly different and meaningful lives into one.

Scott and I would fly to Boca the next morning, and I could sign the papers to finalize the business. I decided to stay overnight at the Florida house. It felt weird—like I had been on a crazy vacation. I was ready to go home to North Carolina.

When I got back to the house in the Hamptons, I grabbed a snack and went to sit on the beach and watch the tide come in. I checked my email and was glad to see a message from Paula. She loved my story about oysters. I was swept by a feeling that all this money couldn't buy a sense of personal accomplishment.

So, now that I had all this money, opportunity, and time, what would I do with it? I needed to give my future a lot of thought. I decided to take the logical approach; which works for most people, even though I hardly ever do anything logically. I decided to list goals, desires, and dreams, which would take some serious thinking and was not a thing to be hurried. I packed up my stuff and walked back up to the house.

I wondered if I needed to clean out the refrigerator. No, it was stocked when I came, so it should be okay. I guessed the worst-case scenario occurred and everything spoiled. I could buy a new refrigerator; after all, I was rich. I laughed and went into the den. My phone rang, and I saw it was Scott.

"Hi," I answered.

"Hi, I have our flight booked for eight a.m. tomorrow. The chopper will pick you up at six and take you directly to the airport. I'll meet you there, and we'll be in Boca by lunch," Scott said.

"Great, I'm beginning to get homesick, as weird as that sounds," I told him.

"This has all been a lot to take in, no doubt. You have handled it all like a pro, and I am proud of you. See you in the morning," Scott said.

"Okay, thank you, see you then," I replied.

I went upstairs to pack my things and go to bed as the morning would come early. I was in love with the Lily Pond Lane house and decided I would keep it. On that pleasant thought, I soon drifted off to sleep.

Four o'clock seemed to come exceptionally early, but as the alarm went off, I crawled out of bed and staggered to the shower. The warm water falling on me felt terrific; what a great way to wake up. I thought about the goals I had set for myself last night. I threw on a pair of jeans, a sweater, socks, shoes, and a jacket.

Goals are beautiful tools, I mused, as long as you remember everything you plan must be fluid as life changes quickly. You have to learn to adapt and change with it or get left behind. Today's affirmation is to remember to concentrate on your goals, not the obstacles. Now that is a challenge in itself!

"Okay, beautiful house, I love you, and I will be back," I said. Then locked the door and got in the car. The time was 4:45, not too bad. I hoped there would be no rush hour traffic. The helicopter arrived promptly at six a.m. The pilot stowed my bags and helped me in. The early morning flight was incredible. The sun was coming up over the Atlantic Ocean, with beautiful shimmers of gold and yellow rising over the horizon casting pink and purple hues onto the ocean's surface. The cityscape soon came into view. The city never sleeps. Plumes of smoke billowed from the factories, and the streets were lined with traffic. The airport came into view, and it was already bustling with planes lined up to taxi onto the runway. The office was just a short flight away.

We arrived at the airport with time to spare. I discovered I loved helicopters! Once at the airport, I checked my bags and went through security to find some breakfast. Biscuit City was a golden discovery. I ordered a sausage biscuit and a Diet Coke, and then I went to wait for Scott. I was anxious to get this legal stuff over and go home, then see the boat!

I found a seat by the window and pulled out my tablet to work on my list of goals for myself while I ate my biscuit. The airport was huge, and I was glad our flight was near the heliport area. I am a goal-oriented person and function better with a list of objectives. But how and where do I start with goals for this life? To plan for the future would take some serious thought.

Scott wasn't long behind me. "Good morning," he said, "I hope you didn't mind the early flight."

"No, I love getting up at 4 a.m.," I said and laughed. Soon it was time to board, and it felt good to be headed south, although I had fallen in love with Lilly Pond Lane.

Once on the plane, Scott asked, "What is that list you are working on?"

"Oh, well, I figured I needed to make some plans about my life since things have changed so drastically," I explained, "You know, to figure out who I am, what I want, and how to combine that with this new life."

"That is great," Scott said. "I was worried about all of this swallowing you up, but you seem like a strong-minded person with her own goals and dreams."

"I am," I replied.

"Is there a guy in your life?"

"Why do you ask that?"

"Well, you are warm and friendly but seem lonely somehow. I just wondered."

"There was once, but that was a long time ago," I said. "Now, the partner in my life is my writing and filming. But someday, maybe."

"When we land, the car will pick us up and take us to my office. My staff has all the paperwork ready for your signature, all the keys to the properties, information, descriptions, and whatever information they think you may need going forward. It should take us about an hour to complete," Scott said.

"Good, I'm anxious to get it all done and finalized," I told him.

"What then?" he asked.

"I'll head back to North Carolina and take a few days to decide my next step. I want to see the boat, and the Jackson Hole property, and take a quick trip to London to check that out. Then there is always LA, I want to take a few weeks sailing to see how I like it. Since it's getting on for winter, I'm thinking of sailing in the Caribbean. After that, who knows?" I said.

The flight attendant brought us snacks and a soda. First-class flying had its perks. We landed in Boca, and the car was waiting, and we headed to Scott's office. In about an hour, the paperwork was all done. Scott gave me the keys to everything, told me copies of the paperwork would be mailed to my home address, and hugged me.

I had arranged for Jim to pick me up at Scott's office and take me to the estate. I got my tickets to RDU, my familiar Raleigh Durham International Airport. It would be great to be headed home once again.

Suzi came into the office to welcome me home. Somehow it felt fake. "Will you stay here for a while now?" she asked.

"No, I'm headed home tomorrow," I replied.

"Home," she said, "where is that?"

"North Carolina is where I live right now," I told her.

"When will you be back in Boca?"

"I'm not sure what I am going to do with Boca," I told her. "It isn't somewhere I would want to live regularly, so I have to decide how much I even need it."

Chip text messaged to ask if I wanted lunch. I sent him a reply that I would be here for dinner and breakfast, and then I was heading back home. It felt great to say, "Going home."

I spent the afternoon rambling around the house. Oddly, I could find very few personal things, only a couple of photos. It was almost as if it was a glorified hotel. Where did Annie hang her hat and call home if that was the case?

I called Scott and asked him. "Hello, did you miss me already?" he joked.

"Well, of course," I answered. "But seriously, I have a question. I can't find anything personal of Annie's at either the Boca house or Lilly Pond Lane. I saw only a few photos at either place," I said. "So, where did she actually live?"

Scott answered quietly, "When she discovered she wasn't going to make it, she donated most of her things to charity. You will find a few things in London and Jackson Hole as she didn't have time to get there to clean them out. In the last three months of her life, she traveled very lightly. She didn't want to be a burden after she was gone."

"I see," was all I could say.

Chip made a delightful dinner—prime rib roast with all the trimmings. "I hope you like it," he said.

"Well, it looks wonderful," I said.

"I roasted it all day just for you; I wanted an opportunity to show off my skills just a little to you," Chip told me.

I sat down to eat that beautiful feast alone in that big dining room. It was cold and lonely.

On impulse, I said, "Chip, please join me for dinner."

"Are you sure?" he asked. "The help doesn't ever eat with the owners."

"Well, in this case, they should. I would love to have your company. This is much too nice a meal for you to not join in," I told him.

As we ate, we talked, and I learned Chip was a graduate of the Johnson and Wales Culinary Institute in Charleston, South Carolina. He had been an executive chef at some of the finest restaurants in the country. Annie and Raymond had courted him before he agreed to become their private chef in Boca.

"Raymond and Annie were extraordinary people to me," he told me. "They would come to my restaurant every weekend to eat and always made me a job offer," he laughed. "I remember it like it was yesterday. Raymond would tell me I had to save him from Annie's cooking!"

"I remember that Annie was never much of a cook when we were growing up," I said.

"I can't believe they are both gone," he said as he wiped a tear from his eye.

"I can't either," I agreed. "On a happier note, this prime rib was magnificent, maybe the best I ever had."

He beamed with pride and appreciation for my compliment.

"Do you like to sail?" I asked.

"Sail?" he said, surprised by the sudden change of subject. "Well, yes, I love the water. Why do you ask?"

"Well, Annie bought me a sailboat. 'Sail around the world and experience all that life has to offer,' was how she put it," I told him. "It is forty-two feet and will come with a crew. I would love to have you join us as our chef. But I didn't even think—you might have a family. If you can't join us, I certainly understand."

Chip smiled and replied, "No, it is just me right now. Let me think about it. For now, just wait till you see dessert!" He hurried off to the kitchen and came back with the most beautiful chocolate cake I had ever seen.

"This is one of my specialties," he said. "It's a five-layer chocolate cake with chocolate mousse, chocolate ganache, fudge, and dark chocolate. There's a milk chocolate filling. I hope you like chocolate," he laughed.

"Oh my gosh, it is sinfully delicious!" I told him. After a couple more bites, I said, "You know, come to think of it, I can't take you sailing with me. I'd get so fat the boat would sink under me!"

"Just wait till you eat breakfast in the morning. You'll be begging me to come," he said as he disappeared into the kitchen.

I was full and knew I would sleep like a log! I melted into the covers and a deep sleep. The alarm rang too soon. I dragged myself out of bed to the shower then got dressed and headed downstairs to breakfast, which did not disappoint. Chip was ready with every ingredient known to man for omelets and pancakes. Bacon was already done and there was fresh-squeezed orange juice. Once again, it was delicious! I gave Chip my card so he could call me directly on my cell phone to discuss sailing.

Suzi was in the office, and the maid was busy somewhere in the house. Suzi and I exchanged greetings and I said, "Suzi, I'll be back here in about two weeks, and we'll discuss the future of the Boca house and staff. In the meantime, continue what you normally do. Put together a report with a detailed listing of what all you the maid, and the gardener do."

"What about Chip?" she asked.

I told her not to worry about Chip. From the look on her face, I could tell she was angry, but she would have time to find another job if she wanted to.

Jim was there promptly at 10:30 to take me to the airport. Jim was a contract driver and had other clients, so I would not have to worry about his future. He would be available when I was back in Boca and needed him. That was a relief, as he was a very kind and thoughtful man.

The Boca airport was small, and primarily designed for private planes coming in and out. I boarded my plane, and we soon took off for good old North Carolina! My Daddy used to say, "You could take the girl out of the state, but you would never get the tar off her heels."

Chapter Twelve

While on the plane, I set up a meeting with Paula for the afternoon after I landed. I was more than ready to get back to work, so I was anxious to see her. We soon landed, and I got my rental car and drove to grab a quick bite at Char Grill. A burger and fries sounded good after all the fancy food I had eaten. I was sure I must have put on ten pounds! Soon I was taking the elevator to Paula's office. The receptionist greeted me as always and said Paula would see me in just a few minutes. Before I could sit down, she was coming down the hall calling out to me, "Stacy girl, where have you been?" We hugged and went into her office.

Paula was a tall, slender woman with striking red hair which today she was wearing down with soft waves that framed her beautiful green eyes. She was dressed to the nines as always and carried herself with the authority of her position.

"I love the story about oysters," she exclaimed. "Love the tie into personal memories and Carolina tradition. So, tell me all about your trip."

"Well, I went to Boca Raton for my cousin's funeral. It turns out she left me her estate," I told her.

"Oh no, you aren't moving to Boca, are you?" she asked.

"Well, it's worse than that," I gave her a brief scenario of what had transpired over the past two weeks. Then told her the estate was valued at $1.15 billion. Gosh, that was the first time I had said it aloud.

"$1.15 billion? With a B?" she exclaimed.

"Yes, with a B," I told her. The look on her face was priceless, and you would have thought I had told her I was pregnant!

"Well, I guess I don't need to ask what your thoughts are on the December issue since you obviously won't be working," she said.

"What, not working? I didn't give you my resignation," I told her.

"Well, I just assumed."

"Honestly, I have no idea where my life will go, but right now, I am a writer, and I don't want that to change.

We talked a bit longer and left it that I was still her feature writer and thinking about December and what she would like to have. I had to get going; there was still a long drive to New Bern and home.

Once I was out of traffic and on the open road, I could think. I needed to talk to someone about all of this, to someone who knew me. I decided to call Debbie, with whom I had been friends since college. She knew me well and we spent a lot of time together. Debbie was an artist and as temperamental as you would expect, but I loved her like a sister. I gave her a call, and we set up a dinner date for soon after I got home to catch up. We would meet at Leo's, a little downtown bar with fantastic food and a great clientele.

Debbie was right on time, and it was great to see a familiar friendly face. I gave her a big hug, and we found a table. "It is so great to see you," I told her.

Debbie Ballard was a petite woman with curly blonde hair and pearly white skin. She had piercing blue eyes that looked right into your eyes. "Wow, you must have had a rough two weeks," she replied.

"Well, it has been an experience," I admitted.

"Let's order. I am starving, and then I want to hear every detail," Debbie said.

"Ok, well, I got a call that my cousin Annie had passed away, and I needed to go to Florida, to Boca Raton, to meet with her attorney and handle arrangements. I am the executrix of her estate," I began.

"Oh my gosh, Stacy, I am so sorry about your cousin," Debbie said.

"It was a shock. We had been very close growing up, together almost every day," I told her. Then, our dinner came, and boy did it smell great! As we ate, I continued with the story about flying down to Florida and meeting with Annie's attorney. I said Annie had been highly successful with her marriage and her business. I knew she was in investment banking, but I had no idea she was so successful. I filled Debbie in on all the details of my inheritance.

Debbie was utterly speechless, something I had never seen. "Wow," was all she could say.

"So, as you can see," I said. "I am exhausted, overwhelmed, and needed to see a friend."

"What are you going to do?" Debbie asked.

As I laid out my plan for the next 90 days she smiled and said, "I think that is very sensible."

Well, that was a consolation; she agreed I was making an excellent decision to sail away, take 90 days, think about it all, and see what comes next. That was a relief.

I went on to tell Debbie I had written a killer story about oysters for the November issue of the magazine.

She laughed so hard she spit her water out when I said that.

"What's that all about?" I asked her.

"Stacy, you are a billionaire, and you're proud that you wrote a story for the magazine. That's precious," Debbie said.

"I know it sounds trite, but I love writing for the magazine," I said.

"Then why don't you start your magazine or magazines?" Debbie asked.

"I always dreamed about it, but making it come true? I don't know," I told her.

"Well, now is the time. You don't need the money, so it won't be a great tragedy if you fail," Debbie pointed out.

"If I started a publishing company, would you come to work for me?" I asked.

"Only if I'm the boss," Debbie said with a laugh.

"That could be arranged," I told her. So again, dreams were being dreamed, and life felt like it was back to normal. What a relief!

We finished our meal and headed out into the street. New Bern is so beautiful it felt good to be home.

As we parted, Debbie looked back over her shoulder and said, "Ok, just let me know when you want me to start."

"You got it," I told her.

When I got home, my house seemed very quaint and small after living in Lilly Pond Lane for a couple of days. I thought—this was a good thing, nothing to be scared of. Embrace it, and go. If only it were that easy. I was exhausted, so I climbed into bed, switched on something boring on TV, and fell asleep.

The following day, I woke up safe and sound in my own house, bed, and old life. Wow, what a journey this has been so far. I decided to begin my day with a prayer. It was always good to know I was not alone. My meditation this morning focused on listening to the sounds here in the country, the rooster next door, the farm animals, and the quiet that country life gives. I felt restored and relaxed. My affirmation for today is to Be Yourself.

I started researching the Caribbean and sailing paths. I was getting excited about this opportunity. I called The Mariners Club Marina in the Florida Keys where my boat was stored and got all the details. The crew was local and on standby for my call. I scheduled an appointment to go down next week and check it out. I also arranged to meet with the potential crew on Friday morning.

Well, I thought, I'll need a place to stay in the Keys. I had never been there, so I was excited to make the trip. I found a spot on the water called Ocean's Edge and I hoped it would be safe and decent.

I decided to invite Debbie to go with me. It would be great to have some company, and I would also like to have her input about the boat, the crew, and all that. I gave her a call.

"Good morning, Miss Thing," Debbie said when she knew it was me.

"I'm headed down to the Keys to check out the boat next Thursday. Would you like to come?" I asked.

"Of course, but I can't afford it right now. I'm between shows at the gallery," Debbie said.

"No problem, the trips on me," I told her.

"In that case, heck yes, I will come," Debbie said. "How many bikinis should I bring?"

"Probably enough for a week or so. I'll make the reservations. Let's plan to leave my house Thursday morning at about four a.m.," I said.

"Sounds like a plan," Debbie replied.

Great, that was settled. So, I set about trying to sort out what loose ends I would need to resolve to be gone for an extended time. I called Jack O'Malley, a realtor friend, to see what he thought my house would sell for and how long that might take.

"Good morning, Stacy," Jack said when I had identified myself, "how can I help you?"

"Could we meet for lunch today? I want to discuss my house with you," I told him.

"Sure, I can do one o'clock. How about the Chelsea?"

"It's a date, thanks," I responded.

Then I gave Scott a call.

"I have a couple of questions if you have a minute," I told him.

"Sure, what you got?" Scott answered.

I told him about my plans to fly to the Keys next week and potentially sell my house.

"I am so glad you are moving in that direction," Scott said. "Why don't you plan to ship your things to the Lilly Pond Lane house? I know you like it, and I will have someone there to make sure everything gets put safely inside for you to unpack," Scott said.

"That solves that problem," I told him.

"Would you like me to join you when you see the boat and meet the crew?" Scott asked.

"That would be awesome, I am bringing a friend, but your advice is always appreciated," I told him.

"I have a house in the Keys if you want to stay there," Scott offered.

"I made reservations at Mariners Club Resort; I don't want to be a bother," I told Scott.

"Okay, I will meet you at Mariners Club about noon, and we can go see your boat," Scott said.

Things were coming together fast. It would be sad to sell my little house, but if I owned a home in New Bern, it would be historic and bigger. When I was a little girl, my Daddy drove us to town, parked about four blocks from the hustle and bustle, and we walked. We always parked just in front of the Blades house, a beautiful Queen Anne-style historic home. It looked like a castle, complete with balconies, turrets, and huge porches. I always dreamed of living there. Maybe one day I will, but that's another day's problem.

I decided to drive down to the graveyard where my mom and dad were buried. I needed to talk with them. It has always been a comfort to me to know where they are buried and feel that I can still be close to them, even if it is only in my mind. The drive down into Pamlico County was lovely, with little traffic. The leaves were just starting to turn a little.

I stopped in town and got flowers to put on the graves. I tried hard to make sure I kept flowers on the graves year-round as a gesture of respect. I sure did miss my parents. Annie's parents were buried in Hobucken, so I decided to get some flowers for their graves as well. Annie would have liked that.

The first stop was Reelsboro at my parent's graves. Reelsboro wasn't much more than a crossroads, but the family cemetery was there. It felt good to tell them all that had happened and my plans. I placed the flowers in the holders, bid them goodbye, and headed to Hobucken to see Annie's folks. I hadn't driven to Hobucken in a long time and wasn't even sure I would remember the way, but it came back as I traveled those old familiar country roads. There was only one cemetery in Hobucken, so their graves weren't too hard to find. The cemetery didn't look like anyone had been there in a long while. The graves were overgrown with weeds and needed cleaning. That is always a problem with country graveyards. The upkeep of the cemetery plot is the family's responsibility but unfortunately, not all families are responsible or even alive.

I cleaned it up as best I could; I hadn't thought to bring any tools. I placed the flowers and told them about Annie. It was a hard thing to do, but somehow it felt necessary. I sat there on the ground for a while and cried. Then I got up and decided to check out the old place where we happily spent our carefree days. The trailer they had once lived in was long gone, but Tripp's Marina was still standing, as was the crab house. I went into the Marina to buy a drink and walked out on the dock. Gosh, the memories I had from here. Mr. Tripp had died long ago, and the grandson who was now the owner wouldn't know me from Adam, but it was a good stop.

The Coast Guard Station was still there. I remember we climbed up the fire tower to see the view and that's where I learned I was scared of heights. We got about two-thirds the way up, and I froze. I couldn't go up or down. Annie had to get someone from the Coast Guard Station to help. It was so embarrassing, and we weren't even supposed to be up there. The nice fellow who helped me get down didn't tell our parents, so we lived to explore another day. I am still terrified of heights; I guess it's Karma.

As I drove back towards town along those old country roads, I had been calling home for so long; the memories began to flood my mind. Those were happy, carefree times. I thought about how much our lives had changed from those days. I always thought I would be married with a half dozen kids and a career by now. I would never have believed all the changes we would go through, losing our parents and now my cousin. I began to put into perspective how short and fragile life is.

Once home, I needed to think about boxes and packing up. I decided it was easiest to hire a crew to come in and pack, ship, and unload. I would need stuff for the boat and a three-month trip to the Caribbean. Unlike most moves when I usually purge things I can live without, this time, it could just all go to the Hamptons. That was easy.

The following day, I got up and puttered around until time to get ready to meet Jack. At The Chelsea, Jack had us a table in the back.

"Hey, stranger," Jack said as he got up to hug me.

"Hey Jack, how have you been?" I asked.

"Good, and you?"

I had decided not to tell anyone else all my business. It was an extraordinary tale, and not many would even believe it. "I have been doing great; I have been working in Raleigh and making the trip up and back," I told him. Well, that was true.

"So, are you ready to sell your place to move?" Jack asked.

"I think I am ready to do just that," I told him.

Jack and I went over comparable properties in the area and established a price. He would drop by tomorrow, take photos, and get the house listed.

"The market is a little slow this time of year with the upcoming fall holidays, but it will sell without a doubt, "Jack said.

"How long do you think it will take?"

"I would guess about 30-60 days."

"Okay, I can live with that," I told him.

I hadn't yet thought about my car. Should I sell it or ship it? It wasn't anything special, a Nissan Rogue, but I loved it. I would have to think about that.

The following day Jack arrived bright and early to take photos. "This looks great, you have taken such good care of it, and the location is excellent," he said.

"Thanks, I love it, but it is time to move on," I answered. My neighborhood was on the outskirts of town; I never was much of one to live in the city. It had three bedrooms with a fireplace and a nice yard. I could see a young family living here.

When I purchased it, I had thoughts that one day my family would live there. At the time, I had been crazy in love with Danny, a Marine stationed in Jacksonville. We met when I was on an assignment writing about the base. Danny was the liaison officer who gave me the tour, history, and information I needed. There was an instant connection. He was ruggedly handsome, with dark hair, blue eyes, tall, and a man in uniform. I was swept off my feet.

We began dating and were inseparable for months. Then one day, I found out that Danny had met someone new and was ready to move on with her, not me. He was getting stationed across the country, and she would be moving with him. Of course, it broke my heart, but I survived, and there hasnbeen anyone since. I didn't want to let anyone in that could hurt me like that again. Maybe it was time for a change in that direction, too. I certainly didn't have any prospects, but I could let down my guard a little now that my future was secure.

After Jack left, I decided to go see my horses. I had really missed them over the past couple of weeks!

Amelia was a longtime friend and fellow horsewoman. We rode trails together and did ranch work together for years. She graciously allowed me to board my horses at her farm where she takes excellent care of them. When Amelia needed to be away, I would reciprocate and take care of all of her animals. Amelia had a breeding facility, and her hard work was paying off this year with a beautiful crop of babies!

Amelia greeted me, surprised, at the barn "hello stranger I thought you were still globe-trotting," she said with a smile.

"Hi, it is so good to be back home, I needed to see the ponies" I replied. As I got out of the car we walked over to the stalls. There were my two beautiful horses. Winston, tall and regal looked over his gate and sweet Ruby almost smiling to see me.

"Amelia, they look great," I told her.

"Well, they are pretty special they belong to a very good friend," she replied.

I took Winston's halter and slipped it over his head and pulled him out for some grooming time. Nothing relaxes your mind and soul like grooming your horse. Slowly stroking their coat and running your hands over them while they bask in your attention, is a connection that is hard to describe, but very addictive. I gave him a big kiss and a treat and returned him to his stall.

Then it was Ruby's turn. Ruby was about 14.3 hands tall so after handling Winston she felt like a pony. She came out of her stall being her usual pushy self, I quickly corrected her, and she settled right in. I gave her a good grooming, kisses, and treats and returned her to the paddock.

Amelia came back to where we were standing saying "You better quit kissing on that spoiled horse,".

"Not today," I replied.

I explained to Amelia all that had happened over a cup of coffee in the tack room. Her response was "I will take care of Winston and Ruby, you go take care of whatever you need to do." Wow, great friends are precious things that you must always look after, I thought. "Thank you, kiss them every day for me," I told her.

"Of course," was her reply.

Now I had to call Kate Langford and catch her up on my good fortune. As I traveled through the country roads, I remembered meeting Kate for the first time. I don't think I slept a wink that night dreaming about going to her farm to ride. Kate promptly answered and I began my story. Her reply was similar to everyone's who knew, "Wow" and of course, I will help Amelia with Winston. I thanked her and promised to see her before I left long term.

Before I knew it was Wednesday night and time to pack for the Keys. Bathing suits—check, beach cover-up—check, beach pants—check, shorts, tanks, and underwear—check.

Cosmetics, hair junk, and deodorant—check; yes, I guess I was ready.

Four o'clock came early. I said a quick prayer and chose my affirmation word for the day – Dream. Debbie was right on time, so we threw everything into the car and headed to RDU Airport. We had to be checked in one hour before departure. We were flying First Class, so I knew Debbie would be stoked. As we made the drive, Debbie was full of questions.

"I can't believe all you have been through in the past weeks," she said.

"It has been surreal," I agreed. "I have a house on the beach in Boca Raton, a mansion on the ocean in the Hamptons, a condo in London, a ski lodge in Jackson Hole, Wyoming, and an apartment in Los Angeles," I told her.

"Oh my, have you seen them all?" Debbie asked.

"No, I've only been to Boca and the Hamptons," I told her.

"What was Boca like?"

"Well, it was beautiful with my private beach and staff, but not to my taste. Annie only stayed there when she came to see her attorney," I explained.

"A staff! Aren't you something," Debbie teased.

"Yes, a house manager, gardener, maid, and chef," I told her. "Oh, and I had a driver."

She laughed loudly and said, "I guess they had seen you drive."

"Ha Ha," I said.

"What about the Hamptons?" Debbie continued.

"Now that is awesome," I told her. I gave her details about the area, the estate, the house, and how magnificent it was.

"That does sound awesome," Debbie agreed.

"I liked that one. I would never have imagined myself living up north, but the Hamptons have something special," I said.

"If you're rich," Debbie said.

"Well, probably," I had to agree.

"I haven't told you the best parts about the boat." As I told Debbie about the boat dating from the 1930s and having been built for a movie producer to entertain, she was speechless once again.

"It sounds beautiful. Is it safe?" Debbie sounded concerned.

"I have seen photos of it, and it's incredible," I said, "all the elegance of that era and 42 feet long."

We finally got to the airport, grabbed our bags, and headed to the shuttle. Security was a breeze as I had become quite the pro. We checked in, and the agent checked our bags.

"Why did she take our bags?" Debbie asked.

"I hadn't told you, but we're flying First Class. The flight attendant takes care of checking our luggage," I explained.

"First Class, oh yeah, that works," Debbie said, affecting nonchalance.

"Are you on a tight schedule to get home?" I asked.

"No, I am wide open till October 15 when I have my next show," Debbie answered.

"Great, I have never been to the Keys; let's stay a few days and have a little downtime. I could use it," I said.

"Sure thing, you could use a couple of nights on the town, drinking, dancing, making whoopee," Debbie teased.

We were shown to our big, roomy seats. Ours were the only seats on our side so we would have privacy. "I love First Class," I told her.

"Bring on the booze," Debbie said. I could tell that taking Debbie was going to make it a party. It could be just what the doctor ordered for me, too.

When the flight attendant asked if we would like breakfast, we agreed that it sounded great. 4 a.m. had come way too early. She gave us a choice of a continental breakfast or a turkey and Swiss croissant. We ordered the croissants and Diet Cokes.

"If this is breakfast in First Class, I pity the poor folks in Business Class," Debbie said.

"I know right," I answered.

Chapter Thirteen

We landed in Miami and switched to a smaller plane to head to the Keys. The water was beautiful! The ocean was shades of blue and green all along the way. There were boats of all types and sizes puttering around. We were too high to see much housing detail, but the road was a mixture of bridges of all different styles and sizes. We landed in Key West and got a rental car. I couldn't wait to see the boat!

Scott was waiting in the lobby at the Mariner's Club. I introduced him to Debbie, and they exchanged greetings. We checked in and dropped our things to hurry off to the meeting about the boat. As we drove up to the dock, there she sat, seventy-five feet of splendor, made of the most beautiful wood with tall masts, precisely what I had pictured. Wind Dancer is my dream.

The Dock Master met us near where the boat was tied off. "Hello!" he called out.

"Hello!" we answered.

"I am so glad you could make it today," he said, "My name is Albert, and I will be giving you a tour of this beauty."

The boat is a 1934 Custom Staysail Schooner. Initially built for a screenwriter/director. From MGM studios. She was primarily used to entertain Hollywood's elite during the '30s and '40s. Bogart skippered this schooner in the 1936 Transpac race to Hawaii. During the Second World War, she was pressed into service, reportedly becoming part of the Hooligan Fleet, patrolling the West Coast for submarines. Following the war, she was returned to Sturges, who then sold her to a billionaire secretly who married an actress on board. Their marriage certificate was still aboard years later. In 1961, John chartered her, sailing from San Carlos, Mexico, to Hawaii and San Juan Island. When her current owners took possession, they commissioned Port Townsend Shipwrights Co-op to do a complete ($1.2 million) restoration! "So, there is her history, now for her beauty," Albert said and gestured for us to board.

The kitchen was pretty good-sized with a banquette of seating in a horseshoe around the table. The living room area also boasted bench-style seating with tables to work from with gorgeous blood-red leather upholstery. There were porthole windows all down the sides with a good desk area in which to work. A beautiful cabinet was mounted on the wall with a solid wood base underneath topped with marble, similar to a China cabinet. There were sleeping berths for the crew, a bedroom for the captain, and a couple more sleeping area-style bedrooms for guests. All rooms came with a porthole view.

Every inch of the boat was polished and shined to the max; indeed, a beautiful piece of craftsmanship from stem to stern. We were ready to go with modern conveniences such as a microwave, freshwater generator, GPS, Wi-Fi, and a General Motors diesel engine. The sails were in top-notch shape. We could tell the boat had just undergone extensive renovation.

The deck area had places to sit down and relax in the sun mixed in among the equipment and the sails. The helm had a comfortable spot for the captain to sit, complete with sonar, GPS, and maps of all kinds. It was perfect in every way.

Scott had a few questions for the Dock Master, and once he was satisfied with the answers, we signed the transfer papers over to me. Wind Dancer was mine!

On the way back to the hotel, we stopped for one last meeting, to meet the boat captain, Alejandro Cortez. Alejandro was tall, dark, and handsome, just like a movie star. He was probably in his late thirties and spoke with a slight accent, not Bahamian, not Spanish, but something beautiful, words rolled off his tongue like silk. He had dark eyes but a very kind and skilled demeanor. I trusted him instantly.

"Hola," Alejandro greeted us.

"Hola," I replied and put out my hand to shake his. Scott and Debbie introduced themselves and shook hands as well.

"Well, I assume you saw the boat," Alejandro began.

"Yes, we just left the dock," Scott told him.

"What did you think of her?" Alejandro asked.

"It looks like everything is in order," Scott replied.

"I guess the real question is, what did you think of her?" I chimed in.

"She is a beautiful vessel, old school in her build. She is sleek and true; I am anxious to get her in the wind," Alejandro replied. "Where would you like to go?"

"I was thinking since it is September and hurricane season, we would just sail around the Caribbean, see the Turks and Cacaos, Exuma, and maybe get down to San Juan," I told him.

"That sounds like a good easy first trip," Alejandro responded. "How long will we be at sea?"

"I have allowed 90 days for the trip," I answered.

"Ninety days is a fair amount of time. Do you want me to take care of stocking the boat?" Alejandro asked.

"I have a chef flying in tomorrow, and he will handle all the food supplies and needs, but everything else I trust you to handle," I answered.

"When would you like to set sail, Ma'am?"

"I am thinking of September 17," I said.

"Okay, that is quick, but we will be ready."

I asked Scott if he had any questions.

"No, sounds like it is all under control," he replied with a smile.

"Okay, then I'll be in touch, and here is my number if you have any questions," I gave Alejandro my card; then Debbie, Scott, and I headed back to the car and on to the hotel.

"Can I treat you ladies, to dinner tonight?" Scott asked.

"Absolutely!" I answered.

"When and where should we meet you? "Debbie asked.

"Meet me in the hotel lobby at about seven. I know a couple of local places I think you'll enjoy," Scott said.

In just a few minutes, we were back at the resort and hurrying up to the room to change into our bikinis and hit the sand. The hotel and beach were beautiful.

"I picked up a brochure in the lobby about all the things to see and do down here. I thought we might look at it while we are on the beach," Debbie said.

"Good thought," I replied.

The resort had chairs on the beach, cabanas, tiki bars, and everything you could ever want to relax on the sand. "When you want a drink or snack, just bill it to the room," I told Debbie. We found a couple of chaise lounges and laid them out.

"Wow, I could get used to this life!" Debbie said.

"Well, I think I could too, eventually," I replied. "What did you think of the boat, Deb?"

"Are you kidding? I think it is paradise," Debbie replied. "When are you setting sail?"

"I am thinking in about ten days. I listed my house in New Bern with Jack, and I planned to have my stuff packed up and shipped to the Hamptons house."

"Are we going to the Sunset Celebration tonight?"

"I don't know. Let's see what Scott offers. We have the rest of the week at least."

"Have you seen Tortugas National Park?" Debbie asked.

"No, but I've heard of it. I always wanted to go spend a day there," I told her.

"Maybe we can day sail there with your boat, and test out your crew," Debbie suggested.

"Sounds like a good idea. I'll check with Alejandro," I answered.

"Time for another margarita, Stacy! Be right back," Debbie said with a wink. Seconds later, she returned with two tall frozen drinks.

"Yum, that is good," I said.

Later we went for a short swim, got a little more sun, drank a little more, and then decided to go up to the room for a siesta before Scott arrived.

We opened the sliding doors to bring the outside inside. The breeze off the ocean was amazing. I grabbed a shower to wash off the suntan oil and sand before I napped. When I got out, Debbie was sound asleep. I settled down into the big comfy chair and was soon dreaming, too.

All too soon, the alarm rang, and we had to get up and dress for dinner. I was glad I had brought a little sundress to slip on. I hadn't had a chance just to cut loose and have fun in a long time. Debbie came out ready to go, and she looked beautiful.

"We are going to dance all night!" Debbie said.

"I am ready, girlfriend," I answered. We met Scott in the lobby, and his jaw dropped.

"Hello ladies, you are dazzling!" Scott said.

"Thank you," I answered.

"We are ready for a night on the town, Counselor," Debbie replied.

"That sounds great; first stop, Parrot's Perch, a local bar for appetizers," Scott said.

We ordered conch fritters, a Key West specialty, and they were delicious!

"Rum is the liquor of the Keys," Scott told us. "So, let's order a round."

"I'm in," I said, "I would like a pina colada."

Debbie chimed in, "Bahama Mama for me."

Soon the drinks with their little umbrellas arrived. The music was as intoxicating as the drinks.

"So, where are you planning to sail away to?" Scott asked.

"I was thinking the Exumas, the Turks and Caicos—nothing too far away since it's September and hurricane season," I answered.

"That sounds like so much fun; we could run away and be pirates," Debbie said with a slightly drunken slur.

"Pirates, huh," Scott said with a smile.

"I just want to get the feel of the boat and sailing again," I told him. "It's been a long time since I was on the open water."

"Well, the captain seems knowledgeable enough to get you there and back safely," Scott said.

"Yes, Annie did well with choosing a crew. She seems to have thought of everything," I replied with a smile.

"Annie had my firm do extensive back-ground checks on each crew member to be sure you would be in good hands and be safe, the Caribbean is no place to be with strangers," Scott told me.

"I listed my house in New Bern and made arrangements to ship my stuff to the house in the Hamptons, we sail in about nine days," I stated.

At dinner at the next stop, we all had various types of seafood and it was terrific! "My sea bass was so good; I haven't had it in years," I exclaimed.

"Glad you are going to take a breather and let all this sink in. I can't think of any better way than out on a relaxing cruise in the Caribbean," Scott told us. We toasted with one more drink, and Scott headed back to his place.

"This is such a beautiful place," Debbie said as we strolled around town.

"Yes, it is," I answered her.

"I cannot imagine all the things you must be feeling inside with the death of Annie, the inheritance, and so much change in such a short time," Debbie said. "I just want you to know that I am here for you; whatever comes down the pipe," she added.

"Thank you, my friend. That means a lot. It has been a lot to absorb. I think I would like to start my very own magazine; if you were serious about coming to work for me. Why don't you come on the sailing trip with me, and we can make plans to get it started." I hoped she'd say yes.

"Really? WOW, okay," Debbie said. "I'll have to cancel my art show, but I think I can do that."

Eight days before we set sail, Chip called. "Good morning," he cheerily began. "I have been thinking about your offer to come sailing and cook," Chip said.

"Great," I replied. "Are you coming," I asked.

"Well, yes. I think I would like to do that," Chip said.

"I am so glad. Hurry up and get your butt down here so you can order supplies. I'll have a ticket waiting for you at the airport."

"Awesome, see you soon."

That was a significant relief; at least there would be one semi-familiar crew member and excellent food on board.

The rest of the crew consisted of Neo and Kosmos, sailors who would handle the sails and work the boat. We all spent the next few days getting ready for the trip, boning up on skills, securing supplies, and ensuring the crew was a go. Chip arrived and soon had food arrangements well in hand. Alejandro and Chip seemed to develop a great working relationship. Debbie and Chip also seemed to have had an instant attraction and were getting along great.

"So much to learn, so many terms," Debbie said.

"I know. I remember some of it from when I sailed with my dad," I answered. Excitement was definitely in the air. I took a walking meditation, a stroll on the dock and around the marina. Walking meditation is always a good choice when you are extremely busy! It gives you a chance to clear your mind and ground yourself in the moment. Life is made up of moments, and if we allow them to pass by without acknowledging them, we lose them forever. My affirmation for this day would be Live in the Moment. My gratitude journal will have new entries today. I am grateful that Chip decided to join us, my crew is trustworthy and exceptional, and I am about to set sail on the adventure of a lifetime.

Chapter Fourteen

Finally, it was the morning we were meant to set sail. Debbie and I arrived at the dock at 6:00 a.m. just in time to see a beautiful sunrise! The crew was already on board, and Chip was in the galley. Debbie and I climbed aboard as Neo loaded our bags. We were traveling relatively light, since we didn't need a ton of clothes, just bathing suits, suntan lotion, and a couple of outfits.

"Good morning, ladies," Alejandro greeted us. "We'll weigh anchor in about 30 minutes, so stow your gear below and make yourselves comfortable."

We climbed down the stairs. "Your room is on this side, and mine is over there," I told Debbie. As I walked into the master's quarters, I could hardly believe this dream of "just sailing away" was about to come true. I hoped Annie was up in heaven smiling down on us.

The boat was terrific in every aspect. The craftsmanship and attention to detail took my breath away. Yes, this was a boat for a rich person to entertain and show off in, and it was all mine. I stowed my gear and went back up top. Debbie soon followed.

Chip came onto the top deck to greet us. "Good morning," he said with a big smile. "Would you ladies care for some breakfast or coffee?"

"After we get underway would be great. I am starving," I said with a smile.

"Okay, just let me know what you would like, and I'll be happy to prepare it for you," Chip said as he returned to the galley.

"Hubba Hubba," Debbie said, "this cruise is going to be a blast. He is cute."

"Yes, he is, isn't he?" I agreed.

The morning fog was just lifting as Neo threw off the bowline and Kosmos threw off the stern. My excitement could barely be contained. The boat headed out to the South Channel; Flamingo Key was at our backs; we would soon pass Cow Key. After that, we would clear the Molasses Reef lighthouse in the Florida Straits, the narrow stretch of water between the United States and Cuba. The water is a beautiful green because it is relatively shallow. Farther out it will turn a deep blue as the bottom drops away to as much as 4,000 feet.

From here we head into Grand Bahama Bay. I remembered from when I was a little girl how it felt when the salt spray gently covered my body stroked by the soft breeze from the boat's motion. Alejandro maneuvered the boat through the shallows as if he had done it a million times.

Memories of sailing with my dad kept floating back. Our boat was nothing like this, just thirty-five feet, but plenty big for cruising around the North Carolina coast. My dad would have some time off from his job, and the two of us would load up the boat and haul it down to Morehead City to put in. We both loved the water, and my dad had spent a lifetime on it. He taught me about all the different kinds of birds and sea life that moved up and down the coast seasonally, the types of fish you could catch, and which ones were delicious to eat, and that weren't. I still remember his big smile as we sailed around the Pamlico Sound and Inland Waterway. I learned the way the weather systems roll in and out and when to be on guard. My dad al-ways said, "A big blow can come up in a few minutes out of nowhere, so you must always watch the sky, Stacy."

As we rolled along on the waves, the birds began to show up— Albatrosses, all kinds of gulls, and an occasional flamingo. It was late summer, so most migratory birds were arriving, and inland the assortment was a birder's paradise. The sun hit my face as morning broke, and the boat could open up, on the way toward Bimini. I got lost in the realization that I owned a boat; I was sailing on that boat, and I could afford to go anywhere in the world! I began to dream about sailing across the ocean to Europe, maybe Spain.

Once we passed Bimini, we were in open water. It was time to set sail and Neo and Kosmo quickly went to work. Once up, the sails caught wind and snapped into operation. In just a few minutes, we were cutting through the ocean waters, entirely powered by the wind. It was a beautiful morning. To my left, there were already two dolphins swimming along beside us with ease. I had forgotten what a lovely sight this was to experience first-hand. The smells, the views, and the sounds filled me with delight.

Alejandro came over to let me know that we would make Eleuthera by evening. "Are there any particular places you want to see?" he asked.

"On this trip, I will leave that pretty much up to your discretion," I told him. "I just want to escape for a while and enjoy the sea and the scenery."

"You have made this journey before?" Alejandro asked.

"Yes, when I was a young girl, I loved sailing and went out with my father regularly. But it has been a long time, too long since I have been on open water," I told him.

"Okay, then I will give you the typical tourist attraction cruise going down and then more local, cool stuff on the way back," Alejandro was firm yet gentle and kind. I felt attracted to him instantly. We would certainly have an exciting cruise.

Meanwhile, Debbie had gone down to the galley to order our breakfast. Chip soon had it ready and sent me a message to let me know. I had decided on a reasonably light breakfast this morning since I hadn't been out to sea in a long time. I didn't want any seasickness to embarrass me. My scrambled eggs and toast were waiting with my usual Diet Coke. Debbie had opted for an omelet and Chip did not disappoint.

"So, where are we headed?" Debbie asked.

"Well, we'll cross close to Bimini, which is the first Bahamian island we will be near. Ernest Hemmingway used to call it his favorite escape," I told her. "We'll dock there for the night and perhaps go ashore. I'm sure the crew will want to check the boat to make sure everything is in prime working order. Then we head towards about 360 other Bahamian islands and cays as we make our way to Exuma."

As I climbed back up to the top deck, I was a bit overwhelmed by my current reality. How could I possibly have buried my cousin and inherited billions of dollars? This situation is insane, but here I am. Now, what would I do going forward, to be worthy of such a gift of trust and love? I wanted to open a magazine. Debbie would make a fantastic editor. What kind of magazine did I want? Perhaps a travel magazine since we have the opportunity to travel pretty much without limits. I would set up a meeting with Debbie to discuss our options and develop a game plan. This trip would be an excellent way to begin a travel magazine and possibly a vlog. It felt great to start to dream and set some goals for my new life while remembering who I am and not losing myself to who Annie was.

But, for now, I wanted to sit in a chair, prop up my feet, and soak in the beauty surrounding me. It was terrific to nap in the sun with the wind floating across my body and a gentle spray now and then. All too soon, Alejandro came over to discuss our first day's trip.

"We will get to Bimini about mid-morning. I will drop anchor a little offshore, so the crew can check out the boat and make sure everything is working properly. I might even do a little fishing," Alejandro said.

"Are there any problems?" I asked.

"No, just a precautionary maneuver. I always tend to err on the proactive side on a boat I don't know," Alejandro said. "The weather conditions are right for us to cross the Gulf Stream, so it should be smooth sailing."

"Will we be able to go ashore in Bimini?" I asked.

"No, the stopover will take just a couple of hours, and I think we would be okay to continue sailing unless there is something you need onshore," Alejandro answered.

"No, that's okay. I wasn't sure how long it would take to get to Bimini," I said.

"It's only about fifty miles from Key West. It makes for a good short test run before we get out in open water," Alejandro told me. "We will be shallow enough for a swim if you ladies would like. We are headed to Eleuthera, which has been described as one of the most beautiful places on earth."

"I can't wait to see how it has changed in the 20 years since I was last here," I replied.

"We have a slip at a deep bay on the south end of the main island where we dock for the night. We can go ashore if you like and tour the island. I know it well," Alejandro said.

"That would be fun; I would like that. It will be nice to have someone who knows the lay of the land guiding us."

Debbie came above deck and settled into the chair beside me. "Wow, this is incredible," she said.

"We're going to dock in Eleuthera for the night, and Alejandro is taking us sightseeing on the island the next morning," I told her.

"I saw a couple of episodes about Eleuthera on the Island Hunter TV show. It was breath-taking," she said.

Chip joined us on deck with some ice-cold bottled water. It was a welcome distraction.

"Alejandro, would you like some water?" Chip asked.

"Thanks, Chip," he answered as he held out his hand.

"Wow, this is beautiful, isn't it," Chip said.

Before long, we were just off the shore of Bimini. Alejandro and the crew moored the boat and began their routine maintenance checks.

"Chip, if you want to get in some fishing, there are rigs and bait below deck in the storage area. I would suggest using a pink and blue jig to see if there is any wahoo about," Alejandro said.

"Sounds like supper to me, folks," Chip said as he headed below deck to get the rods and reels.

"I have a great underwater camera, and the water here is so clear.

Let's take a dip, Debbie, and give it a try," I said.

"Sounds great! Let me change," Debbie said.

As I went to get my camera, I could hear Alejandro telling the crew the routine maintenance stuff to check out. I wondered if everything was okay but couldn't sense any problems. So, I suited up, grabbed my gear, and was ready for some underwater photography.

The boat was outfitted with a dock area that lowered down to the water level for easy diving and swimming. The water was crystal clear, and we could see a few fish and some underwater plants in the ocean below us.

"I have a surprise for you," Alejandro said with a twinkle, Then, he lowered another door on the boat, revealing two brand new jet skis, fueled up and ready to go. "Have you ladies ever ridden a jet ski?" Alejandro asked.

"No, I can't say that I have," I replied.

"Me either," Debbie answered, "but they look like tons of fun."

"Chip," Alejandro called out.

"Yes, Captain?" Chip answered.

"Do you have time to come with me and give these ladies a tutorial on the jet ski?"

"Sure, sounds like fun," Chip answered as he made his way down to the lower deck.

Alejandro and Chip piloted the skis into the water and then motioned for us to climb on. The boat was moored in a beautiful area, about three hundred feet off the island. It was in a deep channel, so the skis came in handy. Alejandro and Chip took the skis close to shore where we could snorkel and get some great photography.

Beneath the surface of the water was spectacular, with a bright sky and clear water we could see right to the bottom. We were in water probably about ten feet deep, and there was sea life everywhere. We photographed sea turtles, a shark, and plant life on the ocean floor.

After about an hour of swimming, we climbed back on the jet skis. This time, Debbie and I drove. It was fun to dart around on the powerful machines. I would be lying if I said it didn't feel good to have Alejandro's arms around my waist holding me.

We drove back to the boat and onto the slips to reload the skis. "What a great surprise. I had no idea," I said.

"I took the liberty of ordering them since we had the built-in slip for them," Alejandro said.

"Good job, Captain," I smiled at him.

"That was awesome, and we got some great shots," Debbie said on the lift back to the main deck.

Debbie and I opted for the top deck lounge area to let the sun dry us and add to the tans we had started in the Keys.

Before long, Chip was catching fish right and left and soon had enough for dinner. Neo and Kosmos reported that everything was in good working order, and we were ready to sail.

Alejandro piloted the boat into Bimini and found our slip. Bimini is the westernmost of the Bahamas and closest to the United States. It is known as the sportfishing capital of the world.

Once we were secured, Alejandro told us we could go ashore so Debbie and I changed for some sightseeing. It would be fun to have a local guide for our tour.

Chip and Alejandro were waiting for us. "Chip, Bimini is the fishing capital of the world, so you might want to visit some of the bait shops in town. Ladies, what would you like to see while we are here?" Alejandro asked.

"I want to stroll through historic Alice Town, and, of course, we must visit the Fountain of Youth," Debbie said.

"Sounds good; just touristy stuff would be awesome," I added.

"Great, the town is within walking distance of the dock so let's start there," Alejandro said.

The streets of Bimini were lined with gift shops, sporting stores, and quaint boutiques. "This town must be the gateway for tourists coming to the islands," I said.

"Yes, it is a small town, about three hundred people, but the real treasures here are below the sea. The reef is amazing, and bull sharks have come to reside here. We can visit the Dolphin Museum if you like," Alejandro said.

"I can't wait to do a little shopping in these tackle shops. Do you ladies mind if I browse?" Chip asked.

"Of course not; we'll be in this boutique while you're looking," I said.

We were delighted with all the cute island clothing in the store, and it didn't take long for me to find a couple of tank tops and a new pair of flip-flops.

"I love these sunglasses," Debbie said.

"Buy them," I told her.

When we went back to the street Alejandro and Chip were waiting. "I see you found something you liked," Alejandro said with a smile.

"Yes, who could resist?" I replied.

"I'm going to do some serious fishing with this new tackle. Look out, ocean, here I come!" Chip light-heartedly said.

"What about you Alejandro, didn't you find anything?" Chip asked.

"No, I try to travel light; my needs are pretty simple," Alejandro replied.

We toured the Dolphin Museum and took in all the sights and sounds of the island town. All too soon, it was time to return to the boat. As we walked down the dock towards the vessel, I couldn't help but take in the splendor of her; she was seventy-five' of beauty! I could hardly believe she was mine.

Chip made us a delightful supper with the wahoo he had caught earlier. I went to my quarters to check emails and catch up with Scott while we had good internet. Scott had asked me to send him frequent emails to ensure we were okay and so he could take care of anything we might need. It was good to have someone on shore who knew where we were at all times. I decided to go up on deck and catch the magnificent sunset that I was sure was coming any minute. I took my camera and climbed up.

Even viewing it from the docks was terrific! There is no other word to describe it. The port was alive with people from all over the world, some just landing here and others preparing to leave. I had never really thought about how life on a boat was a world entirely separate from that of other people. Simple, but complicated too. It was going to be fun to experience this new lifestyle and see if it was for me.

Alejandro sat down beside me in the lounge. "I hope you enjoyed your day," he said.

"Oh yes, it was very nice of you to take the time to show us around."

"It was my pleasure."

"Are we spending the night in port?"

"No, I thought if it were okay with you, we would head out tonight. There is a beautiful wind, and we have seen all Bimini has to offer unless we do some diving. Are you ready to sail on towards Eleuthera?" Alejandro asked.

"Sail at will, Captain," I replied.

I headed down to my quarters. It had been a big day, and I was tired. Sleep came quickly on the boat. The gentle rocking of the waves and the sounds of the wind in the sails soon put me into a deep slumber.

Chapter Fifteen

It was fantastic to wake up to the sun streaming in through my window in the morning. I made time for my morning ritual. Sitting quietly, I meditated to clear my mind. I took time to say a prayer and do my journaling. Today I was grateful for this fantastic opportunity to wake up on a boat and see the sunrise in the Atlantic Ocean. My affirmation for today would be to remember to be present. This life is something that I want to be present for, savoring every moment. It was indeed a generous gift from Annie to buy this boat, hire this crew, and give me this opportunity. I didn't want to miss a minute of it.

Up on deck, I was delighted to look in the distance and see a ship. As we approached Nassau, Eleuthera, I suspected we would see cruise ships up close and realize how small our vessel was in the grand scheme of boats.

We rounded the tip of Spanish Wells in the island chain and headed down the west side of the Grand Bahamas island chain into the deep water. The water turns to a beautiful dark blue, and you realize this is the tip of the open ocean. Basically, Venezuela lies south of us and Africa is to the east. The world suddenly became a lot smaller and easier to traverse, at least in my mind.

The sea life was incredible; birds were fishing in the open water. Now and then, one would dive completely underwater and come up with a fish for breakfast! Dolphins were swimming beside us and talking in their unique language. It was so beautiful and relaxing to just soak it all in, let the wind blow my hair, and allow my thoughts and dreams to run free.

We could see the island shores now as we slowed and dropped sail. Alejandro navigated past Powell Point lighthouse, and soon we were docked. The sun was high in the sky; we secured the boat with the crew and departed for the shore.

Debbie wanted to see the Glass Window and Pink Sands Beach and Chip chimed with "That sounds awesome!"

"All that sounds great, but I am here for the seafood," I quipped.

"You never get tired of seafood," Debbie agreed with a laugh.

"Alright, then," Alejandro said, "let's get a driver to pick us up at the marina, and we will get started."

The driver showed up right on time, in a jeep this time, not a limo. That was a wise change. Traversing the sandy beaches would be challenging in a limo.

The first stop was the Glass Window, a beautiful thin stretch of beach covered in white sand that looks like glass. On one side of the island, the water is emerald green, and on the other, it is deep blue. The bridge crossing the sand is glass, and the strip of land is only thirty feet wide. It truly is worth the stop. Debbie and I took the obligatory photos on the bridge and of the surrounding areas. I brought my good camera and took a ton of pictures to use in our new magazine.

From there we went to Pink Sands Beach. The sand is a soft, beautiful pink made up of the remains of insects that feed on the coral reef just offshore. The sandy beach, considered one of the best in all of the Bahamas, stretches for three miles and is 50-100 feet wide. By now our day was ending and right there was a perfect photo opportunity. I took at least a hundred photos to be sure I captured the peak of the afternoon sunset. The sky was alive, with shades of coral, orange, and red fading to purples and blues.

"I have never seen anything so beautiful!" I exclaimed to Alejandro.

"Nor have I," he said, looking directly at me. The power of that look was like an earthquake! Wow! Get a grip on yourself, girlie, I told myself. This attraction is not a good idea.

I smiled and walked towards Debbie and Chip, who was having a great time running and playing in the waves.

We decided that since we had brought the chef with us, we would have dinner out. Alejandro and Chip discussed where to go and decided we would dine on Caribbean food at a local place called The Front Porch. The menu offered a variety of items such as Callaloo, Jerk, and seafood. I decided on a conch fritter and Callaloo. The drinks of the night were Mojitos, and I must say they were delicious!

We all enjoyed the night out. The food was delicious, and the drinks flowed. Alejandro did a great job babysitting us all, as we might have drunk a little too much, but we all safely made it back to the boat. Once there, Alejandro helped me down the stairs to my quarters, I was a little tipsy as I wasn't used to drinking so much. He opened my door for me and helped me inside. He shut the door, and my heart stopped. Was this where he was going to kiss me? Yes, he kissed me, as I had never been kissed before. Then just like that, he lifted me and put me on the bed and was gone.

Early the following morning, the crew was readying the boat to sail. Dawn was breaking, and I knew Alejandro would be anxious to get into the wind. I climbed up onto the main deck just about the time the sun was rising.

"Ahoy, there! How are you feeling this morning?" Alejandro asked.

"Good morning. I feel just fine," I lied. Deep down, I was thanking God we weren't going to be in rough water today but just skirting the island chain.

"Stacy, about last night, I shouldn't have kissed you. I am sorry. You were so fragile and sweet, and I just got carried away," Alejandro said.

"It's okay. I appreciate you making sure I was tucked in and safe," I replied.

The morning was clear, and the sun was just beginning to show its power burning off the night. You could see the shorelines of the islands as we passed. The locals were getting ready for a day of conch fishing and tourists were milling around the docks waiting for a charter boat trip.

I asked Alejandro where we were headed today.

"Turks and Caicos," he replied.

"The history of these islands and the pirates that frequented them has always intrigued me," I told him.

"Pirates aren't just history; they still exist today," he said.

"Are we in any danger?"

"Mostly, the tourist destinations are safe, but you should always use precautions and remain aware of your surroundings," Alejandro told me.

"What about at sea?"

"The crew and I are no strangers to the use of weapons, and the boat is stocked for emergencies," Alejandro assured me.

Chip made his way topside to tell us breakfast was ready. Alejandro let Neo take the wheel and we went below to eat.

"Debbie sleeping in?" Chip asked.

"I guess. I haven't seen her this morning," I answered.

Breakfast looked delicious! Chip had an omelet station set up and was happy to take our order and make what our hearts desired. A ham and cheese omelet would hit the spot this morning, I thought.

Eventually, Debbie came stumbling into breakfast. "Good morning, Sunshine," I greeted her.

She growled back, "Good morning," so I assumed she was feeling the mojitos of the night before.

"When you feel put together, let's start working on that magazine," I told her.

"Okay," Debbie said and brightened up at the possibility of having something to do.

"Magazine?" Alejandro asked.

"We're putting together a plan to begin a travel magazine, something with beautiful color photos that readers can live vicariously through," I answered.

"So that's why all the photos," Alejandro answered.

"Yes, but we need hundreds more for just one article," I cautioned.

"I know of a few places at our next destination that might work," Alejandro replied.

That was fantastic! I was excited at the thought of being able to go ashore and take photos. However, our photo journey was not just to be taking pictures on shore. Alejandro slowed the boat and anchored just off Cat Is-land.

"Do you dive, Ma'am?" Alejandro asked.

"No, I've never done that," I answered.

"Then I will teach you," Alejandro replied.

"Do we have scuba gear onboard?" I asked.

"Yes, we have enough for four people." Alejandro offered.

"Is it dangerous?" Stacy questioned.

"If you mean, are their sharks, well yes, but I will keep you safe," Alejandro responded.

"Maybe we can start with snorkeling; I can do that," I suggested.

He laughed out loud and said, "Ok, but I didn't take you for the fearful type," Alejandro said.

"Well, I'm not, normally. It's just that this is all so new to me. I'm not sure about it," I replied.

Alejandro and I took the dinghy to shore, planning to snorkel and take underwater photos. We found the reef before we got to shore, so we rowed ashore, secured the dinghy, and swam back out to the reef. It was amazing to see so much sea life swimming in their natural habitat, freely gliding along! So many beautiful colors and species. There were corals of all descriptions and fish galore. I noticed Alejandro swim close to me, and I felt an eeriness as a coral reef shark swam past us. Alejandro gave me a thumbs-up that we were okay, and I was glad he was there.

We took hundreds of shots from beneath the surface and then swam back to the shore. Once there, we took a few more shots of the shoreline and the beach, as well as our sailboat out in the bay patiently awaiting our return.

"That was so much fun!" I exclaimed.

"Were you scared of the shark?" Alejandro asked.

"No, I knew you would take care of me," I said with a slight smile. We loaded our gear, boarded the dinghy, and headed back for some lunch. I hoped Chip had whipped up something delicious!

Sure enough, upon our arrival back at the boat, my chef was on the top deck grilling barbecued chicken. Boy, it smelled good! Chip paired the chicken, with a salad, and fresh pineapple slices with grated cheese. Even the crew commented on how good the lunch was.

"Chip, this is amazing. I'm sure glad you came along on this voyage," I told him.

"Thank you, Ma'am. Me, too," Chip replied.

"Can we get together after lunch for about an hour?" Debbie asked. "I have something to show you."

"Ok, now you have my curiosity up. What is it?" I was curious.

"I worked on our business plan for the magazine, so I want to go over it with you," she responded.

"Great," I told her.

Turning back to Chip I asked, "Do you need any supplies? We will be heading to Turks and Caicos tomorrow."

"Probably wouldn't hurt to get a few refills. I have a couple of new dishes I want to try," he responded.

"Ok, be sure to let Alejandro know," I told him.

Chapter Sixteen

Debbie and I went below to the conference room/office. "Okay, let's see what you got," I told her.

Debbie stood up and prepared to deliver her presentation as if it were in front of a board of twenty executives. I could tell she was very excited about the idea, and that was just what I wanted, passion!

"I thought we could name the magazine Just Sail Away," Debbie began. "We could do this as a monthly issue," Debbie explained, "as a monthly publication for anyone who sails or dreams of sailing. It would be a full-color publication with stories and photos from all the exotic locations in the world. Whoever picks this up won't be able to put it down," Debbie ended.

"I love it!" I responded. "Let's make some projections for expenditures and content."

With a big smile, Debbie said, "Already done; I am a step ahead of you." She then began explaining what her projections were with a January first issue. "I chose January so we could have plenty of time to get going, and what better way to brighten up winter doldrums than to Just Sail Away," she said. We worked out additional details such as publication location, office space, etc.

"How would you like to live in Boca?" I asked.

"Boca, you are kidding?" she answered.

"Well, I have the house there, and it would be a great office spot for the publication, it would give us credentials, as it in itself is an exotic location," I told her. "And, Chip is there," I said with a smirk.

Debbie laughed and said, "That would be phenomenal."

"Okay, let's go for a swim," I said.

We changed into our swimsuits, and I went back to the top deck to ask Alejandro to pull over so we could take a dip.

"Okay, let me make a course adjustment, and I will have you on a secluded private beach in about 30 minutes. Will that work?" he asked.

"Sounds perfect," I said. Debbie came up and we eagerly waited to drop anchor. We rounded a bend, and there was a magnificent private beach, just as Alejandro promised.

"Where are we?" I asked.

"This is known as Ragged Cay, a group of islands that aren't densely inhabited," he told me. When he gave the okay, we dived in. The water was calm and felt good as it engulfed our bodies, salty and warm. It felt refreshing on our skin. As we were swimming and playing in the water, we saw a group of turtles on the shore. I wondered if they were laying eggs.

"Hey, that would make some great shots for the magazine," Debbie said.

"You are right," I said.

Alejandro dove in about that time with our underwater camera. "Hey, did you guys see the turtles up near shore?" he asked.

"Yes, glad you brought the camera," Debbie said.

About that time, another loud splash announced that Chip had decided to join us.

We swam a little closer to the turtles, trying not to disturb them. We got some great shots of them swimming and coming out onto the sand. We even got some photos of them making nests for their eggs. I thought I'd better start a daily diary to record all the stories behind the pictures we were taking. So, we swam, got great shots of turtles, played, and laughed till we were exhausted.

We swam back to the boat, and Neo lowered the dive platform so we could quickly board. This boat was terrific, and it had everything you could need. When we got changed, we were all starving.

"So, what's for lunch, Chip?" I asked.

"Well, I am glad you asked," Chip said. "I threw together a stew with all the leftover seafood we have had over the past couple of days. I put it in the crockpot this morning, and I think you will enjoy it." He dipped us all brimming bowls of stew, and we ate as if we hadn't had a bite to eat in years.

"Compliments to our chef," I told Chip, and the rest of the crew chimed in as well.

After lunch, I wanted to go exploring ashore. "Debbie, would you like to go ashore with me to explore and relax?" I asked.

"That would be awesome. I would love to be able to paint something. I have been itching to do that since we got out to sea," Debbie replied.

"Great, I'll clear it with Alejandro," I told her.

As I went up the stairs, I thought about how good it would feel to be on the beach, just Debbie and I, exploring. Who knows when I have that freedom again?

"Alejandro, Debbie, and I want to go ashore for a couple of hours.

She wants to do some painting, and it would be nice for just us girls to go chill out and have some girl time," I said.

"I don't like for you to go ashore alone, but this should be as safe as anywhere," Alejandro reluctantly agreed.

Neo got the dingy ready and gave me a quick course on how to drive it, and we were off, humming along through the waves. Debbie and I pulled the little boat up onto the beach which was quiet and deserted. We walked up the beach a little way and looked around. We found a beautiful spot that Debbie liked and where she decided to setup her art stuff to paint.

"This is perfect. I can see the ocean meeting the sky and the beautiful pristine beach," Debbie said.

"Okay, then, madame artiste, let's see what you got," I said with a laugh.

She was already in her zone and utterly oblivious to my light-hearted joking. As she set up her easel, I took a little walk on the beach. It was a beautiful bay cut into the shoreline, safe from the ferocious beating of the waves—only soft ripples across the water and a slight sound of the tide as it rolled out to sea. As a child, I always loved to watch the tides roll in and out, and still do now that I am grown. My life seemed so far from that sweet childhood daydreaming. I decided today was the time to enjoy that sweet innocence once again and soak up this bit of beauty and freedom.

The sand was soft and delicate and there was a slight coral tint to it. When I looked closely, I understood why—thousands of pieces of broken shells intertwined with the grains of well-polished sand to make up the beachscape. A few seashells were intact, strewn by Mother Nature along the beach—small scotch bonnets and clams. An occasional clump of seaweed time dotted the shore. Seagulls were squawking overhead, searching for a school of fish to dine on.

I came upon a beautiful piece of gnarly driftwood that would be a prize worth taking home. Into my backpack, it went, mostly. I walked along the edge of the water till Debbie was entirely out of sight. It was nice to be all alone exploring. For the first time in years, I found that childlike wonder, and even found myself giggling from time to time as if seeing everything for the first time. I picked up a sand dollar and it went into the backpack —great treasures to remember this day.

The tide was out about four feet now, and I could see what had been lying beneath the shallow water. The sand rippled from the current. Wait, what is that over there glistening in the sun? As I got closer, I gasped when I saw it, a find indeed, a polished piece of sea glass with pinky-purple hues. Beside it was a piece with blues and greens—more treasure for the backpack.

As I scavenged along, I found a few shark teeth and a couple more shells. Up ahead was a good place to sit and rest for a few minutes. I decided this was an excellent spot to do meditation. I learned how helpful meditation was at combating stress which dramatically contributes to one's overall health, when I was doing a magazine story on the new Zen. Like most people, I had felt that meditation, affirmation, and all that was mainly malarky, but as I researched them, I found I was very wrong. They are easy, valuable tools to use for better all-over health. So, I did not want to get far away from this lifestyle practice from which I had seen great results. I sat down on the shore and began to clear my mind and focus on this beautiful part of the world I had been fortunate enough to spend some time in.

I focused on my affirmation of the day, as every end is a fresh start. I decided to embrace my new beginning with full force and be sure I did not lose the value of knowing where I came from in the process.

After my meditation, I saw a woman walking down the beach. She was brown as a berry with long flowing grey hair—someone local. I could tell by the way she carried herself she was very familiar with this place.

As she drew closer, I gave her a big smile and said hello. She looked at me for a moment studying me, and then replied, "Hello. I see you are a collector.

"A collector?" I questioned.

"The driftwood sticking out of your backpack," the woman replied with a smile.

"Oh, I had forgotten it," I replied. "It's a habit from when I was a kid. I would pick up all kinds of stuff as I explored everywhere."

"So, you haven't lost your childlike spirit, I see." She was still smiling.

"I had lost it, but today I seem to have found it again," I told her.

"The world today is so busy and is very easy to get lost in," she said. "Come, let's sit down and chat. I don't often get visitors." We sat down on the log, and I laid my backpack on the ground beside us.

"I hope I am not trespassing. It is so beautiful here, and I was just wandering and daydreaming," I said.

"So, where are you from?" she asked.

"North Carolina in the United States," I replied. "How about you?"

"Well, I was born not far from here on my farm and have lived on these islands all my life," the woman replied.

"It is beautiful here," I replied.

"Yes, but it is an island. I left once to go to school. My family wanted me to get a good education," she told me. "Seems funny now; living here, you don't need a fancy education. But it came in handy.

"Our island has seen many changes, and our people needed someone to lead them, so I was elected."

"Awesome," I replied. I had no idea what the older woman was talking about, but clearly, she was well-respected and wise.

"Yes, many changes, some good, some not so good, but change is inevitable," she said.

I could see many thoughts rolling across her tanned brow. "Yes, change comes for us all, ready or not," I replied.

"Change can be hard to accept. I have learned to embrace it; when rough waters come, hold your breath and bob. They will soon calm," she said.

"I guess embracing change is the best way to survive it," I said.

"I would like to think of it as a poem, something this piece of ground, our island has taught me.

"Let the winds blow, Let the water rise, Storms will come and go, Yet I will survive.'

"Now, child, you better be getting back down to the beach. The tide will be coming in and your way back will be blocked," the woman said as she stood up. "My name is Neela, Neela Malone. What's yours?" she asked.

"I am Stacy," I replied.

"Well, Stacy, if you come this way again, stop by; I live over that rise. Be careful going back," she said and turned to go.

"Thank you, I never thought about the tides," I told her and picked up my backpack.

"On an island, you learn to live and die by the tides," she said.

I headed back, the way I had come at a little faster pace than before. Just as Neela had said, the tide began to roll in. I got back to where Debbie was painting just in time. "Tides are coming in. We better go," I called out to her.

"I am way ahead of you," she answered. As I walked closer, I could see she had already packed her painting equipment and was waiting for me to return. Her painting was beautiful; I had forgotten how talented she was.

"Can you give me a hand with my bag, while I get the canvas and the easel? It is still a little wet," Debbie said.

"Sure," I replied, and we made our way back to the dingy. We didn't have to pull it very far to be back in the water; the tide had come in fast. The little motor cranked on the first pull, and we were humming across the waves back to the boat. As we made our way back, I told Debbie about meeting the sweet older woman.

"What did you say her name was?" Debbie asked.

"Neela Malone, she was very wise and nice," I responded.

"Do you know who Neela Malone is?" Debbie questioned.

"I just told you," I answered, a little annoyed with this conversation.

"She is only the Governor of this island chain," Debbie answered.

"The Governor?"

"Yes. How did you meet her? Was she alone?"

"I was wandering down the shore, and she was walking alone on the beach. We sat and talked and then went our separate ways."

"You must have wandered onto her estate," Debbie said.

"There weren't any fences, but she said she lived over the rise and to stop by and see her anytime," I responded.

"Wow, only you," Debbie answered with a laugh.

When we returned, I could see Alejandro was worried. We had been gone a long time, and we were out from under his watchful eye.

"Please don't just take off and assume you will be fine. There are places and people here that aren't safe or trustworthy," Alejandro cautioned with a bit of a scowl.

"We were fine," I said.

"This time. You were lucky," Alejandro responded.

I decided not to tell him all the adventure details and went downstairs to recover from the tongue-lashing. Debbie had put away all her gear, and the painting was on the easel to dry.

"Your painting is beautiful," I told her. "I'm glad to see you painting again."

"I am glad you like it. It is a gift for your new house," Debbie said with a smile. "A piece to remember today along with your treasures. I know your backpack must be full," Debbie said with a giggle.

About that time, Alejandro called out for me to come topside. I had a visitor. "A visitor?" I thought.

A well-dressed man holding an envelope stood on the deck. "Stacy, I presume?" the man said.

"Yes," I replied.

"Mrs. Malone requested that I bring you this," and he handed me the envelope. It was beautiful fine linen paper and had the Governor's seal on the outside. As I opened it my hand trembled. I could see the look of worry on Alejandro's face.

"Mrs. Malone would like to invite you and your crew to the mansion for dinner," the man said.

The note said,

> Hello again. I enjoyed meeting you this afternoon and would love for you and your crew to come for dinner tonight. Please RSVP to my courier so that the staff can prepare. I will send a boat for you at about 7 p.m. if that works.
> Sincerely, Neela.

I looked at Alejandro, and he quickly said, "Yes, tell the Governor we would love to at-tend."

"7 p.m. will be fine," I added.

"Brilliant, I will let Ms. Malone know," he responded and got back in his dingy.

After the courier was out of earshot, Alejandro was full of questions, of course. I told him about wandering down the beach and our chance meeting.

"I can't believe you wandered off alone," Alejandro began. "You think you are safe, but now you can see what I was telling you. You didn't even know you were being watched every second, did you? You didn't know that there was probably a rifle pointing at your head in case you moved wrong, while in the Governor's presence. You have to realize and understand that there are dangers here that you are not familiar with. This is not North Carolina!"

"Let me tell you a thing or two, Bud. I am a grown woman. I am not stupid, and I certainly don't need you to tell me when I can come and go. That is my business. I appreciate your concern, but I am not a child. I am going below. Do I need your permission? I asked.

He did not answer but just walked away. I made my way down to the staff quarters to cool down. I sent Scott a quick email to tell him of the meeting and seek advice on proceeding. I knew he would be a good voice of reason.

In answer to Debbie's question about what had happened, I said, "That was interesting. It was a courier from Neela, inviting us all to the mansion for dinner tonight. She is sending a boat for us at about 7 p.m. She invited the whole crew."

"That is a bit odd to invite the whole crew," Debbie responded.

I was afraid she was right; it was odd. I hoped I would hear from Scott before we had to go. I went into the galley and called out, "Chip?"

"Yes, boss," Chip replied.

"We are invited to the Governor's mansion for dinner tonight. They are sending a boat to pick us up at about 7 p.m. Governor Neela Malone and I met on the beach earlier today, and she invited the whole crew," I told him.

"The whole crew? That is odd," Chip said.

"I thought so, too, but that is what the invitation read," I told him.

"I sure wouldn't miss that opportunity. I will be ready," Chip answered.

As I headed back to my room to check my emails, I met Neo in the hallway.

"Ma'am, you look worried," Neo said.

"I am," I told him about the day, the invitation, and my scuffle with Alejandro.

"Ma'am, I have known Neela Malone most of my life. She is a great leader and a fierce woman. She has done many good things for our people. She will be a powerful ally for you, and you can trust what she says," he assured me. "As for Alejandro, he was just worried about you."

"I know," I told him. "Thanks for the heads up about Governor Malone," I told him, then I asked him, "Why did she invite the whole crew to dinner?"

"It is a gesture of politeness to treat us all as her equals, she believes in equality for all people and that we all play a role in the world, not just the rich folks," Neo explained.

I felt better after talking to him, but I would still like to hear that from Scott. I busied myself checking emails and figuring out what to wear—finally, that familiar ding on the computer heralded an answer from Scott. The email assured me that Neela Malone was trustworthy. "How did you manage to wrangle an invitation from the Governor on your first visit there?" he asked.

I laughed out loud when I read it and began typing my answer. It was kind of funny if you think about it. I felt much better about the dinner. Scott told me that Neela's office had inquired about me. They checked the boat's registration, and it led to his office. He did not tell them that I was a new heiress but rather said I was a relative of the owner and enjoying a quick vacation. So at least for now, they didn't know all my secrets.

Chapter Seventeen

The Governor's boat arrived promptly at 7 p.m. I had told Alejandro about Scott's reply, and he was relieved that they thought I was just a relative for now. We all boarded and were treated to a glass of champagne as we made our way up the cove. Neo and Kosmos stayed on the ship to guard it.

As we rounded the bend, there sat the mansion and a mansion it was indeed—a grand plantation, a low country-style big house with a perfectly manicured lawn. The boat took us up to the dock where a driver was waiting at the pier. He had a cute island-style golf cart to give us a ride up the hill to the house.

As we made our way up, the driver told us a bit about the house's history. "It was built in the 1800s and has been in Ms. Malone's family all that time. This was originally a sugar cane plantation, and they made rum. Some of the finest rum in all the world," he told us. It was not unusual to be a sugar plantation or make rum in this part of the world. The house had a grand entrance and a welcoming feel.

Another servant showed us the way to the parlor where Neela was waiting for us. "Ah, you made it," she said with a smile as she stretched out her arms to hug me.

"Yes, thank you so much for the gracious invitation," I told her as we embraced.

"My pleasure, my dear. I don't get company very often," Neela said with a twinkle in her eye. "Now, introduce me to your friends."

"Of course, I am sorry. Here is Alejandro, our ship's captain," I told her.

"Governor, it is a pleasure to meet you," Alejandro said as he shook her hand.

"This is my business partner and best friend, Debbie," I said.

"Debbie, yes, you are the artist," Ms. Malone said.

"Yes, Ma'am, I like to think I am," Debbie said, with a smile.

"Governor, this is Chip, our chef," I said.

"A chef! If I had known you were bringing a chef, we would have upped our menu," the Governor said with a laugh.

"A pleasure to meet you, Governor," Chip said, as he shook her hand.

About that time, an impeccably dressed server came to the door and said, "Governor, dinner is served."

Neela turned to us and said, "Well folks, let's eat. Follow me."

We followed her down the hall and could not help but notice the portraits on the walls. These must be her family lineage. You could tell some were painted in the style of the Dutch Masters. Debbie was, of course, intrigued, and she passed near them to get a better look.

The table was exceptionally long and could easily seat more than twenty people. It was covered with white tablecloths, beautiful fresh flowers, and bone china. Delicate crystal goblets and silverware graced the table. It was a setting that matched the grandeur of the home.

"Well, you may sit wherever you like," the Governor told us and sat at the head of the table.

The waiters pulled chairs out for Debbie and me as Chip and Alejandro took seats across from us.

"What a beautiful home you have, Ma'am," I said.

"Thank you, it has been in my family for two hundred years," the Governor responded. The waiters were busy pouring wine and water for each of us, and the first course arrived—a delicate cold soup made with cucumbers.

"Alejandro where are you from?" the Governor asked.

"I was born in St. Lucia," Alejandro answered.

"Yes, I thought so. I met your mother once, and she is a doctor, correct?" the Governor said.

"Yes, Ma'am, she is," Alejandro responded.

"A charming and brilliant woman," the Governor added.

"So, Chip, you are a chef. Where did you go to school?" the Governor asked.

"I formally attended Johnston and Wales Culinary Institute in Charleston, South Carolina, Ma'am," he answered.

"Very nice. An outstanding school indeed," the Governor commented.

"Stacy, what brings you to the Islands?" the Governor asked.

"Vacation, I hadn't been on vacation in a long time, and sailing away to the islands, well, who could resist that?" I said.

"I see," was all the Governor said.

We continued to make small talk as the meal was being served. The salad course came and finally the main course. A delicious sea bass delicately baked with a vibrant sauce. Delicious indeed.

"Ma'am, I must meet your chef and give him my compliments," Chip told the Governor.

"Call me Neela, son. Of course, you are welcome to visit the kitchen after dinner," Neela said.

We all enjoyed the meal and the wine. Soon dessert was served—a cloud of whipped cream resting on delicate strawberries and a buttery yellow cake. Strawberry shortcake in any language is delicious! This cake was no exception.

"I hope everyone enjoyed the meal. Let's retire to the veranda to talk and enjoy some of our pride and joy, our rum," Neela said.

Everyone followed Neela to the veranda where a servant had already brought in a bottle of rum, and glasses. "My family has been making rum here since the 1830s. I hope you enjoy the shot," Neela said and downed her drink.

We all followed suit and enjoyed the sweet sting as the white liquor hit our throats.

"Very smooth and delicious," Alejandro said.

"I can see a million ways to use this in drinks, food, and pleasure," Chip said.

Debbie and I nodded in agreement.

"Stacy, could you come with me? I want to show you something," Neela said.

I got up to follow her. Alejandro had a guarded look on his face as we passed. She took me down the hall to a library and carefully retrieved a book that was in a box. Neela opened it up and inside some trinket items, stuff like I collect. Neela pulled out a little silver necklace and handed it to me, saying, "This was my grandmother's necklace. She went to the island of the Dominican Republic for her honeymoon when she was married. She was a collector like you and picked up this pretty blue stone she found in the grass and stuck it in her pocket. When she got home, she had it made into a necklace to remember the trip. The bluestone turned out to be larimar. Larimar is only found in one place in the world, and that is the Dominican Republic. I want you to have it.

"Oh, it is beautiful! But I couldn't take it," I said.

"Yes, it is yours. I know there is more to you than meets the eye. Secrets you are not ready to share, but I want you to know that I am your friend, your ally. You can trust me, and if you ever need a haven to call home, you will find it here," Neela said. "Now, put it on, and let's re-join the others."

I put the necklace on, and it was the most beautiful blue I had ever seen. The color was somewhere between the ocean and the sky. I loved it!

The others were all enjoying the night on the Veranda and the rum. "Ma'am, this has been a lovely evening, but we need to get back to the boat. We are sailing early in the morning for Turks and Caicos, so we must get some much-needed sleep," Alejandro said.

"Of course. I enjoyed your visit. Thank you for coming," Neela said. "The boat will be waiting for you at the dock. Please come again," she added.

The butler appeared again with the golf cart. When we got to the pier, the butler handed me an envelope and said, "The Governor wanted you to read this when you get back on your boat. Have a safe trip."

As we rode back to the boat, we were all silent. What a beautiful evening, the stars were out, and the sky was lit up like fireworks—a calm, beautiful Caribbean night. When we got back to the boat, we were all tired.

"Neo, was everything okay while we were gone?" Alejandro asked.

"Quiet and peaceful, Boss, just like we like it," Neo replied.

"I am hitting the sack," Debbie said and went below.

"I'm headed down to the galley to prep for breakfast. Thanks for the evening, and I will see you in the morning," Chip said and disappeared below.

"What did the Governor show you?" Alejandro asked.

"She took me to her library and gave me this necklace. It was her grandmother's," I told him.

"What?" Alejandro was surprised.

"Yeah, she said her grandmother was a collector like me, and she wanted me to have it," I said.

"It is beautiful, and so are you. I am sorry if I was harsh with you earlier. I was distraught," Alejandro said.

"I know. I am sorry, too," I said.

"She also gave me another letter to read when I got back on the boat," I confided to him.

"Well, you should read it, then," Alejandro said. "Would you like some privacy, or is it something you want to share?"

"I can share," I answered and opened the envelope. Inside was a note that reminded me that Neela was a friend and her private contact info if I needed anything.

"You must have made an impression," Alejandro said.

"We instantly hit it off, I had no idea who she was, and perhaps I understand why that touched her heart. I accepted her for herself, not her position. I get it," I said.

"Why don't you go on down to bed? I need to chart our course for the morning and take the first watch," Alejandro quietly said. I went below, anxious to crawl into bed. It had been a long day, and there was a lot to think about, having had dinner with the Governor.

Chapter Eighteen

It was a beautiful morning, and I could feel the motion of the boat and hear the sound of the engine as we chugged out into deeper water. Then came the noise the rigging makes when the sails are being raised. Yep, there it was, the sound when the sails catch the wind. We were on our way to our next adventure—a quick meditation and journaling. Today's affirmation was yes, you can!

I got dressed and made my way to the galley for breakfast. Alejandro came in to let us know that it was about 250 miles to the Turks and Caicos, and we would be at sea for a few days until we reached there.

"I am going to go out into the open ocean so we can make better time. There won't be as much tourist traffic and supply ships, "Alejandro explained.

"Where is the Bermuda Triangle?" I asked.

"Technically, it runs from San Juan, Puerto Rico, to Bermuda, then to Miami, so we are skimming the edge," Alejandro answered.

"Oh, are we safe?" I asked.

"Of course," he replied. He went on to explain that we had already crossed the Gulf Stream, which is like an enormous 45-mile-wide river in the Atlantic Ocean. It flows extremely fast and has strong currents. Sailing through the Gulf Stream with winds that reach twenty knots can be a terrifying experience. An eight-hour sailing excursion through the Gulf Stream can turn into a 13-hour brush with death-with severe weather and high winds.

That night I slept like a log; the salty air was so good for me. When I woke up, we were well underway, with nothing in sight but blue skies and blue water. The sails had caught wind, and the bow wave was lapping against the hull of the boat—salty spray shooting up from the bow and birds were flying along beside us calling. I looked over the rail to see a giant sea turtle puttering along on his way to who knows where just free and happy.

"Good morning, Alejandro," I said.

"Good morning," he replied. "Would you like to start learning how to sail the boat?"

"Me? Sure," I replied. I walked over to the steering wheel, and my lesson began. Alejandro showed me the compass and explained about reading it. I already knew how to read navigational charts from when I was a kid. Not much had changed there. We talked about crossing the tropics, the dol-drums, and storms. I hadn't been through a storm on a boat in 20 years. One time when we were in the Caribbean, thunderstorms had come up with thunder and lightning strikes. But, my dad was confident and protective, so I was never scared.

Heading out to open water was exciting. It had been too long since I had been out that far. Sitting on the deck, no matter which direction you turn, there is nothing but water and sky! Today was a wonderful day, the sun was shining, and it was going to be pretty warm even though it was September and chilly at home, here it was eternal summer.

I spotted a whale off our port side effortlessly swimming and surfacing for air. The enormous creatures are so elegant and beautiful. This one was a humpback whale and it looked like a little one swimming by its mom's side. That is a sight I will never forget, the beauty of a mother and baby. Then I realized it was a pod of whales, maybe four in this group. They swim in this warm water to give birth and mate. I ran for my camera. This sighting was too good to pass up.

When I returned topside, they were still there, swimming effortlessly along; Mother Nature guiding them, pushing them to their destination. The photos were amazing! The whales' migration would make an excellent article for the new publication.

My second sailing lesson consisted of swabbing the deck, polishing the brass, and learning about knot tying. These chores were not as much fun as the first but were necessary items. I liked learning; even though I was rich, I wanted to do things for myself. I liked being independent. I went down below to get out of the sun for a while and do some more brass polishing.

Debbie and Chip were talking in the galley. Those two had been inseparable since we boarded. I was incredibly happy for them. Debbie hadn't had anyone close to her in a long time, and Chip was a good guy.

I went to my room to clean and paid attention to the details and artisanship of the vessel. It indeed was a work of art, built with love and honesty. I was immensely proud to own such a fine vessel.

Kosmos came down the stairs calling, "Stacy."

"Hey, I am in here," I answered.

"Captain Alejandro wants you up on deck, Ma'am," Kosmos said.

"Okay, be right up," I answered.

When I got up on deck, I didn't like what I was seeing. The sky was dark and hanging with black clouds all around us. The wind was picking up, and you could feel the calm before the storm. "Well, looks like we are in for a squall," Alejandro said, with a concerned look on his face.

"A squall, like a quick thunderstorm?" I asked hopefully.

"The weather service says it is a line of severe thunderstorms," he replied.

"So, what do we do?" I asked.

"The line is pretty large, and the land is a good bit away," he replied and explained that we could ride it out or try to power through.

I summoned all my courage and conviction looked him in the eye, and said, "I trust your experience and judgment, so it is your call," I told him.

Alejandro smiled and said, "Thank you, I won't let you down."

"Ok, well, head down below, and you, Chip, and Debbie stay there. Get in a good safe spot as the boat will roll and toss a lot during the storm, but trust that we will be okay," he told me.

"Aye, Aye, sir," I replied and headed below. "Chip, Debbie come here a second," I called.

"Hey, what's up?" Chip answered. Debbie came into the hallway where I was waiting, and I told them of the impending storm. They both looked concerned, and I reassured them that Alejandro, Kosmos, and Neo were experts at this stuff, and we would all be okay. I suggested that we all get a dose of seasick medicine and find a safe, comfortable place to ride out the storm.

As the storm rolled in, the sky began to darken, the hum of our motor was a comfort, and we could feel Alejandro going as fast as she would go away from the storm. His strategy was to try to sail away from it. The wind began to roar, and the boat started to rock. The sails had been put down and secured, and the bow was headed into the waves, which I remembered Daddy had always told me to do. I knew we were in good hands with our crew.

We could hear the wind roaring and see the spray from the waves. The boat had a rhythmic rock to it, and it was good to be in a safe place, sitting down to ride it out. Since I knew Debbie and Chip were nervous, I decided to get them to talk about the magazine.

"I was thinking about our new venture with Just Sail Away," I told them.

"Oh yeah, me too. It's all I think about, it seems," Debbie replied.

"What is Just Sail Away?" Chip asked.

"It's a new magazine that Stacy and I are going to publish," Debbie responded.

"A travel magazine, full-color photos, and stories about our adventures on the boat, and hundreds of others' adventures as well," I added. The thunder was deafening, and the lightning was crackling and striking all around us.

"That sounds impressive, the sailing community is huge, and there are thousands who are sailors at heart," Chip said. The wind picked up, and the waves began to rock the boat vigorously.

"I love that term "sailors at heart," I told him. We heard a loud crack of thunder in the distance. The wind howled so loud we could barely hear each other speak. The lightning was striking the water, but so far had missed us. The rain was coming down in buckets.

"Well, I was thinking it would be great to have a column about cooking at sea," I said. "Chip, would that be something you would like to be involved with?"

"Heck yeah," was his quick response. So as the boat rolled back and forth, thunder cracked, and sometimes we secretly prayed, we formulated the new section for the magazine. "That recipe for the fish stew you made for lunch would be a terrific addition; everyone at sea has leftover seafood," I told him.

"Sounds like a great start. I'll type it up for you," Chip answered.

Then, just like that, the rain stopped like someone shut off a valve. Soon we could see the tinge of blue sky through the window and knew we had gotten through.

Chip said, "I am going to check on my gear and then fix us a fantastic lunch. I am sure everyone is starving after that storm."

"That sounds great," Debbie said, "and I am going to the office to capture all we discussed about the new column."

I headed up top to see if there were any damages.

"How did you fare in your first squall?" Alejandro asked.

"It wasn't too bad." I told him that our new magazine to include a cooking column with Chip, so it kept us all occupied mentally," I told him." You guys did an excellent job!"

"Thank you, that means a lot," Alejandro answered.

"Where are we?" I asked.

He laughed and said, "We are in the Atlantic Ocean."

"Well, duh," I answered back.

Then he looked at me very seriously and said, "Actually, I have no idea, but we can get out the charts and figure it out." After taking some readings and making some calculations, Alejandro decided we were about thirty-five miles off-course south of where he originally intended to go. The National Maritime Weather Service began to ding, and there was an alert waiting. Alejandro quickly retrieved it and looked very worried.

"This is not good," he said.

"What is it, more thunderstorms?" I asked.

"A tropical depression is forming off the coast of Africa," Alejandro answered.

"A hurricane!" I exclaimed.

"Well, not yet, but it looks like it could be," he answered and then added, "We just need to watch it closely."

Chapter Nineteen

Just then, we got the text from below that lunch was ready. "Let's not tell Debbie and Chip just yet. No need to worry them," Alejandro told me. I nodded in agreement. Once below, we were greeted by the happy faces of Debbie, Chip, Neo, and Kosmos.

"The guys here were doing a little fishing right after the storm and caught some beautiful mahi mahi, so voilà, lunch is served," Chip proudly told us. He had prepared us a feast, as usual! Beautifully grilled mahi mahi, a fresh salad, and couscous.

Alejandro smiled and said, "Well, fellas, I guess this beat anything we have been used to with our cooking," and sat down. We all ate hardy and happily discussed the squall line and our good fortune of getting ahead of it.

I could see that Alejandro was worried about the potential for a hurricane. I could certainly understand why. We are in the Atlantic Ocean with an unknown boat, a 3-man crew, and three flatlanders. "Alejandro, can I speak to you for a moment in the office?" I asked.

We headed into the office, the only place on the boat where we could speak freely and in private. "I know our original course was Turks and Caicos and a leisurely trip, but the impending storm changes things," I began.

"Yes, it does," Alejandro replied.

"What do you think we should do?" I asked.

"We can sail further south, down past Puerto Rico. We could visit Martinique, St. Lucia, that area, and we would be far enough south that the likelihood of a hurricane would be extremely diminished," Alejandro said.

"Well, that sounds like a great solution," I told him.

"Yes, we can head to San Juan, Puerto Rico, to fuel up. But sailing through the Mona Passage is treacherous, and it would be better to stay in the open ocean and come in from the west side," Alejandro explained.

"Again, I trust you completely, so whatever you decide is okay," I answered.

"We won't go ashore on the fuel stop. I don't want to take the time if that's okay," Alejandro said.

"Of course," I answered.

"Puerto Rico is an American possession; the crew and I have the necessary paperwork. Do you all have your passports?" Alejandro asked.

"I'll double-check," I said.

We went back to the galley to tell the crew about our course change. "We decided to skip Turks and Caicos, and head straight on down to St Lucia and points south. We can catch the others on the way back up," I told them. "Please check your passports and make sure they are handy and up to date," I said.

Everyone agreed that the plan was okay with them; after all, they were mostly along for the ride.

"I'll need to go into port and pick up some supplies when we get there," Chip said.

"If you can wait, I would prefer to put that off till we get a little farther south, where the waters and weather are friendlier," Alejandro added.

"Sure, but Neo and Kosmos, you might need to do some serious fishing," Chip replied.

"We will be glad to," Neo answered with a smile.

Alejandro called Neo and Kosmos to set sail. The storms were over for now, and we could catch the wind and travel southwest straight toward the island chains. Once we gots to the US Virgin Island chain, we would shimmy down along the shorelines to St. Lucia to ride out any storms.

"How long will it take us to get to St. Lucia?" I asked.

"Two to three days depending on weather, wind, and currents," Alejandro answered.

"Well, I guess we better get this bucket in the wind," I said.

"Yes, Ma'am," Alejandro answered. Neo and Kosmos were already on deck, preparing to sail.

With a substantial portion of the day left, I decided to read one of the books I had brought along for the ride. I got comfortable up on the top deck and settled in for some reading time. I hadn't taken the time to read a book in quite a while. Reading is such a wonderful gift—traveling all over the universe, having adventures, and home in time for supper. You can't beat it. Maybe I would even get time to begin authoring a book myself soon. The book was quite good, a cozy murder mystery. I enjoyed reading these as they aren't too graphic but still filled with suspense. Nothing to keep you up at night just really keeps you guessing. I read steadily for about three hours until I finished it.

I hadn't checked my emails in a couple of days, so I decided to check in below. The first email was from Scott, mostly updating me about corporate business, bank accounts, and life in Boca. He was curious to see where we were since there was a storm brewing. I sat down and wrote back to him to let him know our sailing plans, answer his questions about corporate issues, and check-in. He quickly responded to my email, so I must have caught him in his office. He was glad we were so far south and said it was a testament to Alejandro's skill as a captain, with which I entirely agreed. He also warned me not to let anyone know who I was.

"You are traveling in dangerous waters and some dangerous areas where the long arm of America may not be able to protect you," Scott said. I thought, WOW, I never even considered that it would be dangerous.

He went on to tell me," Don't worry about this, just be aware. Kidnapping happens sometimes, and you could be a prime target."

Now there was something to give me nightmares. I went on through the emails; most were junk. Finally, an email from my editor, Paula. She wanted to check up on me and update me on NC life, fall, and the magazine. She was looking for December story ideas. So, I sat down to think about what would make a relevant story that hadn't been done to death.

Let's see, what would be a family tradition that is commonly done but not thought of as such? Opening presents on Christmas Eve versus Christmas morning, caroling, when to decorate the tree, the house, the yard, Homemade goodies, or store-bought, there were tons of things to consider. I decided an excellent story for the new travel magazine would be Christmas – Should we travel or stay home? That would work for Zest as well. I decided to pitch it to Paula and see.

Debbie had sent me an email recapping our conversations and ideas about Just Sail Away. She is so efficient; I love her! I decided to meet with her and Chip tomorrow while we were at sea to work on the editorial calendar for the upcoming year. I sent them each an email invitation with an itinerary.

I went up on deck and said, "Alejandro, Scott sent me an email and reminded me to be very careful about my identity. He was worried that someone might kidnap me for ransom."

"He is very accurate about it being a possibility; we must be careful about that," Alejandro said. "If we go into port or town, you can pose as my girlfriend, and we will tell anyone who asks that the boat owner is meeting us somewhere in route."

"Okay, that sounds plausible," I said.

"It's no big deal. I am used to being captain for some high rollers, and I trust Neo and Kosmos with my life," Alejandro told me. "Don't worry."

I was glad we had that conversation; I did feel a little better. I went back below to work some more on the computer. I put on some music and made notes about where we were, traveling, ideas, kind of like a journal. I need-ed to begin to document our adventures, expenses, experiences, etc. The photos we took were outstanding. I downloaded them and stored them in the cloud with access for Debbie as editor-in-chief.

I needed to discuss the magazine ideas and plans with Scott to get all the legalities taken care of setup a payroll account for Debbie, etc. That would be tomorrow's work assignment. I caught a little news online about the storm brewing; it sounded pretty bad. I was glad we were well south of the projected path and would not threaten my home. But, home, just exactly where was that? I guess the Hamptons and the boat for now. I could hardly believe all the things that had transpired in the last couple of months! I had gone from living in little New Bern, North Carolina, and a moderately successful career as a writer to being an heiress! The circumstances surrounding me at this moment are the things used to make movies. I thought about how all this came to be. A life that was built for someone else was now mine by default. At times this was overwhelming. I still could hardly believe it, yet here I was, living it.

I took a moment and thought about my cousin, so successful, married, and happy, and then having her life wind up so tragically. Her husband dies in an accident and then she is diagnosed with and dies from cancer. Life is so precious and so short. I must remember to live in the moment and cherish every one of them. Tomorrow is not promised to any of us.

Soon it was time for dinner, and once again, Chip had prepared a feast! Tonight's menu consisted of beef roast, potatoes, carrots, and onions with a dash of mushrooms. Then he added some of my favorites— real mashed potatoes and gravy, homemade yeast rolls, and coconut cake. "Chip, if you keep this up, I will have to buy all new clothes," I said with a laugh, "but, don't stop."

The crew was in good spirits, and everyone was enjoying the trip. Debbie told us she had seen a pod of whales breaching off the boat's port side and had noticed a large ship in the distance. The sunsets were breathtaking every day and could only be rivaled by the sunrise. It was indeed an experience of a lifetime! Dinner was good, and the company was excellent.

As I went to my room, I took a minute to say a prayer to thank God for all my blessings, and to thank Annie for her wisdom beyond her years and her beautiful gifts. Looking out the window at the moon shining on the water and feeling the soft roll of the boat as we chugged along, I knew I would never get tired of this. I could see why sailors were married to the sea. It is so mesmerizing and soothing. I did a short meditation to clear my head so that I could sleep. So much had happened.

I checked my email before bed and there was a message from Donna. It was so good to hear from her. She wanted me to think about the impending hurricane and be safe first and foremost. Then she planted a seed in my mind that when we sailed back, it would be an excellent opportunity to make a documentary about the hurricane, the damage, the people, etc.

It was a great idea, but I felt a little funny about it somehow. It is painful to tell a story about misfortune, but it is also good to acknowledge the suffering and empathize with the victims. I would have to think about it, but it was a valid idea. I decided to answer her back in the morning. I would also send her a few of the photos we had taken to enjoy.

With daybreak, the seagulls were calling as they flew alongside the boat. Breakfast was underway, and I could smell bacon cooking. I got a quick shower and dressed for another day at sea. I had time for my morning ritual, and I wanted to be sure not to drift away from it. Sometimes it was the only sanity I could find. I sat down and meditated about my life and the future, most notably being happy. I had a conversation with God through prayer as to our safety and asked for guidance. Then journaling. There is so much for which to be grateful. I am sure the journal will be so heavy with pages I can't carry it.

Debbie was still sleeping, and the crew was on the top deck, getting ready to raise the sails and catch the wind. I loved watching this and hearing that magic sound when the sails grab the wind and fly!

"When will we get to the port for fuel?" I asked Alejandro.

"We should dock about dusk tomorrow. We will stay there that night where we will be safe from the weather, then head on to our destination the next morning," he replied.

"I have never been to St. Lucia or any of the islands this far south. I'm looking forward to it," I told him.

"St. Lucia is a beautiful island, mostly a mix of French and African cultures," Alejandro responded. "English is the primary language, but with a heavy brogue native to the island. Chip will enjoy all the different culinary versions of foods he is familiar with cooked in new ways. There will also be an opportunity for you all to learn to free dive while we are there."

"That would be impressive; it is such an interesting world underneath the sea," I told him. 'But what exactly is free diving?" I asked.

"Freediving is when you hold your breath and go down. Usually, you can go 10-12 feet under the surface without the restriction of gear," Alejandro answered.

Diving, snorkeling, exploring, and tasty food, I could think of worse places to ride out a storm.

"Remember and be sure and tell Debbie while we are in this part of the world, dress simply, no jewelry, no bling. You don't want anything to call attention to yourself or money," Alejandro reminded me.

"Is St. Lucia dangerous?" I asked.

"It is not the island that's dangerous, but that far south is popular for all types of people, and with this storm coming, pirates and criminals will be looking for easy scores while they are seeking shelter," Alejandro said.

"Do you have a plan if pirates come into play?" I asked.

"Of course, Neo, Kosmos, and I have a game plan," Alejandro assured me.

With a day left at sea, I decided to start my journal about the photos I had taken, and the places and sites we had seen. Good notes were made for good stories later, and our magazine would need great editorial content to intrigue the readership we were targeting. I also made notes about our first storm on the boat and how it felt. Then notes about the impending hurricane and the thoughts and worries I had going through my head. Again, excellent story content and something to occupy my time, so I didn't worry.

I was excited about the prospect of learning to dive. I never thought in a million years that I would be diving beneath the ocean, swimming with the sharks, and evading pirates. Wow, this is grander than my imagination could conceive!

Chapter Twenty

Arriving in San Juan, Puerto Rico, at sunset, does it get any better? The marina dock was alive with people. Boats from all over the world were moored here. Alejandro quickly pulled into the harbor and went to our slip.

"This is beautiful," I said.

"Yes, San Juan is a beautiful town filled with music, festivals, and fun, but it can also be a dangerous place, so we need to all stay close to each other," Alejandro warned.

I told Debbie and Chip to stay close to the boat near the marina and not wander off. They were excited to be in port but understood what I meant.

As we had discussed, I tagged along obediently with Alejandro, not a lousy duty, as he was strikingly handsome and kind. However, tagging along was not my style. The marina smelled of fish and diesel fuel. I could hear all types of languages spoken as we walked around. There was talk of the storm among some sailors, looking for advice from the marina staffers.

Chip was enjoying choosing some new seafood for the boat. Neo was busy getting the fuel, and Kosmos was on the ship guarding it. We moved freely through the crowd, and the marina had a lot to offer. There was a restaurant, a bar, a fish market, a store, and a fuel depot. There were customs officers on duty, but they didn't ask for our papers. English is the primary language, so communication was easy. We got our shopping done and headed back to the boat.

We were all anxious for some downtime but agreed to wait till we were a little further south. We would likely be in St. Lucia for a week waiting for the hurricane to move on through, so there would be plenty of time for vacation then.

Bright and early the following morning I felt the engine fire up, and we were moving.

I postponed my morning ritual to quickly grab my camera and headed up top to see all I could see. The harbor was full of boats of people seeking refuge. I was glad to be headed back out to the open water. Soon we were clear of the harbor and the busiest routes, so we set sails. The morning was beautiful but eerie. You could feel something impending, something coming. The birds were not calling to us as usual and there was no sign of dolphins or whales. Mother Nature knew something was up.

"When will we get to St. Lucia?" I asked Alejandro.

"We are in the Caribbean Sea, and I would guess we would be in St. Lucia about mid-afternoon if we keep a good wind. These are the Windward Islands," Alejandro said. "Famous for pirate lore, rum plantations, and safe harbor. This is my favorite place to sail in the Caribbean. A place to relax, unwind, and explore," he added.

"Well, I am ready for that," I told him.

"A place to find romance," Alejandro said with a grin.

"I am not looking for romance. There is so much to absorb from all that has changed in my life. I can't even think about romance," I answered.

"Well, it has been my experience that you don't find love when you are looking, but actually when you are not," Alejandro said, looking directly into my eyes.

Wow! I am not ready for this yet, I thought, or am I?

I headed below to break the trance and electricity at that moment.

"Good morning, Stacy," Chip called out. "There was a lot of talk about the hurricane on the docks. We made a good move to head farther south."

"I agree; Alejandro seems to know what he is doing," I said.

Chip said, "Yes, he is a great captain. He's also a good man. I have spent a lot of time talking with him."

"Yes, he is," I agreed.

I decided that this might be a suitable time to make sure I did my morning ritual. I meditated for about 15 minutes to clear my head and heart from worry, then had a long prayer with God. My motivational phrase today would be Mindset, which is everything.

I went into my room to check my emails. I had a bunch of weather alerts, miscellaneous stuff, and an email from Scott. He was just making sure I was all right. I answered immediately and let him know where we were and our action plan. I assured him Alejandro had everything under control, and we would be safe unless the storm changed direction. Speaking of that, I decided to pull up the NOAA website and check the storm forecast. It looked like the hurricane would come in just above Antigua and the Virgin Islands, about 226 miles north of where we were. However, the storm was 450 miles wide, so we were bound to get some of it. The hurricane should pass to the north of us tomorrow afternoon.

So even though the weather was still beautiful, it felt eerie, just waiting.

I thought about the hurricanes I had lived through in the Carolinas. Storms were always scary, even though you had a lot of notice that they were coming. Once they got into the Gulf Stream, a lot could change quickly, their wind strength, the amount of rain, and their speed. I thought about the barometric pressure and all that Fish, the weatherman out of Raleigh, had taught us: What to look for and the changes that affected hurricane strength.

One last email from Amelia with a greeting from the horses, saying have fun and they miss me. I had to wipe away a tear.

There was a knock at my door, "Come in," I called out. It was Debbie; she had just got up. "It's a beautiful day. Get dressed. We must sightsee like rock stars today."

"Yay!" Debbie answered back.

I found Chip in the galley. "Good morning, Chip. We're going ashore to sightsee like rock stars. Care to join us?" I asked.

"I'll be ready in ten minutes," Chip said.

I told him, "Take your time. Debbie is just now getting ready." We both laughed.

I went to the top deck to find Alejandro. "Hey, we thought today would be a good day to go ashore and check out Santa Lucia," I said. "Would you be our tour guide?" I asked.

"Absolutely, and I will let Neo and Kosmos know to stay on board and watch over the boat," Alejandro said.

My heart was fluttering; he was coming with us! It was almost like a double date. "Get a grip on yourself," I told myself.

"I took the liberty of calling us a car," Alejandro said.

"Fantastic, we are completely at your mercy. Just take us wherever you think is best," I said.

Debbie and Chip came up top and were ready to go. "Did you get the camera gear?" I asked Debbie.

"Yep, got it, boss," she replied with a smile.

The car arrived minutes later.

Alejandro reminded me, "Remember, you are my girlfriend, so don't jump if I put my arm around you or hold your hand. It is for your safety."

"That shouldn't be too tough," Debbie said with a wink. I am sure my face was a pale shade of red.

"Driver, please take us to the Diamond Falls Botanical Garden," Alejandro told him.

In a matter of minutes, we were pulling up to some of the most beautiful scenery I had ever seen. Alejandro led the way to the ticket booth and purchased four tickets. Debbie was already taking pictures and making notes for an article. She was the right one for the job.

Our tour guide, Alejandro, explained that King Louis XVI of France granted this land to the Devaux family in 1713 to serve the country. The waters were believed to be therapeutic, and the king was so impressed with their analysis that he funded the erection of a stone bath. The waters were beautiful, and of course, we had to stick our feet and legs in for the experience.

We proceeded through magnificent gardens, flowers, and trees that were breathtaking! Beautiful banquettes were set up for visitors to sit down and enjoy the beauty all along the way. Alejandro said, "The Diamond Botanical Gardens sit in a natural gorge that begins at the world's only drive-through volcano and bubbling sulfur springs. The sulfur springs are weak spots in the crust of an enormous crater that collapsed due to a volcanic upheaval some 40,000 years ago. Natural minerals found in the area include kaolinite and quartz and smaller quantities of gypsum, alunite, pyrite, and Geotite."

"This is the largest garden in the world of bromeliads, bougainvillea, and amazing flowers like tuberose,' Alejandro continued. The smell was intoxicating. We continued through the gardens, and we could hear the roar of and then saw an incredible waterfall. We all just stopped and admired its beauty. Debbie took hundreds of pictures and pages of notes.

As we walked and talked, we all got to know each other better. Chip had an incredible sense of humor and kept us laughing the whole time. I could tell Debbie was smitten with him. It was good to see her having fun. Alejandro was dark, mysterious, and profound. He laughed easily and made me feel safe. Debbie and I might come back ashore and work on the magazine and photos. Maybe she would like time to paint.

We headed to the Sulfur Springs Volcano—the celebrated drive-through volcano! I had never seen anything like it. Afterward, Debbie and I got a mud bath that left our skin feeling soft and smooth. Alejandro and Chip enjoyed drinks at the resort while they patiently waited for us.

From there, we had lunch at Dasheen, a restaurant on the property. Chef Ramuc came to our table to talk when he was told we were traveling with the famous Chef Chip from Boca. Together they prepared us a feast, after which we were thoroughly stuffed. Later, Chip told me that the chef had offered him a job to stay on the island.

"Let's go for a hike," Alejandro suggested. We were all feeling lazy but agreed it would be a good idea. We got the car and headed to the Tet

Paul Nature Trail. It was an easy hike and so worth it! By the time we finished, Debbie must have taken five thousand photos and a book of notes. Our first adventure would be well covered.

Even though we were exhausted from our day, Debbie and I had to get in some shopping! We took the car and went back to Castries. The two main streets were filled with shops and boutiques. Most items were duty-free, and it was fun to have some girl time.

Natives use shells and sea glass to make a lot of their wares. I couldn't resist a new bikini and a bracelet. Debbie purchased a couple of outfits as well.

By now, we were all tired. The streets were beginning to come alive with tourists. An island band was just starting to play, and we decided to sit down at a street café for a drink and listen. As we sat there, Debbie and Chip decided to get up and dance. They were perfect together.

Alejandro asked, "Would you like to dance?"

I was completely taken off guard, but I did love to dance, so I said "Yes.

He was leading me around the floor in just a minute, and I felt light as a feather. Alejandro was strong and handsome! The next dance was a Samba; I was so glad I had taken those lessons!

He began to move his body to the music, and I followed the move with him. As I looked around, everyone was watching us. The Samba is a very sexy dance, so I am sure we were quite the spectacle. At least, no one would doubt our relationship after that one.

"Gosh, Stacy, I didn't know you could move like that," Debbie said. "You were impressive!"

"I agree," Alejandro chimed in. After a couple of swallows of our drinks, a slow song came on. Alejandro took my hand and led me to the floor. It felt great to be so close to him. For a few minutes, I could just drop my guard, relax, and just be held, safe, and secure.

When the music stopped, I told him, "Let's go back to the boat. I am exhausted."

He paid our tab and rounded up Debbie and Chip. The car picked us up and drove us back to the dock. Once we got on the pier, we saw a couple of ragged-looking guys nosing around. As we walked down towards our boat, Alejandro pushed me behind him and led the way. When we got up close to the thugs, they showed him a knife and said something to him in a weird dialect. Alejandro angrily answered them back in the same dialect. His stare must have told them he was serious as they moved aside and let us pass, "What language was that?" I asked.

"Patwa," he answered.

We boarded the boat, and Chip and Debbie headed below.

"I want to sit up here and look at the sky and the harbor for a few minutes before I go down," I said.

"I will sit with you to be sure you aren't bothered again," Alejandro said.

I asked him, "What is Patwa?"

"It is a French creole dialect that is used by the islanders instead of English," he told me.

"You speak it very well," I said.

"I grew up here in the Windward Islands," he told me.

"Those guys were scary," I said.

"They were looking for drunk tourists," he told me.

I realized that I didn't know much about Alejandro's past since Annie and Scott had done the background check. "It must have been exciting to grow up in such an exotic place," I said.

He laughed and said, "It wasn't very exotic; it was just home."

We just sat there, taking in the night for a few minutes, when Alejandro drew me close to him and kissed me. It was a kiss like I had never felt before. I melted in his arms, and for a moment, I was lost in ecstasy. "I can't," I said to him as I pulled away.

"What?" he asked.

"I can't; please understand. I don't want this to be awkward, and I am just not ready," I told Alejandro.

"Okay, I am a patient man," he told me with a smile.

"I have had so much happen in such a brief time, and my life has changed so drastically I hardly know if I am coming or going," I said.

"Explain please, I don't know much about you except that you are genuine and beautiful," he said and leaned in to nibble my ear.

I stopped him once again; and said, "Okay, let me tell you, my story." So, I told him about my life before the inheritance, Annie, and what had happened. "So, you see, suddenly I stepped into an entirely different, foreign life," I said. "It is good but different, and I have to have some time to figure out how to live it,"

"Wow, incredible," he said. "No wonder you aren't ready for romance," he added.

"You probably have a fling with all the ladies, but I just don't," I said. "I have never been just anybody's I never will," I told him. "When I give myself to someone, it is for real, it is important, and it is meaningful, I just can't do casual," I added.

"My darling, there is nothing casual about you," he said. "You are special, and you are worth the wait. So, take your time. I will be here if you are interested," Alejandro said and kissed me good night. I went below to get some much-deserved sleep. It had been a huge day!

Chapter Twenty-One

The following day was a complete weather change. The sun could not be found, and the wind was picking up. The storm was still over a hundred miles from us, but you could feel the fury that was moving through the Atlantic. The rain was coming in as bands, and the boat was rolling in the harbor. The birds had disappeared, and there were no dolphins or fish to be seen. Everything knew a storm was coming.

"Debbie why don't you and Chip get some gear, and I'll have the car pick you up and take you to the resort. It's going to get rough, and there is no need for you to suffer through this on the boat," I said.

"Okay, but you should come, too," Debbie said.

I went below to find Alejandro and make the call.

"Stacy, the car will be here to pick you up in about ten minutes. I want you to go into town and ride out the storm," Alejandro said.

"I planned to stay on the boat," I told him.

"Well, your plans have changed. It is not a good idea. Kosmos and Neo will be here with me, and we will be fine," Alejandro said.

"How long will this last?" I asked.

"I don't know; anything can happen in a hurricane. The weather service says it will turn north just after it touches the edge of the Virgin Islands. That's about four hundred miles north of us. The storm is about 450 miles wide, so I am guessing about 3-4 hours. I will come to get you when it is safe," Alejandro said.

Reluctantly, I went below and got my gear. The car came, and the three of us left for the resort. Alejandro had called and made reservations for us for the night. The wind had picked up a lot by the time we got there, and the rain was coming in more brutal bands.

"Stacy, I am scared," Debbie told me.

"It's okay. The storm is about four hundred miles away," I reassured her as we checked in.

"Let's meet in the bar after everyone un-packs," Chip said.

When we got down to the bar, the hotel concierge told us the forecast had changed, and the storm was headed further south than they thought.

"Looks like it is coming over Guadeloupe into the Caribbean and then will turn right back over Haiti," he said.

"What does that mean for here?" I asked.

"That puts the storm only about 150 miles off our coast, so we are going to feel the blow," he said. The hotel had hurricane action plans posted all over the facility. They assured us all that they had backup generators, a strong roof, and hurricane windows. We would all be safe.

"I don't know about you guys, but when someone keeps telling me how safe I am going to be at their facility, I begin to worry," I told Chip and Debbie.

"I agree," Debbie said.

'Me too," Chip chimed in.

Fear struck my heart; the guys were on the boat. I knew Alejandro was clever and would watch the weather. I grabbed my phone to give him a call. "Hi, I just heard the storm was taking a turn for the Caribbean and coming closer to us," I said.

"Yeah, I heard," Alejandro said.

I could hear the urgency in his voice, and I didn't want to bother him, but I was concerned.

"The crew and I are going to batten down the hatches as best we can and come into town. There was only one room at the local hotel, so I checked us in. I will come by and check on you soon. Don't worry," Alejandro said.

"Okay," I said, "Hurry," I added.

Chip knew Debbie and I were both nervous, so he kept us busy with constant conversation, sharing recipes, telling jokes, and even doing a little karaoke. Before long, he had Debbie and me up on stage singing. It was more fun than I had experienced in a long time. It felt good to let go and have fun, even if it was in the face of extreme danger. I had lived through hurricanes many times growing up in North Carolina. However, this was the first time I would be through one on an island. This was scary!

We watched as the staff nailed up boards over the windows, cleared the furniture off the beaches, and rounded up tourists to keep them safe. The wind began to howl, and the rain was starting to pool in the street. Just as the power began to flicker, I saw Alejandro walking across the lobby. A look of relief was on his face to see us. "Hi, guys," Alejandro said and pulled up a chair.

"It looks like it's getting rough out there; glad you made it in," Chip told him.

"I ordered us some dinner as the power will probably go off, and we won't get back to the boat till tomorrow," Chip said.

"Always thinking ahead," Debbie said.

"You know it, babe," Chip said.

The waiter brought our food: fish tacos and coconut shrimp. We ate and talked and watched the storm unleash its fury. The hotel had the weather channel on, and it was broadcasting from Guadeloupe. I was relieved we had come further south.

"Growing up here, it was sporadic for a storm to come this far south or even go into the Caribbean this far south. Usually, the Bahamas get the storms," Alejandro said, adding, "We will be okay. When a hurricane does come this way, it usually isn't so powerful."

Growing up with hurricanes in North Carolina, I knew that areas that rarely got them were usually poorly prepared. Construction wasn't sturdy, and there were no guidelines or building codes per se in the Caribbean. God only knows what the night will bring, I thought.

"Yes, they said this is just a Cat 1," Debbie said.

At about that time, the power went off. The hotel staff told us to stay seated and they would have the backup generator on in a few minutes. Alejandro took my hand so I wouldn't be scared.

The lights popped on, and everyone felt relieved. We were all exhausted, but we knew sleep would be hard to find tonight. I sensed Debbie and Chip wanted to go upstairs and relax but didn't leave me alone. To let them off the hook, I said, "Why don't you guys head on up and get some rest? I will be going to bed myself shortly."

"Are you sure, Stacy?" Debbie asked.

"Yes, I'm fine," I told them.

Alejandro said, "I will stay as long as need be."

Chip decided I was okay and told me, "Call me if you get nervous or need anything."

"I will," I said.

"You look tired," Alejandro told me.

"I am," I answered.

"If you want to go up to your room, I can go," Alejandro said.

"No, I don't want you to go," I said. "I don't want to be alone."

"Do you want me to come up with you? I don't want to leave you alone. I mean to sit by you and watch over you," Alejandro clarified.

"That would be great," I said.

We headed upstairs. I had booked a suite, so I knew there was plenty of room for us both. I put the key in the slot, and we went in.

"Wow, this is huge," Alejandro said.

"Yeah, it was all they had left. A little over-kill, but I am glad to have the room," I said.

We sat down on the sofa turned on the television to the weather channel and watched the storm as it slowly progressed across Guadeloupe and into the Caribbean. Sometime during that passage, I think I fell asleep leaning on Alejandro. As he gently picked me up and put me in bed, I woke enough to hear him say, "Don't be afraid I am going to lie down on the couch until the storm passes."

"Don't leave," I whispered just before I dropped off again.

"I won't ever leave you," Alejandro said and kissed my forehead.

The night had a few bumps and bangs, but every time I opened my eyes, Alejandro was nearby on the couch, so I felt safe. By dawn, the winds had finally died down. The storm had passed us, and for the most part, Saint Lucia was unharmed. The hotel lost part of the roof and a few windows, so we would need to watch out for broken glass.

Alejandro woke me up and said, "Hey, I am going to check on my family and the crew. I will be back soon, wait here for me."

"Okay, but please be careful," I said.

I stayed in bed another hour before I got up and was relieved that we had electricity and hot water. I took a shower, and it sure felt good. I got dressed and waited for Alejandro to return. Debbie and Chip both called to check on me, and we made plans to meet in the hotel restaurant for some breakfast.

Soon Alejandro came walking in with a big smile on his face.

"Was everything okay?" I asked.

"Yes, the family was all good, and for the most part, the town didn't have much severe damage," Alejandro said.

"Have you been to the boat?" I tentatively asked.

"Yes, I took Kosmos and Neo by there so they could tidy up. It looks like everything is in order there too. We were lucky," Alejandro said.

"That's a big relief. I would sure hate to have to stay here indefinitely while we made boat repairs," Chip said.

"Yeah, that would be awful," Debbie chimed in.

"Okay, you two, the trip is far from over; excitement waits around every turn," I said, then laughed.

"So, Captain, where are we headed next?" I asked.

"Since we are well into hurricane season and usually storms follow the same path, I think we should head back towards home. If you want to continue sailing, we can head north," Alejandro said.

"North in the winter, no, I don't think so. Let's head home and put this baby to bed for the winter," I said.

"Home it is, then," Alejandro said.

"Chip, will you take care of our supplies of food for the return journey?" Alejandro asked.

"Of course," Chip answered.

"Okay, then I will make sure everything on the boat is okay and get us ready to sail. Ladies, if you wish to do any more shopping, this would be a good opportunity, you have about two hours," Alejandro said.

"I would like to take the camera and roam around a bit to get some shots of the aftermath for an article. Would that be possible?" I asked Alejandro.

"Yes, but I will need to be with you. There are still a lot of dangers roaming about," Alejandro answered.

"I don't know about you, but I'm ready to get back to the boat," Debbie said.

"Sure, go ahead. I just want to get some shots," I told her.

Chapter Twenty-Two

Debbie and Chip took my suitcase back to the boat with them, and I kept the camera equipment. Alejandro and I set off to roam about a little and take some photos.

I was relieved to see that, for the most part, there wasn't any severe damage, just things you would expect: a few shingles blown off, a piece of roof or furniture here and there. The power would be back on soon, and that was always one of the worst parts as it is sweltering and humid after a summer hurricane.

"Stacy, tell me about living in Carolina. What was it like to have a hurricane there?" Alejandro asked.

"Well, it's much like here, everyone braces for the wind and secures all that they can. Then there is the flooding afterward that sometimes goes as far as 150 miles inland. When I was a kid, the power took about three days to get back on, so it was always guarded. My parents were smart and well-stocked on food," I told him. "I remember our number one hurricane ritual was to fill the bathtub and all the large pots with water," I laughed as I told him.

"We do the same here in the islands, and water is one thing you can't live without," Alejandro replied.

I took photos of the debris and folks scurrying around to make repairs. Those, coupled with good notes, would suffice for the story's beginning, but the reporter in me wanted more. "Could we sail into the islands that were hit harder so I can get more of the story?" I asked Alejandro.

"Sure, but we will have to be careful. Desperate times make desperate people," he reminded me.

Just then, as I was walking down the beach, the sun came out, and the birds were back. It is amazing how Mother Nature takes care and lets her creatures know when it is safe and when it is not. You just need to get in touch with it, watch it, and respect it.

When we got back to the boat, Alejandro seemed sad.

"Are you sure everything is, okay?" I asked.

"Yeah, I just dread getting home and docking for the winter," he told me.

"Aw, sailing is in your blood, I know," I laughingly told him.

"No, it is not that," Alejandro said.

"Then what?" I asked.

"It means I won't see you again, at least not soon," Alejandro said.

"I don't know about that, you never know when I will want to Just Sail Away, "I said.

He looked up and smiled. "Where are you headed when we get back into port?" Alejandro asked.

"Well, I put my North Carolina house up for sale and sent all my stuff to my estate in the Hamptons," I said.

"You in the Hamptons?" Alejandro said.

"I know, I speak a bit Southern to live there, but the house is magnificent, and it's on the Atlantic Ocean," I said.

"Oh, I see," Alejandro said.

"I also have a house in Boca, on the ocean," I said.

"That is cool, one for winter and one for summer," Alejandro said.

"Well, that isn't all. I have a lodge in Jackson Hole that I haven't even seen yet, and condos in Los Angeles, Manhattan, and London," I said.

"How rich are you?" Alejandro asked.

"Very. You see, before Annie's death, I had an okay job, a middle-class house, and a used car. The death and inheritance have been quite a lot to get used to," I said. I explained that Annie bought me the boat to fulfill my childhood dreams of sailing away.

"I had no idea. No wonder you aren't romantically interested in me," Alejandro said.

"What? I never said I wasn't interested. I said I wasn't ready," I reminded him.

"I am nobody, just a boat captain for hire. I have nothing to offer you," Alejandro said.

"I would prefer to be the one who makes that decision if you don't mind. It's not about money, even if I didn't have money," I said.

"I know, and I hope you know that is not why I am attracted to you either," Alejandro said.

"I do," I said. "I'm glad your family was ok."

"They were doing just fine. The hurricane hadn't bothered them much," Alejandro answered, smiling.

"You must miss them a lot," I said.

"I do, but an occasional visit is enough. My parents are very opinionated about my career choice," Alejandro answered.

"I get it. My folks thought I was crazy to want to be a writer," I told him.

"Sometimes, they just don't remember the passion for chasing your dreams is yours, not theirs," Alejandro said.

"This is true. I hope if I ever have children, I will encourage them to follow their dreams, throw caution to the wind, and go for it," I said with a smile.

"Is that how you live?" Alejandro asked.

"I didn't, but I just might in the future. Who knows? "How much damage was there to the boat?"

"Not too bad, a couple of pieces of electronic equipment are on the fritz, and one of the jibs has a tiny hole," Alejandro answered.

"Can we sail with that stuff torn up?" I asked.

"Yes, we could, but I am going to get it fixed while we are here. The harbormaster has time to do it and the necessary parts. It will only cost us one more day here if that's okay with you," Alejandro said.

"If you think that is what we should do, of course, I agree," I told him.

"Good, while they are working on the boat, it would be a great opportunity to gain experience in free diving. After a hurricane comes through, the bottom is all stirred up, and there is no telling what we might find," Alejandro said.

"Okay, I'm game," I answered.

"Let's go out to the boat and see if Chip and Debbie would like to join us," Alejandro said.

When we got to the boat, Chip and Debbie were in the kitchen working on dinner together. "Hey, Alejandro and I are going to do some freediving. Would you like to come," I asked.

"That sounds incredible, but I have a ton of work to do to get dinner and put away the supplies, so I will have to pass," Chip said.

"I guess I will stay here and help Chip. You two go and have fun," Debbie answered.

"Neo and Kosmos will be here in case there is any trouble so that you will be safe," Alejandro told them.

I changed into my suit and threw on a coverup, and we were off. Alejandro knew the island like the back of his hand. We walked through the streets for a while and finally got to a beautiful, secluded cove.

"Here we are," Alejandro said with a smile.

"This is beautiful. Have you swum here a lot?" I asked.

"Almost every day as a boy. My family's property begins about one hundred yards up that way," Alejandro answered.

"Okay, Mr. Instructor, tell me what freediving is," I said.

"Well, you hold your breath and dive down deeper than you can go with the snorkel. We wear snorkels and a mask to help you keep your breath. We will dive down about ten to twelve feet. Time will be short because you will have to practice learning to hold your breath for longer times," Alejandro said.

"Okay, well, I think I can do that," I said.

"Once we are in the water, follow my lead. If you see a shark or a barracuda, don't panic. I will be right there," Alejandro said.

"I will do my best," I told him.

We walked over to a rock with a smooth surface and slid into the water. It was a little cool as it had been churned up pretty heavily. Once in the water, Alejandro said, "Take a deep breath and head down."

I followed his instructions and just under the surface was a whole new world. I thought I had seen some beautiful things when we snorkeled, but this was quite different. There were distinct kinds of fish, different types of vegetation, and shells. It was beautiful. After a couple of minutes, Alejandro gave the signal to the surface, and I followed.

"Well, what do you think?" Alejandro anxiously asked.

"Oh my gosh, it's incredible!" I answered. "It's beautiful and different from anything I have seen up to now."

"You're doing great, now just get another breath, and we will go back down," Alejandro said.

I took a deep breath and headed under the surface. This time there were tons of fish playing and swimming around the rocks. I saw an eel peek out from behind a rock, but he quickly retreated when he saw us. As I was swimming along, I saw something odd and shiny on the bottom. I dove down to take a better look. It was round and glossy, so I picked it up. Just then, Alejandro gave us the signal to surface, so I carried it to the top.

"What did you pick up," Alejandro asked.

"I don't know what it is. It just looked out of place down there," I said and showed it to Alejandro.

Alejandro's face lost its color, and he quickly said, "Give it to me and tell me where you found it."

"Almost straight below us. What is it?" I asked.

"You stay here. I will be right back," and just like that he disappeared under the surface.

Alejandro returned to the top and said, "We need to go back to the boat right now.'

"But this is so much fun. Did I do something wrong?" I asked.

"I will explain it when we get back on the boat," Alejandro answered.

We climbed out of the water and saw someone coming down the beach. It was a man walking like he was looking for something. When we got up close to him, he said, "Hello, have you two been diving down there?"

Alejandro looked him right in the eye and said, "No, we were snorkeling further up the beach, but my girlfriend saw a shark and got scared, so that ended our fun."

He looked at me and said, "Scared of sharks, are you? Well, you better be careful where you go around here. You might wind up supper for some of them."

Alejandro took my arm, and we walked on past him, and he didn't respond.

Once back at the boat, I knew something was wrong. "What was that all about?" I asked.

"That thing you brought to the surface was a marker for somebody, for the dope they dropped off in the ocean," Alejandro said. "It puts off a beacon, and the drug dealers track it down. The storm must have washed it into the cove," he added.

"Oh my," I said.

"I would never have taken you there to free dive if I had any idea that it would even be a remote possibility that we would stumble onto that," he said and gently touched my hair.

"It's okay. You managed it very well," I said.

"Hopefully, that guy won't come snooping around," said Alejandro. Then, turning to Neo, he said, "Stand a close watch this evening. Trouble may come calling."

"Boss, if trouble comes, I am ready," Neo answered.

"Go on down and change your clothes. Dinner will be ready soon, and I am starving," Alejandro told me.

I went downstairs and changed my clothes. I was hungry, too, though, with the excitement, I hadn't noticed it. The Caribbean is a beautiful and mysterious place, but not somewhere I want to spend a lot of time. I decided not to mention the beacon to anyone. I didn't want to scare them.

Chip had made a beautiful dinner and everyone else was in a good mood, laughing and joking with each other. I put on my game face and joined in. When we finished dinner, I went to my room to catch up on my emails, and soon I was sound asleep. It had been another big day.

Chapter Twenty-Three

The following day was beautiful, and Alejandro and Neo gathered up the small sail to repair it. While they were gone, I decided I would go for a walk. I climbed down to the dock and headed towards shore. I was walking towards the shops enjoying a beautiful morning when a man came up to me and asked me for directions. I explained that I wasn't from there and couldn't help him. A second man appeared and grabbed me by the arm and pulled me into an alley. They put a cloth over my face, and that was the last thing I remembered.

When I woke up, I was tied to a chair in a dark, run-down room. There were two men in the room with me, one I recognized from the beach yesterday, and the other had red hair.

"Oh, you are finally awake. Well, that's good because I have some questions for you," the taller man said.

"Where am I?" I asked.

"That doesn't matter, and I will be asking the questions, lady," the red-haired man said.

"You and your boyfriend were diving in the cove, weren't you," the tall man stammered.

"No, we were snorkeling further up the beach. I don't know how to dive," I answered.

"You're lying. I was watching you," the red-haired man said.

"Why would I lie, and what difference does it make to you?" I angrily spat out.

The tall man slapped me hard and said, "You better tell me the truth, or there is worse coming for you, lady."

"Did you find something odd on the floor of the cove?" the tall man asked.

"I told you we were snorkeling, looking at fish and vegetation," I answered. Another slap, this time a little harder!

Tears were running down my face. What was I going to do? Nobody even knew I had left the boat. Everything Alejandro had told me was coming true. Would these men kill me, I wondered.

Back on the boat Alejandro and Neo had returned and were ready for breakfast. While Neo went to store the sail, Alejandro went below. "Good morning," he called out.

"Good morning," Chip answered.

"What's for breakfast this morning, Chef?" Alejandro asked.

"I can whip up an omelet and some toast or pancakes if you prefer," Chip answered.

"Has Stacy eaten this morning?" Alejandro asked.

"I haven't seen her yet," Chip answered.

"That's odd. She's usually bright-eyed and bushy-tailed about daybreak."

He got up and knocked on her door. "Stacy, are you awake yet?" Alejandro called out.

No answer. He opened the door and could see that she had slept in her bed and dressed but wasn't in her room. Next, he knocked on Debbie's door. "Debbie?" Alejandro asked.

"Good morning," she answered and opened her door with a smile.

"Have you seen Stacy this morning?" Alejandro asked.

"No, I figured she was off somewhere with you," Debbie answered.

Alejandro ran up on deck to find Kosmos. "Kosmos, have you seen Stacy this morning?"

"No, Captain, I thought she was sleeping in," Kosmos answered. "Is she missing?" Kosmos asked.

"Yes," Alejandro answered with worry all over his face.

Chip and Debbie had come on deck. "Should we call the police?" Debbie asked.

"Ma'am, it doesn't work that way here on the islands," Neo said.

"Before we do that let's see if we can find her," Alejandro said. "Chip, you, and Debbie stay here with the boat in case she comes back. Neo, stay here with them. Kosmos, let's head into town and see if we can find any trace of her."

Alejandro went below to get his pistol. Kosmos was armed as well. When they returned topside, Alejandro took Kosmos and Neo aside and explained about the beacon Stacy found. "I am afraid one of those drug dealers took her to see what she found."

"I'll stay here and protect Debbie and Chip, but if you need me, send me a text and I'll be right there boss," Neo said.

"Thanks," Alejandro said, and he hurried to catch up with Kosmos on the dock.

"Any ideas, boss?" Kosmos asked.

"Let's walk into town and look around for a few minutes. We can ask around if anyone has seen Stacy. I will recognize the guy from the beach if I see him," Alejandro said.

The port had been busy with all the folks in town during the storm and no one remembered seeing an American woman, Alejandro and Kosmos combed the streets, and went back to the cove. They spoke to folks they thought might have answers, but nothing. Not a trace.

Back on the boat, Alejandro was sick with fear and worry. "Why didn't I check on her before I left and remind her to stay on the boat?" he fretted.

"Boss, even if you had, she would do what she wanted to, anyway. She probably just went for a walk. Surely, she's back on the boat by now," Kosmos tried to reassure him.

Stacy had not come back, and Debbie was frantic. "Oh my God, someone has taken her! How did they know who she was?"

"Let's not jump to conclusions just yet," Chip said.

"When Stacy and I went freediving, she found something on the cove floor, a beacon. When we surfaced, she showed it to me. I grabbed it, dove under it, and put it back. But a man walking down the beach saw us and asked us about it. I told him that we had been snorkeling up the beach and not diving. The beacon was a transmitter that the drug lords used to find their drugs when they were dropped in the ocean. It had washed into the cove, and he was looking for it," Alejandro told them.

"Oh, my God! Drug dealers!" Debbie exclaimed and burst into tears.

"Are you sure we shouldn't contact the police?" Chip asked.

"Not yet, she's only been missing a few hours, and they won't do anything for 24 hours," Alejandro said.

"Boss, we need a plan," Neo said.

"You're right, Neo".

Back in the dingy room, the red-haired man looked at me and said, "You sure are pretty. Maybe I will keep you as my muse, and he brushed my hair back with his hand."

"Lady, you have five minutes to answer my question, or I am going to start getting rough with you," the tall man grabbed me by my ponytail and snatched my head back. "Do you understand me?"

"I already told you all I know," I said, and he slapped me again.

By now, bruises were starting to rise on my face, and my eye was swollen and painful. I overheard the men planning to ask for ransom for me.

"Well, she doesn't know anything, but maybe her boyfriend does," the tall man said.

"Yeah, she is pretty; maybe we can get a couple of thousand dollars out of him to get her back," said the red-haired man.

"If not, we will take her to G13. She'll bring a handsome reward from the slave traders," the tall man said.

"Where's your cell phone?" the red-haired man asked.

"Why do you want that?" I asked.

"Are you going to tell me, or do you want me to search for it? the tall man said with a nasty smirk.

Oh no, I thought, they'll figure out who I am if they get my phone. "I dropped it when you grabbed me back in the market," I said.

"Well, let's leave her here and go to the dock. I'll recognize the guy she was with," the tall one said.

"Here, put this over her face to knock her out so she won't scream while we are gone," the red-haired man said.

I struggled, but they put the smelly cloth over my nose, and I was out.

On board the ship, Neo and Kosmos talked to Alejandro about what to do. "Boss, I have some dark connections in the area. Let me make a couple of calls and see what I can find out," Neo said.

"Sure, whatever you think we can do that would help," Alejandro answered. He was visibly shaken and scared.

"Boss, I am going to call Neela Malone. She will be able to help us. She has deep resources, and she liked Stacy," Kosmos said.

"That's a great idea. Neela is pretty far away, but as you said, she has deep resources," Alejandro answered.

"Boss, when we find where they have Stacy, you stay with the boat. Neo and I will do whatever is necessary to get her back," Kosmos said.

"I'll come with you," Alejandro said.

"No, it's better if you don't," Kosmos said.

Neo spied the two crooks walking along the dock and thought they looked suspicious. He climbed onto the dock and bumped into one of them. "Oh, excuse me," Neo said.

The tall man replied, "You better watch out who you are running into, buddy."

"Really? And just what would you be wanting to do about it?" Neo asked.

Hearing the exchange Alejandro went on deck and recognized the man confronting Neo. He climbed down onto the dock. The men saw him and started towards him.

"Aren't you the guy I ran into at the cove?" the tall man asked.

"Excuse me?" Alejandro asked.

"Yeah, you had that girl with you and were messing where you don't belong," the tall man said.

"I don't know what you are talking about," Alejandro answered.

The red-haired man said, "Well, you better remember if you want to see that pretty young thing alive again."

"That's right, our boss has her and he wants $5,000 to give her back," the tall man said.

"That's right, and you got one hour to get the money and meet us at the cove," the red-haired man said.

"And come alone," the tall man added.

"I can't get that kind of cash in an hour," Alejandro said.

"You better," the red-haired man answered, and they walked away.

Kosmos had managed to slip unseen off the boat and was waiting to follow them.

Neo got a text from Kosmos shortly, and told Alejandro, "Boss, I'm going to meet up with Kosmos. We have a plan."

"I'm coming with you!" Alejandro said. "I'll get the money from my mother and be there in time."

"Boss," Neo said, "you know they ain't going to bring Stacy to the cove and give her back. You go to get the money and wait for my text. Don't worry, Kosmos and I have done this before," Neo added.

Neo headed up the dock and disappeared. When he met up with Kosmos, Kosmos said, "They're in that hotel, Room 7. I heard from Neela, and she said they may be planning to sell her to the sex traders in the G13 gang. We have to act fast."

"They approached the boss about a $5,000 ransom, and I guess they plan to line their pockets with a little extra before handing her over to G13. I told Alejandro to get the money and wait for our text. I thought it would give him something to do," Neo said.

"Okay, I'll reconnoiter the room and see if she is in there. They didn't see me so that they wouldn't be suspicious," Kosmos said.

"Once you're sure she's there, give me a sign. We'll wait till they head out to collect their $5,000, and we can get her out," Neo said.

"Yeah, and then we will head to the cove and help the boss take care of them," Kosmos said.

It wasn't long before the abductors headed to the cove. Stacy was still out from the chloroform. Once the coast was clear, Kosmos picked the lock of the room, she was in. He gave Neo the sign, and they went in to get her. She was slumped over, bruised, and beaten, out cold. They looked at each other, fearing the worst. Neo felt for Stacy's pulse. "She's alive," he said.

Kosmos cut her loose, picked her up, and they headed for the boat.

"Chip!" Neo called out in advance.

"Yes! Oh my God, is she alright?" Chip said as he saw Stacy's condition.

"She's been drugged with something and knocked out, but she is okay. Take her below and have Debbie stay with her. There's a forty-five under the mattress. Do you know how to use one?" Neo asked.

"Yes, no problem," Chip replied.

"When did Alejandro leave for the cove?" Kosmos asked.

"About five minutes ago," Chip said.

Alejandro had called his mother and told her everything. She told him to come to the house, and she would have the cash ready. "Thank you, Mom," Alejandro said as he took the money.

"Be safe and keep Stacy safe. I can see you care deeply about her," his mother answered.

Alejandro gave her a quick kiss and was gone. In minutes he was at the cove.

Kosmos and Neo were hustling double-time as they made their way to the cove.

Alejandro was sitting on a rock near where they had been freediving. He had a million thoughts running through his head, wishing he had never brought Stacy there when he saw the men approaching.

"Did you bring our money?" the tall man asked.

"Yes, where is she?" Alejandro demanded.

"The money first," the red-haired man snarled.

Alejandro saw Kosmos and Neo coming up the beach behind the men. To stall them just a couple of minutes longer he said, "No! I need to see her before I give you any money!"

"You don't get to make the rules, lover boy, I do," the tall man answered.

Neo came up behind him and put a large blade to his throat. "No, I make the rules," he said with a smile. Kosmos had made short work of the red-haired man and had him tied and gagged.

"We got her boss. She's safe," Kosmos told Alejandro.

"Now, I believe these boys have business with the St. Lucia police, so let's be getting them on down to the jail," Neo said.

Alejandro ran back to the boat. "Where's Stacy? Where is she?"

"She's in her room. Debbie's with her, but she looks bad," Chip said with a worried look.

When Alejandro saw her frail figure in the bed, he collapsed in tears.

"She hasn't come to yet, but she doesn't seem to have any other injuries other than her face," Debbie said. "I have been putting on cold compresses to help with the swelling." She got up from the bedside chair and gestured for him to sit there. "I need to get some more supplies," Debbie said, sensing he might need a moment alone with her.

Alejandro took Stacy's hand and cried. He said a prayer of thanks that she was alive and bent down to kiss her cheek. "Stacy, I love you so much. I am so sorry that this happened," Alejandro said.

After a while, I opened my eyes and said, "Where am I?"

"You're safe on the boat with all of us," Alejandro said.

Everything came washing back over me. "Those men! I've got to get up," I said.

"My darling, those men are in jail. Neo and Kosmos rescued you and dealt with those two," Alejandro said. "You are safe. You are safe."

Kosmos popped in to check on them and saw Stacy was awake. "Welcome back, Ma'am, don't you worry about those two. They ain't ever gonna hurt anybody again," Kosmos said.

"Thank you," I said in a weak voice.

"Stacy, are you hungry?" Chip asked.

"Not right now, but thank you," I answered.

Debbie poked her head into the room, and when she saw Stacy's eyes were open, she began to cry softly. "Oh my God, I thought we had lost you," Debbie said. "Thank God the fellas got to you, and you're okay."

"The doctor will be here shortly to take a look at you and make sure everything is okay. So, you get some rest," Alejandro told me.

"Don't leave me alone," I said.

"Don't worry, I will be right here. Now rest."

About an hour later two visitors came to the boat. It was Neela Malone herself and a doctor. "Hello, everyone," Neela said as she boarded. "I was in the neighborhood and thought I would check on our girl."

"Governor, thank you for your help," Kosmos said.

"Think nothing of it. I am always glad to help," Neela replied as they went into Stacy's room. "Governor!" Alejandro said with a start. "It's good to see you, and thank you for everything,"

"No need to thank me," Neela said. "Now, may I have a minute alone with Stacy?"

"Of course," Alejandro said and stepped into the galley.

"Stacy, I am so thankful you are okay. You were a fortunate young lady," Neela said.

"Yes, I was lucky," I answered. "What are you doing here?"

"Kosmos is an old friend, and when he told me you were in trouble, I sent him a little bit of info to help him. I also brought my physician to give you an examination. I didn't think you would want any of this to be public information," Neela said.

"Thank you," I said.

The doctor helped me sit up on the side of the bed. He gently cupped my chin in his hand and tilted my face up so he could see. "Well, young lady, you took a few hard whacks to the face," he said.

"Yeah, my hands were tied so that I couldn't fight back," I said.

The doctor laughed out loud and said, "Probably a good thing you were. You wouldn't have had a fair chance against those thugs."

He listened to my chest and heart, and then he said, "I know this might be a little embarrassing, but those men didn't force sex or touch you that way, did they?"

"No sir, thank God," I answered.

"Good, well, I think you are going to make a full recovery physically. Give it a little time for your mind to recover. You have been through a terrifying situation. I am going to leave you some tranquilizers and sleeping pills in case you have any problems. If you need me, just call," the doctor said.

On the upper deck, Neela was talking with everyone about the incident. "Those two hoodlums had contacted the G13 and planned to sell her into the trade. Just lucky Kosmos and Neo rescued her when they did. So often this stuff happens, and before the girls can be found, they are sold, and then they vanish almost into thin air," Neela said.

"We took them to the police, and they were arrested on kidnapping charges. Luckily, they were just small-change crooks trying to score," Kosmos said.

"Will Stacy have to testify at their trial?" Alejandro asked.

"No, I will take care of that. We can do a video affidavit and keep this private," Neela said.

"You are a Godsend," Debbie said.

"No, I just care about people and am here to make sure they are okay," Neela said with a smile. "Chip, there is one thing I need."

"Sure, anything. How can I help?"

"I am starving," Neela said, "Will you make me something for dinner?"

Everyone laughed, and Chip responded with, "At your service,

Ma'am."

Chip went to the galley, Debbie went back to Stacy's side, and Alejandro talked with Neela, Kosmos, and Neo on deck. "I have never been so scared in my life," Alejandro said.

"Yeah, it could have been a lot different, but we were able to act quickly, and the crooks were stupid to come here in person," Kosmos said.

"Governor, would you like to stay over on the boat tonight?" Alejandro asked.

"No, I appreciate your offer, but my helicopter is on the island. I'll head back home, but not till after I eat. After all, I can't pass up a meal from Chef Chip," Neela said with a laugh.

"Ma'am, you won't be sorry. He is a fine cook," Neo said.

Everyone went down to the galley for dinner Debbie came in with Stacy. "What are you doing out of bed?" Alejandro scolded Stacy.

"The doctor said all my injuries are to my face, my legs are fine, and I'm hungry," I told them.

The conversation was primarily light, and we were all thankful for the outcome. All too soon, it was time for Neela to go.

"Stacy, if you ever need me, remember I am only a phone call away," she whispered as she hugged me goodbye.

"Thank you," I said. "I'll remember."

It had been a long and emotionally draining day, and everyone was anxious for some sleep. Neo took the first watch, and we all headed to bed. Debbie tucked me in and handed me a sleeping pill. "Here you go, take this. You need a solid night's sleep. If you need me, I am right next door," Debbie said.

A few minutes later, Alejandro came in to say goodnight. "Stacy, I was so scared! What if I had lost you?" He asked.

"Me too," I answered.

"Do you want me to stay?"

"Yes," I said as I drifted off to sleep.

Chapter Twenty-Four

The sky was much clearer in the morning, still a little windy, but that made it a wonderful day to sail. Kosmos and Neo fired up the motor and headed up to the marina to fuel the boat.

Afterward, we headed out to open water, navigating in and out of the boat traffic. Once in open water, we set the sails, and I heard that familiar sound of "pop" as the sails caught the wind. We were on our way. Alejandro steered northwest, and we were underway. The birds and the dolphins had returned, and the world felt right again. We decided to stay out to sea far enough to keep out of traffic so we could make good time. We wouldn't need to stop again until we got to Bermuda.

However, we decided to make stops in Jamaica, the Cayman Islands, Cancun, and Key West. There were no storms on the radar, and the forecast was for smooth sailing for the next ten days.

Our estimated sailing time was about 20 days from St. Lucia to Key West. Out on the open water, you could smell salt in the air, and the sun was warm, flowing down on us like honey.

"Oh, I could live at sea forever! What a beautiful day," Debbie said as she crawled into a lounge chair beside me. "So glad to see you up and around this morning."

"It is gorgeous, isn't it," I said.

Suddenly, Alejandro was beside me and said, "Come look, whales and their calves."

We hurried to the bow and the humpback whales were making their way gracefully through the waves, calves at their sides. One whale breached, bringing her whole body up out of the water and landing with a huge splash. It looked as if she were playing. Another whale breached, and it made our hearts sing to see them frolicking and enjoying life with their babies. They were without a care in the world! If only our lives could be that simple!

The whales moved on out of sight, and Debbie and I settled back into our loungers for a nap. Alejandro was ever vigilant at the wheel, watching the waves and the sky, keeping us safe. Chip was down below, preparing a fantastic lunch for us.

We would be at sea for three days before we made landfall again. In some ways, it was a beautiful thought of total escape. In other ways, it was eerie and forbidding. I went downstairs to check my email one last time because we would get no signal out in the open ocean. Amazing that with today's technology, we can get an internet connection at all.

I knew I would have to tell Scott what had happened, but I dreaded it. I got out my gratitude journal and added today's items. I am incredibly grateful for the pod of whales we saw as well as the dolphins, birds, and turtles. What wonders of nature they all are! I am also thankful for being spared by the hurricane and for the beautiful weather that followed. I am beyond grateful for this fantastic group of friends who risked their lives to save me. I am thankful I am alright. I gave up a quick prayer and checked my emails.

There was one from Scott, ever vigilant. I promptly answered to let him know we were okay, and what our course would be. He was pretty upset about the incident with the thugs and said we would discuss it at length when I got into port. There were a couple more emails from friends making sure I was okay. Amelia had sent another photo of the horses and had enjoyed the photos I had sent to her. It was good to remember home. Then I went back up to the main deck.

Alejandro came over to see how we were doing. "You know that if we turn left, we will go to Venezuela, and if we turn right, we'll be headed to Jamaica. Both are dangerous areas of the Caribbean. Venezuela has the second-highest murder rate in the world., It would be hazardous for a tourist to go there," Alejandro said.

"My sister has friends in Venezuela, and they are all on the run seeking to get out of the country," Neo added.

"Violent crime and the collapse of the economy there have become ripe territory for people smugglers, kidnappers, and robbers," Alejandro said.

"So that is why we are sailing far from shore for the next three days," I speculated.

"Yes," Alejandro answered.

"I received a memo from Scott that Venezuela was a Level 4 warning, and our government advised no travel by US citizens there," I told the group. Haiti, Honduras, and Nicaragua were Level 3, and the memo strongly advised rerouting. "I guess they don't have Pirates of the Caribbean for nothing," I said.

"I sure hope we don't see any pirates," Debbie said, and you could hear the fear in her voice.

Kosmos pointed out a group of enormous sea turtles off the port side. That effectively lightened the mood. Sea turtles are such amazing creatures. They swim along for miles in the ocean.

"Have you ever really watched a sea turtle swim?" Alejandro asked.

"Of course," I answered.

"No, I mean have you watched how they move?"

"Well, no, not really," I answered.

He said, "Sit here and watch, focus on the turtle, how freely he moves through the water, the way he propels his body. It is almost like a bird flying with wings."

"Wow, you're right. It almost looks as if the turtle is flying on the water," I answered.

"You need to learn to appreciate the beauty and details that the sea has to offer you. It is truly a new frontier, an amazing frontier," Alejandro told me. I knew, right then and there, that the sea would always be his first love.

Before long, Chip was ringing the dinner bell; lunch was ready. Alejandro put Kosmos at the helm, and the rest of us went below to feast on whatever was creating that tantalizing smell that was coming from the kitchen!

"Chip, what's for lunch? It smells delicious!" Debbie said.

"Chilean Sea Bass with lemon parmesan sauce and creamed spinach," Chip answered.

"Oh, my goodness, I think I have died and gone to heaven," Debbie commented.

"Chip, if you keep cooking like this, I will have to cut the doors larger," Alejandro added.

"Come, sit, and enjoy," Chip said with delight. We were all eating and smacking our lips, enjoying every morsel when Kosmos suddenly came to the door and asked Alejandro to come up top. The situation didn't look good; I could see the worry on his face.

Alejandro jumped up and bounded up the stairs. In a flash, he returned to tell us to all go to our cabins and lock the doors. "Don't open them unless I come to get you," Alejandro said.

"Alejandro, what is going on?" I asked.

"Not right now, just trust me," Alejandro replied. We immediately locked ourselves in our cabins. I could hear another boat coming pretty close to us, so I peeked out the window. I could see the boat coming dangerously close to us.

"Ahoy, there, mates," I heard one of them call out. The guy on the boat looked rough and dirty, wearing ragged jeans and covered with scars. There were more men on the boat with him—all dirty, and all with guns!

"Hello," answered Alejandro. I couldn't see him, but I could hear the conversation.

"Our boat is giving us some trouble. We need to turn off our engine and tie up to your boat to let ours cool off," the gruff-looking guy said. Two of the guys started towards the side of the boat to board us. All the men had weapons and looked ready to fight.

"No, mate, you are not boarding our boat, and you are not tying up to it," Alejandro told him.

Kosmos said, "You back on away now, and you can live, mate. "Kosmos was pointing a high-caliber rifle at the man's head.

Then I heard Neo chime in, "That's right, get the heck away from here. You won't be boarding this boat today." Then Neo fired a warning shot above their heads. "Move, now," he shouted.

"I didn't mean you any harm. We'll be on our way then," the gruff guy said. Their boat pushed off away from ours, but they traveled very slowly. I had a terrible feeling this wasn't over just yet.

"Neo take down the sails, and Kosmos, get the engine fired up. I'll be right back," Alejandro directed. "Is everyone down here doing, okay?" Alejandro called out.

I cracked open my door and told him we were all fine, just a little scared. "Alejandro, what do we do if they come back?" I asked.

"Don't worry about that right now. We'll use the engines and put some miles between us and them," Alejandro assured us.

Once the pirates saw the sails drop, they knew we'd soon be gone, and they started shooting at us. Luckily, they were lousy shots. Neo and Kosmos never backed down and continued with their preparations.

In minutes I heard those big engines come to life and felt the boat surge into a solid forward motion. She could do twenty-five knots, and that had to be faster than the pirate's boat.

The pirates fell in behind us and tried to catch us, but they were no match for us. I heard more shots, but they couldn't hit us now. I guess they were just showing their prowess. The other boat faded into the distance as we made full speed ahead toward the Cayman Islands. I eased out of my room and went up top. "Hi, is it okay to come out now?" I asked.

"Sure, I think we are okay for the moment," Alejandro said.

"For the moment?"

"Well, they don't usually give up that easily, so I am taking us into the shipping lanes where there will be other boats and patrols," Alejandro said. I noticed Neo had binoculars and was keeping a careful eye on the horizon to ensure we weren't being followed.

"You know, boss, they looked more like dope dealers than pirates," Neo said.

"Well, either way, I am glad they gave up," Alejandro said.

After about an hour, Alejandro cut the engine and had the sails raised again.

"You know, when I dreamed of sailing away, I don't think my dream included pirates," I told him with a nervous laugh.

"I bet not," Alejandro replied. "Seriously, Stacy, I must keep you stashed away and safe. If they had any idea that you were on board, you could be in serious jeopardy," Alejandro told me.

"I never thought about that being an issue," I said. "The paparazzi don't even know I am alive yet," I told him.

"No, but when they do, we will have to be very careful about your comings and goings," Alejandro told her.

Kosmos and Neo joined the conversation. "Ma'am, don't you be fretting about them, pirates. I won't let them hurt you," Neo said. Neo had a big warm smile and the heart of a warrior.

"Thank you," I replied.

Neo and Kosmos were once mercenaries and had trained with the Brazilian Mossad. Either could do what it takes to keep us safe and secure. Debbie and Chip had come up top to see what was happening and what was next.

"Way to go, guys!" Chip told the crew.

"That was insane," Debbie added.

"It's not unusual for pirates to go after boats here in the Caribbean, but it is the shortest way back to Key West," Kosmos told us.

"I think we will be safe for now; we will keep sailing all night, taking turns on watch and piloting the boat," Alejandro said.

"Kosmos, you and Neo take the first shift, and I will be up at midnight to relieve you."

"I am going down to fix dinner. Debbie, do you want to come help me?" Chip asked.

"Sure," she said.

"Alejandro, what is our next stop?" I asked.

"The Cayman Islands are about two days out from here. We'll stop there and refuel, pick up anything we may need, and then head towards the Keys," Alejandro told me.

"Doesn't that route take us around Cuba? Can we stop in Cuba?" I asked.

"Why yes, it does. But not this trip. I don't know if Cuba had any damage from the storm, and the last thing I want to do is dock somewhere that is desperate for supplies and a way out," Alejandro said.

Wow, desperate for supplies and a way out, I hadn't thought about it, but he was right. I could see tons of danger in us docking at any island that had damage. I was so stupid to ask if we could dock just so I could get pictures. "Alejandro, I'm sorry I asked to stop so I could get pictures of the damage. I never thought about the danger," I told him.

"I know you didn't think about it, but you need to start thinking in those terms. You are a celebrity now, and that status has inherent risks and dangers," Alejandro said.

"One of the big downsides to all this fame and fortune," I said.

Chapter Twenty-Five

It was hard to sleep that night. The boat had its usual gentle tossing, but I couldn't get the events of the day out of my mind. I couldn't help but think this inheritance and instant riches weren't what they were cracked up to be, and I began to cry. I heard a soft knock on my door and called out, "Come in."

It was Debbie. "I thought I heard you crying," she said. "Oh no, you are crying!"

"It has been a very rough day; I can't help but think about what if," I told her. "What if they knew I was on this boat? What if they had kidnapped me?"

Debbie put her arms around me and said, "That didn't happen. Alejandro, Kosmos, and Neo won't let anything happen to us."

"Yes, today we were lucky," I answered. "But what happens when we get back home, and the press figures out who is the heir to Annie's fortune? The paparazzi will be stalking everything I do," I said and began to cry again.

Debbie, always knowing what to do when I have a meltdown, looked me straight in the eye and said, "Okay, when we get home, just sign over all the money to me. Problem solved."

I couldn't help but laugh.

"Now that's better. There's the Stacy I know," she said. "Now, you get some rest. We are safe for now," and walked out the door.

I got up and took Dramamine, which would make me sleepy. I brought them with me for seasickness, but, knock-on-wood, so far, I hadn't needed them. I walked up on deck to clear my mind.

"Hello, Ma'am," Neo greeted me.

"Hello," I answered.

"Ma'am, have you been crying?" Neo asked.

"Maybe a little," I replied.

Neo was a big guy and certainly tough as nails, but his face softened, and he hugged me. He whispered in my ear, "Please don't fret. I won't let anybody hurt you."

I hugged him back and thanked him for his bravery and concern. "It just really scared me to think of what might have happened," I told him.

"Well, now you know Kosmos, Alejandro, and me, we are Superheroes, and we will protect you no matter what," he said with a laugh.

"Neo, what kind of yarns are you spinning tonight?" Alejandro said as he came up on deck.

"I was just reassuring Stacy here that she was in good hands with us, boss," Neo replied.

"Yes, she is," Alejandro said. "Now you go on down and get some sleep. I need you fresh and alert in the morning. We will be passing by Cuba."

"Good night, Stacy, boss," and just like that, he disappeared below deck.

"What are you doing up at this hour?" Alejandro asked.

"I tried to sleep, but it just wasn't working. It's been a big day, and I guess it all caught up with me," I said.

"You look like you have been crying. Are you okay?" Alejandro softly asked.

"Yes, I am okay," I told him.

"Sit up here next to me. It's cool in this night air, and let me hold you," Alejandro said.

"Gladly," I said as I scooted up next to his warm body.

Alejandro put his arm around me and snuggled me up close to him. It felt good to have someone close to me again. As we sat there quietly, I thought about my life. Was I ready for romance? If I were, he would be a perfect fit. He is strong, caring, brave, and sweet, all rolled up into one.

The Dramamine began to work on me, and I couldn't keep my eyes open. I slumped over his shoulder, and he didn't move. He let me sleep on his shoulder, in his arms.

All too soon, Kosmos came up to relieve Alejandro. "Boss is that Stacy?" he asked.

"Yes, she was pretty shaken up after today, so I let her rest on my shoulder," Alejandro told him.

Kosmos was smiling from ear to ear and said, "I believe you are falling for her, Boss, and I can't blame you. She is beautiful, friendly, and honest. Go for it."

"You are right. I am falling for Stacy," Alejandro answered him. He picked me up and carried me downstairs. He opened my cabin door and brought me inside. He gently placed me on the bed and leaned over to kiss my forehead.

I was very dizzy, but I felt his kiss, and I heard him say very quietly,

"I am falling for you."

I slept very soundly for the rest of the night. The following day the sun was shining, and the seagulls were chattering as they followed along behind our boat. I got out of bed, threw on some clothes, and headed to breakfast.

"Good morning, Sunshine," Chip said.

"Good morning."

"Does an omelet sound good to you, or would you prefer something else?" Chip asked.

"An omelet would be fabulous," I replied.

Alejandro suddenly appeared for breakfast. "Can I join you?" he asked. He looked like he hadn't slept much the night before. His hair was ruffled from his hands running through it, and he had big bags under his eyes.

"Sure," I told him.

"Did you get any sleep last night?" he asked.

"Yeah, after a bit," I replied with a sheepish smile.

"I slept like a log. Yesterday was intense," Chip said.

"Yes, it was. I don't want to experience that kind of drama again anytime soon," Debbie said.

"Yes, that was very strange," Alejandro said.

"Strange, how?" I asked.

"Well, it was strange," Neo chimed in as he came down the stairs. "Breakfast smells delicious, and I am more than ready for it this morning."

"Well, normally, pirates don't give up and go away that easy," Alejandro stated.

"Yeah, Boss, which was weird when they came up close. I just knew we were in for a fight," Neo said. "I was ready though; I had my AK locked and loaded for them."

"Thankfully, it didn't come down to that…. this time," Alejandro said.

"I'll say! Have you ever been in a situation where you had to fight?" I asked.

"Yes," Alejandro answered, "And it wasn't a good outcome." Then he changed the subject. "So, is everyone up for a stop in the Cayman Islands tomorrow?"

"I have always heard about the Cayman Islands and their loose banking practices," I said with a snicker.

"Au contraire. The Cayman Islands has one of the most secure banking systems in the world," Alejandro said. "That is why so many major wealthy businesspeople put their money there," he added. "Yes, I was thinking about opening up an account there myself,"

Debbie laughed and responded, "That sounds like a plan."

"What else is there to do in the Caymans?" I asked.

"Ma'am, you will love it there. It is beautiful and offers all types of hikes, snorkeling, horseback riding, and beaches," Neo said.

"Well, it sounds like just what we need after this trip, some time to relax and have fun," I told them.

"Well, I better be getting back up top so Kosmos can come down and eat," Neo said, "He gets cranky when he gets hungry," he added.

"Chip, are you up for some fishing today? I know a great spot where we can take a break and catch some fresh seafood," Alejandro said.

"Always, my friend, just say when," Chip answered.

In about an hour, the boat slowed down, and Neo dropped the sails. The water was beautiful, the sea was calm, and the wind was softly blowing. "Okay, fellas, get those hooks in the water and catch us something good," Alejandro said.

"Boss, you don't have to tell old Kosmos that twice," Kosmos said with a laugh and grabbed his fishing gear. Neo was right behind him. Chip came up on deck saying, "Well. It feels like fishing time, "and quickly went to cast a line.

It was calming and reassuring to see the four of them fishing and so relaxed and patient, but it wasn't long till Neo hollered, "Fish on," and everyone sprang into action. When fishing this deep, there was no telling what we would catch, and this first catch did not disappoint. Neo pulled up a big wahoo! Soon they were all getting a workout when a school of tuna came through. Kosmos landed a small yellowfin tuna, and we knew we would be eating well that night!

The ocean was beautiful as the sun was setting, calm wind, and it was one of the most beautiful sunsets I have ever seen! I decided it would be an excellent time for some much-needed meditation. Today's focus would be on making sure I don't lose sight of being happy. I sat on the deck in the lounge closed my eyes and cleared my mind. As I soaked in all the sounds around me, the birds, the fellas talking and laughing, and the sounds of their reels when they got a fish on, I realized that happiness was all around me. All I must do is see it, smell the salty air, watch the fish as they were brought on deck for our supper, and know that these people were my friends and would support me as I support them. After meditation, I thought about all the things that I am grateful for, and there are many. A quick prayer and I was done. Wow, that always revives me and makes me stay focused on the right path. My thoughts were interrupted when Alejandro spoke,

"We should be pulling into the marina at Grand Cayman in about three hours, so just after lunch, we can go ashore and have some fun! Does that sound like a plan?"

"Heck yeah," I answered. "I would love to lie on the beach for a few hours and just be still."

Debbie said. "Me too." Chip added, "And have some of those umbrella drinks."

"I would love to go horseback riding. I have always dreamed about the waves splashing under my horse's hooves," I told them.

"Okay, then done and done," Alejandro said.

The sun would have been sweltering except for the wind from the boat's motion. The sails were all open, and we were gliding across the ocean smooth as silk. The dolphins were swimming beside us, playing and talking to each other. Occasionally, a sea turtle would venture by on his slow and steady journey somewhere.

Funny, when a childhood dream comes true, and you think it was something you always wanted, and then you realize that it isn't. When I was a kid, I loved to be on the boat, on the water, almost anytime I could be. It was a particular time with my dad. I dreamed of having a big fancy yacht and sailing around like the rich people who came to the dock in Hobucken. But Hobucken and that time of innocence were a long way away now. In that dream, there weren't pirates, hurricanes, or danger. Just beautiful sunny days spent idling away the summer. I had enjoyed this trip through the Caribbean only to a small degree. It was nice to take the boat out, get to know the crew, and explore, but was it worth the boat's upkeep, the crew's salaries, and the hassle? I wasn't sure. I would have to talk to Scott about it. The ship was too big to do the minimal amount of sailing that would make me happy. I could do with a boat half its size or less!

But if I hadn't had this opportunity, I wouldn't have met Alejandro. Handsome, honest, sweet Alejandro. Could he be the one? I could easily fall in love with him, that much I was sure of, but this new life had just begun, and I didn't even know where I was headed. Maybe this wasn't a good time for a romance. Perhaps I was just seduced by the sailing adventure and the loneliness that wealth creates. Time tell.

Suddenly Neo hollered, "Boss!"

Alejandro ran up on deck asking, "Neo, what is it?"

"A boat off our port side. Looks like it's deserted and drifting," Neo said.

Alejandro dropped the sails and switched on the engine to try to get up close to the boat. "Be careful, Boss. It could be a trap," Kosmos told him.

As we got closer, we could see a man lying on the deck bleeding. "Ahoy, mate," Alejandro called out. "Do you need help?"

The man raised his head a little and said, "Please." He was so weak we could barely understand him. The guys jumped from our boat onto his to see what the problem was. "Oh no, Boss, it is a fishing accident," Neo said.

"What?" Alejandro asked.

"Looks like this swordfish jumped right on this deck and took revenge on this guy for catching him," Neo said.

Alejandro climbed onto the man's deck to see for himself. The man had been cut severely, and the swordfish was lying beside him. "Kosmos, get me our first aid kit and some bandages," Alejandro said.

"Kosmos, what's wrong?" I asked.

"An injured fisherman. He needs our help, bad, Ma'am," Kosmos answered.

"Neo, call the Coast Guard. Have them meet us and tell them we are headed into the harbor," Alejandro said. The fisherman told Alejandro that when he hooked the fish, it sailed up in the air and right onto the boat. When it flounced, its sword sliced open the fisherman's leg.

I could hear Neo on the radio with the Coast Guard explaining what happened and what we found. Alejandro managed a field dressing for the man's cut with the precision of a doctor. I was sure he had been on many trips with his mother and obviously learned a lot.

Once the wound was dressed and the bleeding was under control, Kosmos tied the boat behind ours, and we headed toward shore. "I will stay here and take care of this wounded man, Kosmos. You take the helm and head us towards the Cayman port. We should run into the Maritime patrol soon," Alejandro said.

In 30 minutes or so, we saw the Coast Guard boat. They came alongside us and quickly evaluated the wounded man. "Alejandro, great work; you are your mother's son," the captain said with a smile. "Thank you, sir; she taught me a lot," Alejandro replied.

The patrol checked the fisherman's identity and learned his name was Tommy Caruthers. They loaded him onto a gurney and moved him to the patrol boat. "We will take Mr. Caruthers's boat to the dock and put it in a slip for him if that's alright with you," Alejandro volunteered to the Coast Guard. "I will give the Harbormaster his information.

"Mr. Caruthers, be well. Your boat will be safe," I told him. The Coast Guard thanked us all for our help, and then his boat heeled away from ours, heading for shore with its siren wailing.

Chapter Twenty-Six

Soon we were approaching the marina. Cayman's beaches were beautiful! Sparkling water, white sand, and high-rise hotels. Tourist dreams. The marinas were all shiny and new, with everything polished and clean. You could tell that theirs was a high-end business. Alejandro pulled into the slot at the marina, and Kosmos and Neo tied us up. They would stay with the boat while we went ashore.

Alejandro directly went to the Harbormaster and told him what had happened. "We docked the Caruthers boat in the slip next to ours," Alejandro told him.

"Thank you, Alejandro. I will take care of it," the Harbormaster assured him.

When Alejandro returned, he said he had called for a car to meet us at the dock. "Do you all have your passports?" Alejandro asked.

"No, shucks, hang on," and Chip ran downstairs to grab his.

Alejandro explained that we could go straight through customs as we had nothing to declare. I reserved a room at the Grand Cayman Resort to use their towels, beach, and showers. We didn't have to take anything ashore with us. We could pick up suntan lotion and miscellaneous items at the hotel store.

Customs were a breeze. The car took us to the resort, and we checked in. I was glad Scott had given me an American Express card as it was widely accepted. I didn't know how much the hotel room was, and I didn't ask. It didn't matter because we all needed some time to unwind. Debbie and I stopped at the hotel store and bought suntan lotion and a couple of magazines. The hotel concierge assigned us a cabana spot on the beach.

I had never been to such a high-end resort. This place was amazing! The cabana had four lounge chairs, a couch, chairs, a television, and a waiter! Towels, robes, and throws were also available. All of this is right on the edge of the ocean. The waiter was at our disposal to get us drinks, snacks, or whatever our hearts desired. Now, this part of being rich was nice! There were kite surfers off to the left and families swimming off to the right. The beach in the center was privately reserved for us.

"Alejandro, what a terrible accident. Have you ever seen anything like that before?" I asked.

"Unfortunately, I have. Fishermen get so excited about landing a big one that they don't take necessary safety precautions. He would have died if we hadn't come along when we did," Alejandro said.

"Enough about sadness, just look at this place!" I exclaimed.

Debbie and I went in for a swim and the water was excellent! "I saw in a brochure that the ocean here stays about 82-84 degrees all winter long! I could get used to this," Debbie said.

"Yes, this part is fabulous," I replied. Soon the fellas were in the water, too, playing and frolicking like kids. The water was a perfect 82 degrees, and it was late September! We decided to rent some snorkeling gear and check out the bottom.

The masks and breathing tubes opened a whole new world to us. The first thing I noticed was how clear the water was. To my left, I could see a giant starfish, not the kind you find on the beach dried up, but a real-live starfish. It was creeping along the bottom with each point of the star-like little legs. Then a beautiful stingray came past at an elegant, peaceful winged pace, like a bird coasting through the water. Its back was black, and the underside was a stark white in contrast. Then suddenly, there were tropical fish everywhere. I held out my hand, and they came out of curiosity to see what I was. Fish in all colors of the rainbow. There were some in beautiful hues of blue and yellow! I believe they are called blue and stoplight parrotfish. There was also grouper and snapper and we even saw a moray eel.

The underwater plant life was extraordinary, too. All different colors, shapes, and textures of plants living along the reef, everything from blue to yellow to pink and green. The reef itself, was a living, evolving creation, home to all types of marine life. I liked Angelfish best. A conch went inching its way along the bottom, tiny crabs were milling along, and a slow, steady sea turtle swam past me. I looked over at the others who were signaling me to surface when I realized a couple of small sharks were swimming amongst us. I didn't think we were in any real danger, but the sharks scared away the beautiful fish, so it was time to take a rest.

On the surface, Debbie was alive with chatter. "Oh my gosh, I have never seen anything like this," she squealed. "I got tons of fabulous photos. I love this underwater camera!"

"Beneath the surface is a whole separate world, alive and working oblivious to all the chaos going on above the water," Chip said.

"Well, folks, let's head up to the cabana and get some lunch. "Race you!" Alejandro challenged. Everyone took off running as best we could in the waist-deep water. We exited the water laughing and huffing and puffing, out of breath. And swimming makes you hungry.

The hotel's service was worthy of its five-star rating. We ordered a full meal delivered right to our beach chairs, and it was delicious! "Well, after that meal, I need a siesta," Chip told us.

"I think we all do," I said.

"Well, I guess a short nap won't hurt anything. Why don't you guys sleep while I check on the boat and arrange our horseback riding for the afternoon," Alejandro said.

Soon everyone was napping in their chairs. I decided to take a walk up the beach by myself. Once I got past the resort area, the beach was deserted. I meandered along the shoreline, picking up an occasional seashell. Always the collector, I saw a beautiful piece of something green sparkling in the water. It was sea glass. Now there was a treasure! I picked it up, a beautiful triangular shape in shades of blue and green, polished smooth from the movement of the waves. I suddenly realized I had wandered pretty far down the beach and had better head back. Alejandro would have a fit if he came back and I was gone. The resort and our beach were in sight. I hurried back and dropped into my chair just as Alejandro stepped into the cabana.

"Okay, it's time to rise and shine, crew," he said. I lazily rolled over and tried to open my eyes to look at him. He was incredibly handsome with his dark hair and dark eyes. He was looking down at me so gently and softly that I couldn't help but melt.

"I think I would rather sleep than ride a horse," Chip said with a yawn.

"Oh no, you aren't getting off that easy," Debbie told him. "I've always dreamed of riding horses on the beach near the ocean, and I need a partner."

"Okay, okay," Chip said as he sat up. I was already up and getting my flip-flops on. "I can't wait," I exclaimed.

The car was waiting for us at the hotel door, and away we went. We headed to Barker's Beach and the stable where horses and a tour guide were ready for us and soon, we were on our way. My horse was a black and white medicine hat painted with beautiful markings. Debbie was riding a chubby palomino with a flaxen mane and tail. Chip a paint horse with a perfect heart-shaped marking on her belly. Alejandro was riding a big bay gelding with a white face.

We headed down to the most pristine, beautiful beach I have ever seen. There wasn't a person in sight for miles. The horses knew the way and needed very little guidance from us which was good as I hadn't ridden bareback in a long time. Our guide was Jack, an island local. He told me he had been with the stable for about five years and fell in love with the horses from the first opportunity to work with them. "I love caring for them. They have become my family," Jack said.

"I can see why they would. They are impressive," I told Jack. As we rode along, Jack and I talked about island history, the horses, and home. As an orphan on the island, Jack had lived a hard life. He had found a home at the stables and a new family.

We got to the spot where the horses swim, and they were glad to have arrived. They willingly walked right into the ocean, out deep enough that the water came right up to our saddles. It was amazing to feel the cool water and the warmth of the horse's bodies beneath us. The horses' strength as they swam effortlessly along was terrific. They seemed to enjoy the swim and not mind the riders on their backs. Surprisingly, it was easy to stay on and just submit to the moment and relax. I had forgotten how much I loved riding.

"Are you enjoying this ride?" Alejandro asked as his horse swam up beside me.

"Oh yes, it's everything I had hoped it would be," I told him.

"Awesome," he replied.

Debbie and Chip had fallen a little behind us but seemed to be in a world all their own.

The horses knew their limit and swam back toward shore until they could walk to the bottom again. The sun was hot, beating down on us, and by the time we got back to the stables, we were all dry but scaly with salt.

"I am so glad we rented a room," I said.

"Me, too," Debbie agreed. "I look a mess."

"You shower first, I need to do my ritual," I said.

"What is this ritual?" Debbie asked.

"Well, I try to sit down each morning and take a look at my life. How can I be a better person, a better friend, a better businesswoman? Then I meditate to focus on the things that I need to improve. Afterward, I say my prayers. The last step is my affirmation word or phrase. I once thought this was extremely silly, but I learned it is a powerful tool. My ritual helps keep me balanced and focused," I explained.

"Wow, will you teach me to meditate?" Debbie asked.

"Sure, it's straightforward. Most people get so hung up on meditating that they make it hard, but it isn't. You find a quiet place, close your eyes, and think about what you wish to happen, such as being a better friend.

Then clear your mind of all the other thoughts and just think about that one thing, focus on it, and before you know it, it will become a reality," I told her. "There are all styles of meditation walking meditation, music, chants, and so on but, I have found that simplicity is best for me."

"Wow, I can see where that would be so helpful. I'm going to try it," Debbie said.

"I can't wait to get in the shower," I said, and then it hit me. "We didn't bring any clothes," I said with a laugh.

"Shopping trip!" Debbie said with a smile.

The hotel was close to the downtown area, and we could easily meander around and browse the boutiques.

"We could go back to the boat and get a change of clothes," Alejandro said.

"We could, yes," I said, "but these stores have such cute stuff," I told him. I finally decided on a cute flirty strapless sundress and some sandals.

"This will be perfect for dancing the night away," I told Debbie.

Then Debbie spied her outfit for the evening, a red gauzy shirt and wide-legged beach pants with a floral top. "I just love red," she said. We made our purchases and headed out the door. Chip and Alejandro opted to go back to the boat and get some clothes while Debbie and I showered at the hotel.

"Deb let's see if we can get a spa appointment. I could use some spoiling," I said.

"Heck yeah, that sounds great," she agreed. The hotel had an opening, and we got right in. I hadn't been to a spa in a long, long time, well, actually never, but I had always dreamed about going to one. "So, what services would you ladies like to try?" a beautiful, svelte redhead asked us from behind the desk. At that moment, I felt like the country bumpkin that I am. I thought I should ask for a menu.

To my surprise, Debbie, who reads every brochure known to man, knew just what to request. "Well, we would both like a hot stone massage with essential oils, maybe lavender, to relax us," she said. "We have had a big day of swimming and horseback riding, and I don't want to be sore tomorrow," she told the hostess.

"Fantastic, let me show you to your rooms," the redhead said.

She looked at Debbie and said, "You are in 7A right here, and you" she said to me, "are in 7B across the hall. If you need anything, dial extension eight. Enjoy."

My masseuse in 7B was a very athletic-looking lady in her mid-forties. "Welcome, please step into the dressing room and remove all your clothes.

Here is a towel for modesty's sake," she said in a thick French accent. So, I did as she asked. The towel was generous, thank heavens, and when I stepped back out, she said, "Just climb up on the table, lie face down, and loosen your towel. I am going to pull it around and drape it over your butt." So, I did as I was told and got into position.

She began by warming up my muscles with her hands, and it felt amazing! I had never had a massage. I always felt it was too expensive a treat, but boy, was I wrong. Yep, I should have been doing this regularly. It felt good to let go of stress and relax. Then came the hot stone part. I was a little apprehensive because it sounded like torture. She began placing these wonderful warm stones on pressure points all around my back and shoulders. The stones' warmth was soothing, almost like a heating pad, but with just enough weight pressing on those points to release them. I was pretty sure I was in heaven. The skilled lady worked her way down my leg muscles to my feet, and by the time she was done, I was a dishrag. It was amazing. Then she said, okay, you are all done, I will step out, and you can get dressed now.

Debbie was waiting in the lobby.

"That was amazing," I told her.

"I know, I had never had a massage, but boy, I want that on my expense account," she told me with a wink.

"Expense account? You must think I am rich," I responded. We were both laughing as we went up the elevator to our room and got dressed.

"So, are you and Chip an item?" I asked Debbie.

"Well, we have been seeing a lot of each other," she answered.

"Is he, you know, the one?" I asked.

"Well, I like him a lot, but I'm a long way from settling down, so we will have to wait and see," she told me. "What about you and Alejandro?"

"I could easily fall in love with him, but my life is so twisted right now I don't feel like I can make any type of commitment or long-term plans about love," I told her.

"I know what you mean. You know we have both gotten more than we dreamed of and now all of a sudden, what do we do with it?" Debbie told me.

"Yeah, we have some growing pains to live through, no doubt about that," I agreed. "But, for the here and now, let's go have some fun."

When we were ready, the men were waiting in the hotel bar.

Chapter Twenty-Seven

"Wow," was all Chip could say! "You both look stunning and ready for a night on the town."

"Well, I don't know about you, but I am going to wear out these feet dancing the night away," Debbie said.

I could see from his facial expressions that Alejandro was impressed. "Yes, you both are exquisite beauties," he said. Then he took my hand and kissed it. I felt like a princess!

"So, what are you guys in the mood for, for dinner?" Chip asked.

"I would like a big juicy steak," I told them.

"Italian sounds pretty good," Debbie chimed in.

"Of course, I would like something different. How about something with an island flair," Alejandro said.

"So, let's walk around a little and see what hits us," Chip said. We headed into town which was alive with people—folks from all over the world walking around the different restaurants and shops.

"What is that fantastic smell?" asked Debbie.

"Smells like grilled mahi mahi with some island seasonings," Chip said.

"Well, it smells like heaven. Let's find it. I am starved," I said.

"Fish Shack," Chip said, "that's it."

We were seated pretty quickly at a great table on the water. The soft lights from the city reflected beautifully in the water. It was very romantic and a fitting scene for our final night in paradise.

Chip ordered us a nice pinot to go with our dinner. Yes, as always, he was one hundred percent spot on with his culinary smells and tastes. That magnificent smell was indeed grilled mahi mahi with an island seasoning blend. The restaurant is called Mahi Mahi Cayman. We all decided to try it. The warmth of the atmosphere and the wine were working. We were relaxed and unwinding. The meal was delicious, and the presentation was impeccable. Being ultra-rich does have its rewards, I thought.

After the meal, we walked back towards the hotel, looking for a club to dance in. Alejandro asked us, "What type of music and dance do you guys like?"

"Something hip, young, and fast," Debbie spoke up.

"I agree," I said.

"Well, then you want Obar," Alejandro advised us.

"How do you know so much about the party scene here?" I teased.

"Well, I might have partied here a few times in my life," Alejandro admitted.

Obar was incredible, right on the main strip, and the music was blasting. The bouncer at the door took our cover charge and let us in. The bar was packed, and the dance floor was getting hot.

"This club has everything you could ever ask for," Debbie said.

We made our way to a table, and a scantily clad waitress took our drink order. I ordered my favorite Bahama Breeze, and Debbie seconded that notion. Alejandro was a rum and Coke kind of guy, and Chip decided to try the local craft beer.

It didn't take long till we were all on the dance floor having a blast! I hadn't danced so much since I was in high school. We danced to every song the band played, and then they slowed it down. Slow dancing with Alejandro was like floating on a cloud and very sensual. I wondered if he thought he would get lucky, or maybe it would be me who got lucky, but who cared? Tonight, was about fun.

The evening was a blur, and suddenly the bar announced the last call, and it was time to crawl back to the hotel. Chip and Debbie said they would catch up with us at the boat as they wanted to stop for a late-night breakfast.

"Debbie, I want to talk to you about something," Chip said.

"Okay," she answered and wondered if Chip was getting too serious about her already.

They found an all-night diner and went in for a bite.

"I need your advice about something," Chip began. "I have missed the restaurant business ever since I agreed to be a private chef for Annie and Raymond. I have dreamed of owning my very own restaurant for as long as I can remember. One of the reasons I took the job with Annie was to make enough money to save up and buy a place."

"I can understand that everyone has dreams," Debbie said.

"The problem is I like Stacy, and I don't want to let her down," Chip said. "But I need to begin to make my life, get my business established, perhaps settle down and have some kids."

"I think Stacy would be happy for you and understand completely. You just need to tell her," Debbie said.

"Okay, when the timing is right, I will," Chip said.

"In the meantime, you should begin moving forward with your dreams so that when we get back, you can achieve them," Debbie said.

"I appreciate your advice on this. I am enjoying getting to know you and hope you feel the same," Chip said.

"I am enjoying getting to know you as well," Debbie said.

Then the food arrived, and the mood was lost. "Well, let's eat," Chip said.

Chapter Twenty-Eight

Alejandro had gone back to the boat, and I crawled into bed to reflect on the day's events. Wow, what a day it had been, real fun: something I hadn't taken time for in my life in an exceptionally long time. Swimming and playing in the water, snorkeling, lounging around, and then horseback riding. How could I have asked for more? I hadn't ridden a horse since I left New Bern, but that draw was still there. I wanted to see my horses again. I wanted to ride. That is something I was going to make time to do in my life, no matter where my riches took me.

Of course, there was a change in direction with Alejandro, the boat, and the crew. When I got back to the States, I was sure that the media would have discovered that I inherited Annie's fortune. I was nervous about how that would go and how I could become a recluse. But having seen Neo and Kosmos in action I knew they would be excellent bodyguards.

Then there was Alejandro, himself. I admitted my feelings for him, my need for him, and I was willing to face them unafraid. Now that was a massive step for me. I was so happy that he seemed to feel the same way about me. I hoped it was not just infatuation on his part, but I couldn't think about that. I had to trust in the here and now, moving forward to love. With so many thoughts dancing in my head, I drifted off to a very sound sleep.

I heard a loud banging on my door at 7:45; it was Neo. "Neo, good morning. What are you doing here?" I asked.

"The boss sent me to escort you back to the boat just in case you were oversleeping," Neo said.

"Oh no, I did oversleep! I'll be ready in ten minutes. Did you wake Debbie yet?"

"Yes, Ma'am, Ms. Debbie, and Mr. Chip are awake and will meet us in the lobby," Neo said with a smile.

"Right," I answered. "Be right there, Neo."

When I got down to the lobby, we all piled into a cab to the dock. Alejandro and Kosmos were getting the boat ready to go when we arrived. We all hurried down the pier and boarded.

"Good morning," Alejandro greeted us.

"Morning," I said. I think I was still half asleep.

"I'll head down to the galley and get us some breakfast," Chip said.

"I am going to bed," Debbie said.

I went to my room, showered, and put on some fresh clothes. When I went back topside, we were motoring out of the harbor. I could hardly wait to get to the open sea. The harbor was a hive of activity. People were working on their boats, scurrying around the docks, and filling up with fuel. Gulls were flying and squawking at everyone as they buzzed past. As soon we were out in the open ocean, Neo and Kosmos put the sails up, and in just a few minutes, I heard that old familiar sound of the sails catching the wind.

"Let's just enjoy this last bit of our trip and see where the future carries us," Alejandro said.

Kosmos shouted, "Thar she blows!" and pointed off the starboard side at a humpback whale and her calf. How beautiful! The sea is such a wonderous frontier. It's hard to believe that there is an entire universe just under the surface.

Chip poked his head up through the stairwell and hollered, "Breakfast is ready!"

I headed to the galley. "You don't have to call me twice," I told Chip. "I'm starving."

In just a few minutes, Kosmos and Alejandro made their way down as well. Chip had outdone himself; he must not have had a hangover at all.

"I have prepared for your dining pleasure pancakes, applewood smoked bacon, and scrambled eggs," he said. "We also have a selection of fresh fruit."

He dished up pancakes and passed the plates down the line. "Oh, I forgot the fresh-squeezed orange juice," Chip said and got up to fetch it.

"This is so good!" I told him.

"Fresh oranges were available in port," Chip confided.

"Alejandro, how long will it take us to get to Key West?" I asked.

"About a day and a half. We will stay in the shipping lanes to avoid any hassles, and the weather forecast is perfect."

"What is our route?" I asked.

"We will head northeast and cut through by Guantanamo just north of Jamaica. There are a lot of small islands and then the Keys," Alejandro explained.

"Awesome," I said.

"Then we will head West and swing by the Bahamas," Alejandro said.

"Will we stop anywhere?" I asked.

"Not unless you need something," Alejandro said.

"No, I was just curious."

Alejandro and Kosmos headed back topside, and Neo came down to eat. "Well, I hope everybody is done because Neo is here, and I am starving," he laughingly said.

"Enjoy, it was delicious," I told him and headed up top. I settled down in the lounge and pulled out my planner to make some notes about the magazine.

"A penny for your thoughts," Alejandro said as he sat down beside me.

"I hate for this trip, this moment, to end," I told him.

"Me too," Alejandro said. "But why are you so worried looking?"

"The closer to the States we get, the more real my life moving forward is becoming. I dread dealing with the paparazzi and media frenzy that is sure to follow me," I said.

"You should not worry, my love. You have the best protection force in the world at your disposal," Alejandro said.

When we made the turn around Cuba, there was a boat shadowing us. "Alejandro, have you noticed that boat following us and watching us?" I asked.

"Yes, as a matter of fact, I have."

I have a call into the Maritime Security at Guantanamo to alert them. They are also observing us."

I let out a big sigh of relief, "I knew you would be taking care of us."

"I came this way because pirates have been very active lately, and I wanted to be sure we had an extra big brother if we needed it," Alejandro said.

I went below to check my emails and itinerary. I let Scott know what time we would be making port and be back in Boca. He responded that he would be glad to see me and asked if I could set up a meeting on the coming Wednesday. Well, I would be getting "home" on Tuesday afternoon to Boca, so why not? I emailed him that I would be there, and he offered to treat me to lunch. It would be good to see him and catch up on what's been happening in the real world. So yes, we were on for lunch at the Yacht Club in Boca at 1 p.m.

Debbie knocked on my door and asked, "Hey, can I come in?"

"Sure, I was just going to send you an email," I told her. I have a meeting with my attorney on Wednesday in Boca. Let's get together before then to discuss the magazine and devise a loose plan to present to him then."

"Absolutely," Debbie said. "Let's do it Wednesday morning when we're back to reality and normalcy. That will give me some time to get some notes together for you. Does it feel good to get back into business mode?"

"Yes, actually it does," I told her. "Paradise has been wonderful, but I have a big mountain to climb, and I have to be focused to manage it."

"So, what about Alejandro?"

"I have deep feelings for him, and he does for me, but we both decided that we're not ready for a meaningful relationship. My life is so uncertain, and his love is the sea," I told her.

"I see the same sort of dilemma with Chip and me. I adore him, but who knows where this wonderful opportunity will take me," Debbie said.

"Will you be okay with Chip working out of the house?" I asked Debbie.

"Well, he has to talk to you about that. He has been saving money to open his restaurant in Boca. I think he is ready now," Debbie said.

"That is so awesome because I don't need a full-time chef or even a full staff in Boca. But that can be your decision since you'll be living there," I told her.

"Don't let Chip know I told you," Debbie said.

"Of course, I won't," I assured her. "Oh, and don't say anything about sailing north yet because we haven't talked to Kosmos and Neo."

We went up on deck to relax in the sun. It had been a long couple of days, and I was ready for some downtime.

"Ma'am! Look on the port side—a pod of Orcas" Kosmos yelled across the boat.

I had never seen Orcas up close. They were beautiful. They moved through the water effortlessly and their size was incredible! There were so many! I could count at least twenty-five! They averaged about twenty-two feet in length and Neo estimated most of them to weigh at least 10,000 pounds.

"Oh my gosh!" Debbie exclaimed and ran downstairs to get the camera.

"They are something, aren't they?" Alejandro said. "You can't get that in North Carolina," he teased.

"No, you sure can't," I agreed with a laugh.

"Orcas hunt in pods, sometimes as many as forty of them. Have you ever seen them hunt?" Alejandro asked.

"No, I bet it's amazing," I said.

"It is, to think that so many of these killer whales come together, sometimes as a family, sometimes just for the ride. They carry out coordinated attack patterns so that the pod can eat. Science has only just begun to tap into their intelligence," Alejandro said.

"How do you know so much about them?" I asked.

"One of the deadliest things for a sailor is to collide with one of these big boys. He can total a boat without even trying," Alejandro said.

Debbie was back and snapping photos like a madwoman. She was going to be perfect for this new position. I had chosen well.

"What if they decide to eat us?" I asked.

"They won't; people are too sweet," Alejandro said with a chuckle.

In just a few minutes, they were gone on their journey to wherever they were headed. What a special treat, I thought.

Chapter Twenty-Nine

As night began to fall, Neo and Kosmos dropped the sails and switched over to our engine. The Bahamas would be off the port side about daybreak. The ocean was beautiful this evening, slick as glass, with no wind, but the sunset was incredible.

"In honor of our last night aboard this fantastic sailboat, I have prepared Crab 5 Ways for your dining pleasure," Chip told us with a twinkle in his eye. He had made every effort to impress with tablecloths, candles, wine, and a magnificent dinner.

"We have eaten at some fantastic spots over the past few weeks, so I decided I needed to remind you guys who is the king," Chip said with a laugh!

We all raised our glasses and toasted Chip and his culinary skills. As the meal went on, each of us took turns making a toast. When the meal was over, we wandered off to our special spots to be alone and reflect on this journey.

I went topside to relax in the lounger. The air was fresh and cool, and the moon was up and sparkling. Stars flooded the sky. Neo was at the helm, and the big diesel engine was humming.

"Good evening, Ma'am," Neo said.

"Good evening."

"Are you glad to be going home, Ma'am?" Neo asked.

"I'm not sure where home is," I told him. "I inherited a house in the Hamptons, so that's where I'll be living," I told him. "Have you ever been that far north?"

"Yes, Ma'am, once or twice. It was freezing and busy!"

"Now, tell me a little about you. We haven't had much time to talk,"

"Well, old Neo's story ain't much Ma'am. I was rowdy when I was young and married the most beautiful woman in the world," Neo told me. I could see his eyes deep in thought and memory. "We were so in love, and we moved to the island of Antigua. We had a big earthquake followed by a tsunami, and she swept away while I was at work."

"Oh Neo, I am so sorry," I said.

"Yes, it was a terrible thing, but ready or not, life moves forward, so here I am," Neo said and tried to force a smile.

May I join you?" Alejandro asked.

"Boss, I am going to take a break, if you don't mind. I will be back shortly," Neo said.

"Of course, take your time. I will be up here for a while," Alejandro answered.

He sat down and leaned back on the cushions. "This sky is magnificent, isn't it?" Alejandro asked.

"Yes, I don't remember seeing it so clear and beautiful before," I said.

"The equinox has come, and we are now officially in fall. The sky is crisp and clear in the fall and winter. It's my favorite time," Alejandro said.

"Fall is my favorite season, too. I love everything about it."

"Are you ready to get back to reality?"

"Yes, I think I am," I told him. "I'm anxious to figure out what my role is in this life, how to integrate my old life and grow into new things."

"You will do well, whatever you tackle," Alejandro said with a smile.

He leaned in for a kiss, and his arms around me felt so right. Then unexpectedly, I moved to kiss him. As usual, Debbie with her impeccable timing came bouncing up the stairs to see where I was.

"Oops," she said and turned to go back down. I didn't stop her. I wanted to be alone with Alejandro tonight.

We sat there enjoying the night, talking about anything and everything, and drinking wine until well past midnight. Finally, I was too sleepy to continue and fell asleep on his shoulder. He woke me up to tell me to go to bed and get some rest. We said our good-nights, and I went downstairs. Sleep came easily. I was exhausted.

I was up by 8 a.m. I did my morning ritual and looked forward to the new day! My affirmation phrase was Don't call it a dream; call it a plan. It had been an exciting time at sea. We had gone through our first journey, a hurricane, a potential pirate attack, incredible beauty, snorkeling, horseback riding, eating fantastic food, and romance. How would the everyday world ever compare? I said a silent thank you to Annie for this opportunity and this unique boat and went to the galley for breakfast.

"This morning's breakfast is just Continental; I was pushed for time," Chip apologized.

"This is fine. After that meal last night, you have nothing to apologize for," I told him. I grabbed a Danish and a glass of Chip's famous fresh-squeezed juice and went up on the bridge to see how things were going.

"Good morning," I said to the crew.

"Good morning," they all replied.

"We will be in the harbor in Key West in about 30 minutes. We had a wonderful time last night," Alejandro said.

"Awesome, I'll call for the car to meet us."

"I already took care of it for you," Alejandro answered.

"Anxious to get rid of me?" I asked.

"No, it is just me taking care of you," Alejandro answered with a determined look in his eyes.

"Before we get into port, I would like to speak with the three of you for a moment," I said.

Everyone looked very serious at my statement.

"I know you don't know much about me, and that's because I don't know much about me, either. That sounds odd, I know, but I inherited a couple of businesses, some money, houses, and this boat from my wealthy cousin. I was just a typical woman trying to make a living and doing okay for myself. Now I find myself catapulted into a very different life, and I don't know what it will bring. I feel kind of alone and scared. Going forward, I may need protection from strangers. There will be loads of media and paparazzi. I need to know the boat will be a haven at a moment's notice, with you three on board to keep me safe," I said. After a couple of moments for that to sink in, I asked, "Would you be interested?"

Alejandro was, of course, the first one to speak. "You know I am in," he said.

"Where would we live, Mam?" Neo asked.

"Well, I have a house in the Hamptons, a lodge in Jackson Hole, a condo in Manhattan, a place in California, a flat in London, and a house in Boca, but whenever I am on the boat, you would be here with me," I said. "When I'm away, you can be home with your families or live on the boat and remain on my payroll wherever you live."

"What exactly do you want us to do?" Kosmos asked.

"Well, I want you to protect me, be my private security force, crew the boat when we're sailing, and keep me safe," I told him. "The job will pay handsomely. I value each of you.

"Ma'am, I don't have a family anymore or much of a home, so if you will have me, I am in," Neo said.

I threw my arms around him and gave him a big hug, "Of course, I will have you," I said with a smile.

Kosmos answered, "Can I think about it a little, Ma'am? I am honored to be selected for this position, but I need to discuss it with my family."

"Of course, take whatever time you need. We can always work out something on an as-needed basis so you could live at home part of the time as well," I told him.

After an overnight stay in the Keys to fuel up and to clear U.S. Customs we headed up the coast to Boca Raton.

Chapter Thirty

We pulled into the harbor, and Jimmy, my driver, was waiting. Jimmy greeted me with a smile until he saw my tears, then he handed me his handkerchief. "Welcome back, Ma'am," he said quietly.

"Thanks," I told him. We got in the car and drove away.

The house at Boca was a welcome sight. I needed a place to crash and think. Debbie and I went up to our rooms. Chip went to the kitchen to take inventory.

"I think I'll take a nap," I told Debbie.

"Okay, sounds like a plan; see you in a little while," Debbie said.

I put my suitcase down and climbed into that big old comfy bed. My phone lit up with a text from Alejandro. It was sweet, a sad face with a quick note "Miss you already." I answered with "Me too," and that was it. I fell into a blissful sleep. About an hour later the phone woke me—Chip letting me know lunch was ready.

I pulled myself together and headed downstairs. "What's for lunch?" I asked.

"I ran up to the local market and got some fresh chicken salad, I know the chef, and it is quite good. Then I whipped up some chicken noodle soup and fresh bread," Chip said.

"That sounds delightful," I told him.

Debbie was right on time for our meeting. "Well, are you ready to get started?" she greeted me.

"Yes, Ms. Editor, I am," I told her, and we went into the office. She had made tons of notes, projections, and plans and had a hit list for potential advertisers. She had beautiful photos and story ideas. "I prepared a report for you to share with Scott," she told me and showed it to me and explained it. It was great to be working!

"Looks like you have a great vision for our new venture," I told her.

"I had a lot of time to think about it on the boat, and I know it will be a big hit," she told me.

Chip approached me in the hall and wanted to talk for a few minutes. "Sure, come in."

"As you'll remember, I have been saving for a long time and looking for a place to open a restaurant," he began. "While we were on our sailing trip, a realtor contacted me, and the ideal place has finally become available," he said.

"Where would you locate it?" I asked.

"A building here in downtown Boca, in a trendy section has just become vacant," Chip said.

"That would be a suitable location for sure."

"I know you don't need me here at the house, heck you are hardly ever going to be here, and I have feelings for Debbie that I would like to explore. It would be uncomfortable for me to be an employee of hers if we were dating," Chip explained.

"Yes, it would."

"So, I'd like to give you my notice and go for it with my restaurant."

"Chip, you know you'd always have a job with me if things don't work out."

"Thank you, Stacy, that means a lot."

"Are you looking for investors?" I asked.

"Of course," he answered.

"Well, then put together a proposal for me to consider, and I'll see what I can do. "He gave me a big hug and thanked me over and over.

Oh no, it was almost time for Jimmy. I dashed upstairs and got ready for Scott. I put on a business outfit, grabbed my bag and briefcase, and headed downstairs. Jimmy was right on time.

"Good afternoon," Jimmy said as he opened the car door.

"Good afternoon."

"You look like things are going a little better for you today," Jimmy said.

"Definitely," I told him. He gave me a big warm smile in the mirror.

Scott had a table and as I approached, he stood up to greet me. "Hi, world traveler," he said with a smile. "How was your trip?"

"Well, it was interesting," I replied.

"Interesting isn't exactly the word I expected," Scott said.

"The boat was magnificent; the crew was great. We rode out a hurricane on an island to the south of the storm. We almost had a pirate altercation and had to end the trip early because of the additional possibility of hurricanes," I told him.

"I see," Scott said.

"How is everything else?" he asked.

"Well, I decided to start a magazine about sailing," I told him. "I'm a magazine editor by trade and I've asked one of my best friends to run it for me from here in Boca, probably out of the house here for now. I have here a presentation that she put together for us to review," I added.

"That sounds good. I am glad to see you're finding your way," Scott said.

"How are all the investment businesses doing?" I asked.

"Everything is perking along just fine," Scott told me.

"Good, because I know nothing about that business, so I am happy it doesn't need me."

"I also decided not to dock in the Keys. I'll take the boat up to the Carolinas and dock it somewhere up there. Then I can sail when the weather is nice," I told him. "I'll keep the crew on my payroll on stand-by status for whenever Debbie or I need it. I know you had them checked out, and they are competent, and I would feel better knowing I have a safe place to escape. Unfortunately, I have to assume that a bodyguard or two will be necessary in the future. The media are bound to learn who I am." I told Scott.

"I think that is a wonderful idea, Stacy. I hope you will never need them, but most wealthy clients always travel with some type of security personnel. I don't honestly think you could find anyone more capable or loyal," Scott added.

"When we berth the boat, I'm going to head up to the Hampton's house. I had my things shipped thereafter I arranged to put my house in New Bern up for sale. So, I am sort of anxious to get there and make it home," I told him.

"Good, it's beautiful there, and I know you'll enjoy it."

"I think I'll be at the Hamptons house for about a month and then go to Jackson Hole to check out the lodge, do a little skiing, and learn something about that business."

"It's a beautiful place and I think that would be a great idea," Scott said. "I'll let them know to expect you in early November."

"Fantastic," I replied.

"When you get time, stop by the office. I have some more papers for you to sign, nothing important, just routine stuff," Scott told me.

"Okay, I'll come by before I head back to the boat. Do you have plans for Thanksgiving?"

"Well, not at the moment," Scott said.

"Why don't you and your family come out to the lodge and spend Thanksgiving there?" I asked.

"That would be fun. Let me check with my wife," Scott said.

"Awesome," I replied.

Lunch, as always, was delicious!

"How is the island resort idea coming along," I asked. Scott had pitched the idea of investing with some other business folks to buy an island and turn it into a five-star resort. He had sent me pictures and ideas which I fell in love with. A great investment idea, I agree.

"Well, the island has been purchased, and the developer is with the Architect to get a final drawing for us to approve. I think it will be ready when we see each other at Thanksgiving," Scott said.

"Great! I love the idea of owning an island," I said.

"Well, you could easily buy one for just you if you wanted to," Scott said.

"I know, but this way, I don't have to do anything but sign papers. I am getting the hang of this heiress stuff."

"Stacy, I know this is none of my business, but are you and Alejandro a couple?" Scott asked.

"Alejandro and I have feelings for each other, no denying it. However, I am uncertain about what I want and how my life will look in the coming months. I don't think it would be fair to pursue our feelings at this point," I said.

"Probably a smart answer, but let your heart tell you if it is the right answer. You're young, you have plenty of time, but people don't always wait," Scott said.

We chatted a little more, then it was time to leave. "Thank you for lunch, Scott, it was good to see you," We hugged each other, and I went out to meet Jimmy.

On the way back to the house, I texted Debbie asking her to meet with Suzi, the Boca house manager, and me when I got back. When I got back to the house, I set up a meeting with Suzi. I knew this would be dicey, so I was happy to hand her off to Debbie's experienced hands.

Suzi was her usual pushy self, asking a bunch of questions about "the new house guest," so I took pleasure in explaining that Debbie would be her new boss and she was at Debbie's disposal. She didn't like it, but she also didn't want to lose her job. Debbie quickly took charge and gave Suzi a list of things to prepare for her to review. Yep, I knew that was a good call.

"Hey, how would you like to go bum around Boca with me and check out the marinas, dive shops, and other stuff related to our publication?" Debbie asked.

"Great idea," I told her.

We called for the car and Jimmy was right on time. "Hi, ladies," he opened the doors. "Where are we off to today?"

"Jimmy, this is Debbie Ballard. She will be heading up a new magazine about sailing for me and living here at the Boca house," I told him.

"Pleased to meet you, Ms. Ballard," Jimmy answered.

"Please, just Debbie. We want to check out the stores that cater to boats and boaters," Debbie told him.

We spent the afternoon sizing up the marina area, and Jimmy had good suggestions about additional avenues for advertising, such as high-end real estate and car dealerships. Debbie would have plenty of fodder to get this thing off the ground, and I knew she could do it.

"When you are back on the boat or traveling to the Hamptons, do you think you will feel like writing a couple of stories for our first edition?" Debbie asked me.

"I would be delighted," I answered. "Do you have the editorial calendar ready for the first issue?" I knew that was a dumb question. Debbie probably had the entire year done.

"Well, yes, Ma'am, I do. I have the entire year laid out," Debbie answered.

"I knew you would," I teased her. "Email it to me to check when I get on the boat, and I will work up something great for you."

"I get it. Life is going to be a wild ride but be sure you don't lose Stacy in the process. Also, travel slowly. Love can be a dangerous game," Debbie said as she reached over and hugged me.

Back at the house, Chip had been busy preparing our dinner. He was so excited, he messaged me to see him when I got in, so I went straight to the kitchen.

"Hi," he greeted me.

"Hi, what's up?"

"I got the architectural drawings back for the restaurant, and I wanted you to see them."

"Wow, now that is big news! Okay let's have a look," I said. Chip rolled them out on the dining table and began to explain his vision. It sounded like a good sound plan.

"What type of capital do you need from an investor?" I asked.

"I was hoping you might see the value and do seventy-five thousand dollars," he said.

"Okay, I have to get it approved by Scott, and I have no idea how that will go, but write up the proposal, attach a set of the drawings and anything else you might have, and I will see what I can do.," I told him.

"Great," he answered, "let's eat." He messaged the rest of the crew that dinner was ready, and they slowly meandered down to the kitchen.

Chapter Thirty-One

Suzi had left for the day, and the maids were gone, so it was just Debbie, Chip, and me.

"I made for your pleasure tonight something very American and simple like home cooking," he said with a big smile. The anticipation was building. "Hamburger steak, gravy, mashed potatoes, and corn on the cob," he exclaimed!

"Oh my God, Chip, I love you," I told him.

"I second that," Debbie said. It was the perfect meal for our return home.

We talked about the new restaurant, the new magazine, and where I was headed next. I told everyone goodbye at the dinner table as Jimmy was on his way to take me back to the boat.

Before Debbie and I said our temporary goodbyes, we made plans for her to fly to meet with me every two weeks wherever I was. "The magazine is off to a good start, and I have every faith that you will do an amazing job!" I told her. "Scott will draw up an employment and partnership agreement for you and send it over this week,"

"Partnership? I'm confused," she said.

"Don't be. If you are going to work hard enough to make this successful, it is only right for you to have a share of it."

"Wow," was all she could say.

Jimmy, as always, was right on time. He loaded my luggage and we pulled onto the highway and headed back to the boat.

"It sure has been nice to have you here for a little while, Stacy," Jimmy told me. "Remember, anywhere you are if you need anything, call ol' Jimmy."

"I appreciate that. Thank you," I said.

Before long, we were back at the docks and Alejandro was there to meet me. "Hi, glad to have you back," he said as he hugged me.

"Great to be back.," I told him.

"So, how did Scott take the news about all of us?" he asked.

"He thought it was an amazing idea and supported it one hundred percent," I said.

As we walked down the dock to the boat, the moon was out, it was a warm night, and the harbor was softly lit from the streetlamps and vessels. It was magical and beautiful, and I said as much to Alejandro.

"Yes, it is, but don't get too comfortable. You are headed into frigid weather very soon," Alejandro said with a smile.

"I will be simply fine. I'll have memories of you to keep me safe and warm," I said as I snuggled a little closer.

"Yes, as will I," Alejandro replied. "Now off to bed, you go. You have had a big day."

"I'm not sleepy just yet. I'll put my things away and come up top with you and the crew.".

"Okay, whatever you say," Alejandro answered.

I went down to the galley, and that sweet, wonderful Chip had left us all kinds of sandwich items, bread, soup, and snacks for our trip. I sure was going to miss his cooking but was so proud of him and his new venture. I put away my things and headed topside.

Up on deck Kosmos and Neo were with Alejandro waiting to talk. "Hi, guys," I greeted them.

"Glad to have you back aboard, Ma'am," Neo answered.

"Ma'am, I spoke with my wife, and I would like to accept your offer," Kosmos said.

"That is awesome. I feel better already," I told him.

Then it was Neo's turn. "Ma'am, I don't have any family, so I too, would love to accept your offer and work for you."

"Oh Neo, I am so happy, thank you, thank you all," I said.

"Oh, I almost forgot! I have to go back to Scott's office tomorrow morning before we set sail, I have to sign some papers," I said.

"No worries, I will wake you by 8 a.m., and you can go while we finish with the supplies," Alejandro said.

Promptly at eight, there was a loud knock on my door and Neo called, "It's me, Ma'am, Neo.

"The boss sent me down to make sure you were up and ready. Jimmy will be here in about 30 minutes.

"Okay, thanks," I told Neo. I got up, got dressed, and went into the galley. Kosmos was in the kitchen.

"Well, boy, do I miss Chip this morning, no chef. I guess the glamorous life is over." I said.

"No, Ma'am, the glamorous life is just beginning. You see, I double as the boat's cook," he said with a big belly laugh. "Now, how do you like your eggs?"

"Kosmos, you never cease to amaze me, scrambled with cheese, please," I said.

Alejandro joined me in the galley. "Good morning. How are you this morning?" he asked.

"I'm doing great! I didn't know Kosmos could cook," I said with a laugh.

"Well, if you can call it that," Alejandro said with a wink.

"Good morning, Captain. What would you like for breakfast this morning?" Kosmos asked.

"What are my choices, sir?"

"Well, there is bacon and eggs or eggs and bacon, whichever you prefer," Kosmos told him.

"Jimmy will be here any minute. I better head up to the dock," I told them.

"Okay, see you later," Alejandro said.

Chapter Thirty-Two

Jimmy was at the dock, patiently waiting for me. "Good morning, Stacy," he called out as he opened the door.

"Good morning; sorry I am late," I said.

"No worries, Ma'am, we are right on schedule," Jimmy replied, and we drove off.

At Scott's office, his receptionist offered me a Diet Coke and it was very welcome this morning. "Thank you so much," I told her.

"No problem, it's how I start my day, too. Scott is in this conference room waiting for you," she said.

"Good morning, Stacy," Scott greeted me.

"Well, let's address the elephant in the room. What in the heck happened down there?" Scott asked.

"Alejandro and I went freediving near his parents' property. I saw something odd on the bottom. picked it up and swam to the surface with it. It turned out it was a homing beacon for a drug drop. I had no idea. Alejandro took it, dove right back down, and replaced it where I got it. A man coming down the beach must have seen that. He confronted us but let us pass. The next day I went for a walk alone in town. Nobody knew I was going, which was a huge mistake on my part. The man from the beach and his partner grabbed me and beat me up to find out info about the beacon. Kosmos and Neo rescued me from where they had me hidden. Alejandro went to meet them with ransom money so Kosmos and Neo could get me. Neela Malone helped with intel for the guys. They rescued me, got the bad guys, turned them into the police, and that was that" I said.

"Holy Mackerel! I can't believe you went through all that," Scott said.

"I learned a valuable lesson about my future safety once I recovered from that experience. It won't happen again," I said.

"Well, you look bright-eyed and chipper this morning Thank God you're okay," Scott said.

"Well, I am. The crew agreed to work for me and protect me. So, I am all set, I think," I told Scott.

"That is perfect," Scott replied. "You know there will be a lot of social events coming up in the next few months that you will want to attend so folks can get to know you," Scott said.

"Like what?" I asked.

"Well, the season is usually kicked off in early November with a ball at the home of Donna McCartney, fashion designer. Then a little soiree at Martha Stewart's bungalow near you. Then in New York, there will be parties galore, some sponsored by the bank's clients, so it is always good to at least make an appearance. I will send you a list." Scott said.

"Do I have to go?" I asked.

"No, you don't have to, but it is a good business practice to make appearances, at least at some of them. If it is an important event, I will message you and send a chopper. How about that?" Scott said.

I could see that I wasn't going to get out of these events, so I said, "Okay."

"I worked up a partnership agreement for you and Debbie regarding the magazine," Scott said. "I made you the sixty percent owner to retain control and Debbie is forty percent. I set up a generous salary and bonus plan for her."

"Great, she'll be thrilled, and I know she'll do a great job," I said.

I signed the documents, got my reports to read on the boat, and headed down to meet Jimmy. Once in the car, a sigh of relief escaped my lips. It was good to be able to retreat from this for a while longer.

"Are you okay, Ma'am?" Jimmy asked.

"Yes, it's just that sometimes all of this is a bit overwhelming," I told him.

"I can only imagine what a change and a shock this has all been for you," Jimmy said.

"Yes, it is taking a lot of adjusting," I replied.

"You know Ma'am, your cousin Annie: I loved her like a daughter. Whenever she was in town, the two of us would just drive around for hours to be alone. We would go to Burger King, her personal favorite, or get take-out Chinese and ride around, eat, tell jokes, talk about music, and laugh. Sometimes she just needed to be normal is how she would put it," Jimmy told me.

"Really? I can see her doing that," I said with a chuckle.

"So, if you ever need a confidante or just a buddy, Ma'am, I am always available, even by phone," Jimmy said. "Well, we are here unharmed. You just remember, if you need ol' Jimmy, I'm only a phone call away. You take care now." Jimmy gave me a hug when I got out of the car.

As I walked down the dock back to the boat, I was thinking about my life. After all, today was a big step, almost like the first day of my life. Oh my, how life had changed! A few short months ago, I was worried about the magazine's November story, and now I am a billionaire. I have a boat and am starting my magazine. Wow, things are going well.

Kosmos spotted me coming and called out "Ahoy Ma'am!"

"Ahoy, Kosmos!" I replied.

"Welcome aboard. Can I help you?" Kosmos asked.

"I'm fine, thank you," I answered.

"How was your meeting?" Kosmos asked.

"Good, I think I'm done with legal stuff for a while now," I answered.

Hearing all the talking, Neo came up on deck.

"Welcome back, Stacy," he said.

"Thanks."

Alejandro came up from below, and his face lit up when he saw me.

"Hi, glad you are back," Alejandro said.

"Me, too."

"Should we prepare to sail?" Alejandro asked.

"Whenever you are ready, Captain," I answered.

"Cast off the lines, Neo, and let's begin our new adventure," Alejandro said.

"Aye, aye, Sir," Neo replied.

Alejandro was an expert at piloting this massive boat in and out of tight spots. The marina was packed today, but he made it look easy. It was a beautiful October morning, and here in Boca Raton, it was still hot—at least 87 degrees. The sky was beautiful, and the gulls were squawking at all the tourists in their domain. The water was dark and a little murky, but I knew as soon as we were just a little way offshore, it would turn a beautiful shade of aqua. I was anxious to feel the spray on my face and the winds of freedom in my hair.

"Stacy, have you looked at the sailing routes, or do you have anything in particular in mind?" Alejandro asked.

"Well, no, I haven't had any time, and that is your area of expertise," I said.

"Okay, I have plotted a course I think you will enjoy. The water along the coast is shallow and treacherous, so I am going further out to deeper waters. If you need the internet, you will have about an hour of it available," Alejandro said.

"Sounds good. I know you picked a safe route."

"So, what were you and Scott dealing with this morning?" Alejandro asked.

"Scott was reminding me of parties coming up for the holidays, some of which I will be expected to attend beginning in November," I added.

"Ah, becoming quite the socialite," Alejandro teased.

"Don't laugh. You might be my plus one," Stacy teased.

"You haven't lived until you have seen me in a tux," Alejandro said.

I laughed right aloud and said, "Do you own a tux?"

"Well, now that you ask, no, I don't," Alejandro said. "I have to buy some clothes. My wardrobe pretty much consists of shorts, t-shirts, swim trunks, boat shoes, and flip flops."

"Oh my gosh, you're right. I hadn't thought about that. In thirty days, we'll go from about eighty-seven here to probably forty degrees up there. I better do some shopping as well," I said.

"Well, there should be great shopping in Charleston, South Carolina, with an easy place to dock. They should have winter clothes in stock there by now. Does that sound like a good stop for you?" Alejandro asked.

"Yes, Charleston is a big enough city to have everything we will need."

"Okay, then I will chart our course and head that way."

"I'm going below to check my emails and work on my December writing project. It is due any day, and I haven't even started it," I said and headed down the stairs.

Chapter Thirty-Three

It felt good to be back in front of the computer. The email tab was pretty full. There was an email from Donna who wanted an update on the progress of the documentary. I would need to address that one soon. Paula had several emails inquiring about the status of the December story, which is a priority. Then there was an email from Scott.

"Good morning," he began. "I hope you are doing well on your trip. I just wanted to let you know that Suzi has resigned as of tomorrow. I assume Debbie will just take over those duties as I can't see a need for a manager other than Debbie at this time. Is that okay with you? I also took the liberty of ordering a car for you, courtesy of the corporations. It's a beautiful sapphire blue Mercedes SUV and will be delivered to the Hamptons estate on or about November 1. I trust you will be happy with it,"

I immediately responded, "That sounds great. I'll let Debbie know about Suzi, and who wouldn't be happy with a Benz? LOL."

I wrote a short email to Debbie and advised her to get the checkbook and other information from Suzi ASAP so the transition would go smoothly. I knew she could manage whatever Suzi threw at her.

I emailed Donna, my friend who had suggested the possibility of a film about the hurricane, and explained that the storm did too much damage to the island I was on. With so much going on, I would have to put that on the back burner for a while.

Now for Paula. "I am working on the finishing touches for the story today," I typed. "I will have it to you in the morning." I was hoping that this would prove to be true. So now, what would I write, St. Nick? No, that's been done to death. How do you choose a tree? So many people use artificial trees these days so that might not appeal to the masses. The lighting of the Christmas tree in small-town celebrations? Yes! That would be a great topic and something I can do out at sea with internet access. I went up on deck to ask Alejandro how long we would be in touch with civilization.

"Hi, how long will we be able to get the internet?" I asked.

"Well, how long do you need it? I can sail close to the coast or go further out to sea to make time, whichever you prefer," Alejandro said.

"I need it for a couple of hours. I have a story due in the morning, and I will need to Google some info to write it."

"Okay, I will keep us close enough to shore for you to get internet, and we will put into port in northern Florida, probably Jacksonville, for the night," Alejandro said.

"Awesome, thanks," I replied and bolted back downstairs.

The story was going to be great. I would chronicle a variety of small-town celebrations and remind our readers how much fun such a small-town Christmas can be! The story just rolled off my fingertips, and the information I gathered sounded like so much fun. I knew Paula would love it.

Before I knew it, I was done. I sent it off to Paula before dinner, and an early story is never a disappointment.

I went up on deck and took a look at the scenery. It was cool enough now for a jacket. It is incredible what a difference a couple of hundred miles makes in the temperature, and of course, it was late afternoon now. Kosmos was at the helm, Neo was cleaning equipment, and Alejandro worked on our path in the captain's quarters.

"Oh, Kosmos, the water, the smells, the scenery are all so different here I can see the changes already," I said.

"Yes, Ma'am, it doesn't take long to lose that beautiful tropical feel when you head north." Kosmos

"I'm glad I have this light jacket with me."

"Yes, Ma'am, I am gonna have to buy some long britches! I have worn shorts so long I didn't even own any long pants" Kosmos said with a laugh.

"Oh no, are you cold?" I asked.

"No, Ma'am, I am okay, but it won't be long before we start seeing frost and ice trickle in the air," Kosmos said.

"We will see about picking up a couple of outfits in Charleston when we stop there," I told him.

"Yes, Ma'am," Kosmos answered.

Neo came up on deck with a worried look on his face.

"What's wrong?" I asked.

"Weather radio picked up a strong storm a little bit ahead of us. We probably need to adjust our course. Is Alejandro up here?" Neo asked.

"I am now; I just saw it come through," Alejandro said.

"Is everything okay?" I asked.

"Well, we don't know these waters, and we are pretty shallow here.

Are you finished with the internet?" Alejandro asked.

"Yes, thank you," I said. "Can't we just go into port?"

"No, there aren't any places big enough to handle this boat till we get to Jacksonville," Alejandro replied. Turning to Kosmos he said, "Let's head out to deeper water where we will be safer. Take us on out, Kosmos, and I will check to see if we can go around it. Neo, check to see that everything is battened down. Drop the sails; we will be diesel-powered for a while."

"This sounds serious," I said.

"They don't call this coast the Graveyard of the Atlantic for nothing, the water here is shallow. I know that sounds like it would be safer, but it isn't because shallow water can get nasty quickly. There are sandbars, shipwrecks, and all kinds of stuff in the water, so I will feel much better if we are deeper. It takes deep water a little longer to get angry. We will be fine, I am just being proactive," Alejandro explained.

"Okay, what should I do?" I asked.

"Go below and monitor the weather channel. Let me know immediately if there are any substantial changes in this system," Alejandro said.

I went down to the captain's quarters. Once in front of the weather monitor, I could see why he was worried. This storm was massive and packing some punch; winds were gusting at 60 m.p.h. There were reports of hail and lightning. The last place you want to be is on a boat in a flat ocean with lightning striking all around you. The wind was already picking up, and the sea was rolling. I could hear thunder and see lightning in the distance. I was worried.

Up on deck, things were already getting interesting. The waves were getting bigger, and Alejandro took over the helm.

"Kosmos, get the life jackets out and make sure everyone is wearing one," Alejandro said.

"Aye, aye, Sir," Kosmos answered and hurried off.

"If you guys have any cold-weather gear you might want to get it on. It is going to be a chilly rain with a cold wind," Alejandro said.

"I feel the chill in the air," Kosmos commented when he returned with the life jackets.

"Kosmos, I have to admit it scared me when you handed me a life jacket."

"Ma'am, Captain says we have put these things on, and if you have any cold-weather gear you should change into it., The temperature is dropping fast," Kosmos said.

"Okay, I'll do it. This storm is massive," I said.

"No need to be scared, Ma'am, we got this," Kosmos reassured me.

"I know," I said and tried to muster a smile.

I went to change into something warmer and was glad I had some long pants and a light jacket, at least. The temperature was still dropping. I could hear the thunder getting closer, and I was scared. It had been a long time since I had been on a boat in a thunderstorm, but I knew I was in capable hands. I tried to quell my fears and put on a brave face as I sat down in front of the weather monitor.

Alejandro appeared to check on me. "Are you doing, okay?" he asked.

"Yes, I'm fine," I said.

"I plan to sail through it on the southern tip and go around it out in the open water. It is a widespread storm, but I think we saw it in time to do this. It will get a little rough, but we aren't in any danger unless we get hit by lightning. So, stay down here and try to relax. Oh, and unplug your computer and any electronic devices you see down here."

"Aye, aye, Sir," I said with a smile.

Alejandro went back on deck, and I remembered once when my father and I got caught in a horrible Northeaster. I was sure we would capsize. Dad was an experienced sailor, so he knew just how to position our boat to keep it from taking on a lot of water and being rolled by the waves. I was scared and excited at the same time. The power of one of these storms is immense and excites me as much as it scares me.

The waves were getting stronger now and I could hear rain pelting the boat. I was glad I wasn't up on deck as those raindrops sting when they come with so much force. As I watched out the porthole, Alejandro expertly positioned the boat for maximum sustainability in the waves, just like my dad did. I knew we would be safe.

Then the hail came, the lightning was crashing around us, and the waves were rolling. I knew the guys up on deck were getting pelted hard with rain and hail. Just then, I heard the loudest explosion I have ever heard! I knew we had been hit by lightning. Oh my gosh! How badly would we be damaged? Would we sink? I knew better than to run up on deck. It would be dangerous, and I would only be in the way. I could hear the guys hurrying around on deck, and then Neo popped in the doorway.

"Ma'am, are you alright?" he asked.

"Yes, just terrified. Are we okay?"

"Yes, luckily, this boat has some high-powered lightning protection, and we only suffered minor damage, we think," Neo said. "Stay down here, Ma'am, till we are out of the storm, okay?"

"Okay, I will look around down here and make sure everything is okay," I said. I didn't notice anything out of place, but I had unplugged almost everything down here.

Kosmos came down to inspect the galley. "Looks like the freezer is shot from the strike, but everything else in the galley seems okay," Kosmos told me.

"If that's all we lost, I will be delighted," I said.

Finally, the rain and wind subsided, and I could see the sunshine again. I went up top to evaluate the damages. "Well, how are we doing after that strike?" I asked Alejandro.

"Looks like most things survived. Kosmos said we lost the freezer, and I am fairly sure our navigation system is fried," Alejandro said with a serious look on his face.

"Oh no, how will we know where we're going?" I asked.

Neo laughed loudly and said, "Old school, Ma'am, we will chart our course by the stars and handle what comes."

"You can do that?" I asked Alejandro.

"It has been a while, but yes, I can do that," Alejandro said.

"Ma'am, it is simple if we head that way, we will come to shore in the United States. If we head that way," he pointed in the opposite direction, "we will come ashore somewhere in Europe," Kosmos joked and laughed loudly.

"Well, that sounds simple enough," I said and found myself laughing as well.

"These are pretty costly repairs that we can't get done just anywhere, so tonight I will chart where we are and figure out the closest repair harbor to head to," Alejandro said.

"This storm has made me hungry. I'm going below and see if I can scrounge us up some supper," Kosmos said.

Chapter Thirty-Four

As night began to fall, the sky was beautiful, and one by one, the stars started to light up the sky. Dusk was always one of my favorite times at night; without lights from the towns, you could vividly see the night sky. Alejandro was at the helm. Without the navigation system, we couldn't set the boat on autopilot, so somebody had to be always on watch.

"Beautiful, isn't it?" I said to Alejandro.

"Not as beautiful as you," Alejandro replied.

I could feel myself blush. I managed to summon a soft "Thank you" and walked up close to him. Kosmos was making dinner, and Neo was getting some sleep to take the night watch. Alejandro pulled me closer to him and just held me in his arms. His embrace was strong and made me feel safe and secure.

"I have a surprise for you when dinner is ready," Alejandro said.

"A surprise?" I asked.

"Yes, it is extraordinary and something I am sure you have never experienced," he said with a twinkle in his eyes.

My mind was racing now. Was Alejandro thinking we were going to have sex? As much as I would love to strip off all my clothes and just freely enjoy those pleasures, this indeed wasn't the time or the place.

"Now go below and wait for me. I will come to get you in a few minutes. I have to prepare for the surprise," Alejandro said.

"This is really weird," I said.

"Just go with the flow and trust me," Alejandro urged.

"Okay," I said and went below.

I immediately went to look in the mirror and wished I hadn't. After a day of heavy storms, lightning, wind, and rain, I was a mess. Boy, did I need a shower! Just then, I heard him gently knock on my door.

"Okay, come, my lady," Alejandro said.

We climbed the ladder to the upper deck. All I could say was "WOW! Alejandro had set up a table for our dinner complete with candles, wine, and Kosmos as the waiter! "Oh my gosh," I said with tears trickling down my face.

Alejandro pulled out my chair and I sat down, and then he sat down across from me.

"For your dining pleasure tonight, I have prepared for you some fresh sea bass, cabbage, and potatoes. I am no Chip, but I think you will like it," Kosmos said. "I will be in the galley if you need me," he added.

As he disappeared down the stairs, all the boats' lights went off, and we were in complete darkness except for the candlelight. In all my life, I had never seen anything so beautiful. I enjoyed being on the ocean on my boat under the stars and having a lovely candlelit dinner.

"Do you like it?" Alejandro asked.

"I am speechless," I said.

"Well, that is a first," Alejandro said with a chuckle.

"You were right. I have never experienced this before," I said.

The meal was delicious, the wine was affecting me in a good way, and I was at total ease for the first time in a very long time. Instead of worrying about us drifting aimlessly at sea, I decided to live in the moment and soak up every second of this. I knew I was in competent hands times three.

We sat up on deck eating and drinking for hours. It was great to have time to be alone and get to know each other.

"So, tell me all about you," I said.

"There isn't much to tell," Alejandro said.

"I doubt that; every day, I find a new layer," I said. "Come on, where did you grow up?"

"I was born in St. Lucia on February 17, 1980. My father was a Merchant Marine captain and sailed from the islands to England, France, and Italy. His name was Victor Cortez, and he was originally from Spain. My mother, Maia, was born in St. Lucia and is a doctor on the island. She and my father lived in St. Lucia all their lives. My father passed away last year, but my mother, as you know, is alive and well." Alejandro said. "Now you."

"Okay, I was born in New Bern, North Carolina and my father had been a career naval officer. I used to sail with him on our little boat on the Inland Waterway and Pamlico Sound. He passed away about eight years ago. I have a million memories of my time with him and all the things he taught me. My mother was from New Bern, and her family had been farmers. I guess that's where I get my love for the earth, growing things, and animals. New Bern is a small town, and after graduation, I went to college in Boone, North Carolina. I always loved the mountains, so that is why I picked that school," I said. "So, your mom was a doctor. That must have made for an interesting life."

"It did. I can remember a million times traveling with her to remote villages to treat folks, deliver babies, and deliver medicine," Alejandro said.

"Okay, tell me more."

"St. Lucia, as you saw, is a tiny island, and my mother passionately believed in a good education regardless of what you planned to do in life. So, she planned for me to go to college at Oxford University in England. Then I transferred to the University of Hawaii at Hilo to get my degree in marine biology."

"How did you wind up a ship captain?" I asked.

"My father was a merchant marine captain, as I said, and he took me sailing with him when I was a kid. I fell in love immediately with everything about the sea, hence the marine biology," Alejandro said. "My mom would not hear of me becoming a sea captain without a "Plan B" as she put it, so I agreed to get a degree in Marine Biology so she would be assured I would always have a job. I feel silly telling you this stuff, I don't usually let anybody this close, but with you, I am a fountain of personal information," Alejandro said with a sheepish grin.

"I want to know every detail," I assured him.

"Okay, but first let's learn some more about you. What made you become a writer?"

"Well, I took a class on writing in college and loved it. It was mostly researching subjects and writing a synopsis of the subject. When I submitted my computer story to the editor, and it came back as a newspaper article in a couple of weeks, I was hooked. I will always be a writer but why didn't you want to become a doctor?"

"That was my mother's "thing," and I wanted to be different. I thought seriously about veterinary medicine, but the sea had my heart, so marine biologist won out," Alejandro said.

"No wonder you know so much about fish in the sea," I said.

"Okay, what about your past boyfriends?" Alejandro asked. "Is there a chain of broken hearts in North Carolina?"

"No, afraid not. I was in love once. I thought I would be a wife and a mom, but after being together for a couple of years, he decided to move on with someone else and was transferred to another duty station. He was a Marine and a nice guy, but I never saw this double life thing coming."

Alejandro gathered me closer to him and whispered, "What a fool he was."

"What about you? Did you leave a chain of broken hearts all over the world? Do you have a girl in every port?" I asked.

"Well, I have done my share of dating, but I have never been in love before you. They were casual affairs that lasted from one night to maybe two weeks, then I moved on. Until you," Alejandro said.

I snuggled close to him and felt safe and loved. We sat close for a little while and then remembered we had to chart our course by the stars. Alejandro got up and got out the compass, the sextant, and the nautical charts. He explained that celestial navigation uses "sights," or angular measurements taken between heavenly bodies—the sun, the moon, a planet, or a star. Navigators can use the moon, a planet such as Venus, Polaris, or a bunch of other navigational stars whose coordinates are tabulated in the nautical almanac and air almanacs. Navigation by stars is a lost art that is vastly underutilized.

After we sighted the moon, Mars, and a couple of constellations, Alejandro calculated our position on the map. We were here about 350 miles off Charleston and about four hundred miles off Bermuda. So, if we headed west, we would sail into Charleston harbor in about 15 hours under diesel power.

"Do we have enough fuel?" I asked.

"Close, we will use sail tomorrow if the day is nice and get under diesel power to jump the Gulf Stream," Alejandro said.

"Now you know how to calculate your course the old-school way," he added.

"Nope, not even close, but I don't need to. I have you," I said.

Alejandro went below for another bottle of wine, and I sat back down on the bench. "One last bottle of this delicious nectar," Alejandro said.

"Oh no, good thing we are going to port tomorrow," I said with a laugh.

We finished that bottle and learned more things about each other until the wee hours of the morning.

"Alejandro, how do you feel about kids?" I asked.

"Kids, I like them. I would love to have a few," he answered.

"Me too, I think," I said.

"You think?"

"Well, my life has just been spun around, and I have no idea where I am headed. I'm already in my early 30's, so the clock is ticking. I don't know if I will have time," I said.

"Stacy, we make time for the things that are important to us," Alejandro said. "You can't lose yourself in Annie's old life, you are a beautiful woman, and you deserve a life, too. So, are you sleepy yet?"

"I am, but I hate for this magical night to end."

"I am glad we are taking this time to get to know each other, you know, really know each other," Alejandro said and kissed me. "Now off to bed with you, and I will wake Neo for his turn to man the helm."

I reluctantly went down the stairs to my quarters. I put my pajamas on and crawled into my bunk. In a few minutes, I fell asleep; between the magic of the night and the potency of the wine, I could not keep my eyes open.

The morning seemed to come early, and I dragged myself out of bed and up to the top deck. The sun was shining brightly, and we were having an excellent time. The wind was up, and the sails were full. We were headed towards Charleston, our backs to the sunrise.

Kosmos came up from below to let me know breakfast was ready. "Ma'am, I made a quick breakfast this morning. Yours is in the microwave so that it would stay hot." Kosmos

"Thank you," I said and went back below.

Alejandro was in the galley eating his eggs when I walked in. "Good morning," he said.

"Good morning," I replied.

"Did you sleep okay?".

"Like a log, the wine zonked me out.".

"I slept like a log, as well," Alejandro chuckled.

"You aren't familiar with that phrase?" I asked.

"No, in the islands, we say 'I slept like a brick'," Alejandro laughed.

"No way!"

"No, I am teasing. We say log, too," Alejandro admitted.

"Have you ever been to Charleston?" I asked.

"No, I have always wanted to go and tour the historic district and eat seafood, but I have never made it this far north before."

'It sounds so funny to hear of Charleston as 'this far north'," I said with a laugh.

"It's a beautiful day today, so I think we will be safe to jump the Gulf Stream, so we should be there this afternoon sometime," Alejandro said. "We can dock at the port, and we can get a car so we can go to town. I am sure we will be there a couple of days for the necessary repairs," Alejandro said.

"The guys need to go to town as well. They both need some winter clothing. It's soon going to be getting cold as we go further north," I said.

Chapter Thirty-Five

The morning was full of sunshine with a light wind as we approached the Gulf Stream. You could see the difference in the water's color and the current flowing north. It was incredible to see first-hand. The gulf water is much warmer and pushes north in a swift treacherous current. We planned to jump into the stream, ride it north a few miles then jump out on the other side to head into port in Charleston.

The bird activity increased around the Gulf Stream, and once we were in it the dolphins were quick to escort us. Occasionally we saw whales swimming along with the current, making their migration to the colder waters north to breed and calve.

Once inside the current, our speed picked up and we were traveling nicely. "I think we will be in port just after lunch. Do you want me to rustle up something for us to eat or wait for fancy city food, Ma'am?" Kosmos asked.

"I would love some of your cooking; fancy food just doesn't cut it anymore," I said.

"Yes, Ma'am, coming right up," Kosmos said and disappeared below.

"We should be close enough to land now to get internet if you need to do anything on the computer," Alejandro said.

"That sounds good. I think I'll go down and eat lunch then check my emails," I said.

I went down to the galley, and the smell was fabulous. "Kosmos, what is that smell?" I asked.

"Ol' Kosmos is cooking you up a fish stew, it is a favorite around the Carolinas. I haven't made one in a long time, but I haven't lost my touch." Kosmos said.

"When will it be ready?" I asked.

"We can eat in about thirty minutes," Kosmos replied.

I decided that would be just enough time to check my emails and catch up with everyone. The first email, of course, was from Paula. She loved my story. That is always a great feeling and great to hear. I emailed her back to let her know where we were and that we were doing great.

There was an email from Debbie, filled with excitement and plans for the January issue. Of course, she was wondering what story I would like to write for that. We have had so many experiences on the boat, from hurricanes to jumping the Gulf Stream, that I would have to give that some thought. I sent her a response that we were almost in Charleston and that I would get back to her soon. Scott was checking in with the routine updates on the business. He had forwarded my first party invitations for a holiday mixer with Donna McCartney on November 12 at her home in the Hamptons.

I Googled Charleston quickly to find where to shop and do fun things. I wanted to take Alejandro to the City Market in downtown Charleston and there were great boutiques and restaurants. We just had to do a carriage ride through historic Charleston and then a quick jaunt to the mall for winter clothes. The car had been arranged and would meet us at the harbor. We only needed to call about ten minutes before we wanted him to arrive. The day was shaping up to be perfect.

Everyone but Kosmos came down to the galley to eat lunch. He took the helm while we ate.

"What is that smell?" Neo sniffed appreciatively as he came into the galley.

"Fish Stew," Alejandro answered.

"It's delicious," I added.

"Then hand me a bowl. I am starving!" Neo said, then added, "Boss, what is the plan for Charleston?"

"After I meet with the dockmaster, Stacy and I will go into town to shop for some winter gear. When we get back you guys can head in for a shopping trip. I am cooking a romantic dinner for the two of us tonight here on the boat, so you guys take your time," Alejandro said. "Then tomorrow Stacy and I will do the town,"

"Hopefully, the boat will be fixed, and we can get under sail by Monday morning," I said.

"I think that will be easily done," Alejandro said.

"I can't believe how good this stew is. I should ask Kosmos for his recipe," I said.

"Kosmos don't share no recipes, Ma'am. He doesn't write anything down, it's all just out of his head as he goes, but he is a pretty good cook," Neo said.

"Well, that was good, now let me get back topside and get us into the Charleston harbor," Alejandro said and hurried up the stairs.

"You know he is over the moon for you, Ma'am," Neo confided. "He doesn't give his heart easily, but he has fallen for you, so please be gentle with him. He is a good man."

"I know, and I am pretty 'over the moon' for him too," I said.

"Good, you make a nice couple, and two good people need good people to love. That one special person may only come around once in your lifetime. Mine did. So, hang on tight," Neo said.

"I will, and thanks for the advice," I said. As I went topside, I wondered if I was doing the right thing in letting Alejandro go.

We could see the Charleston skyline coming into the horizon. As I sat down on the bench on the upper deck, I couldn't help but think about all the history that Charleston held. A busy seaport was established in 1670, I believe, by the English settlers. The first shots of the Civil War were fired right here in this harbor at Fort Sumter. Yes, there was a ton of history here and things to see and do. I can just imagine what the skyline must have first looked like back then, no high-rise buildings, just a few homes and businesses on the street, and Fort Sumter standing proudly in the harbor. It was a beautiful city that I was anxious to explore again.

Alejandro maneuvered the boat into the slip at the harbor and met with the dockmaster to arrange the repairs. Kosmos was making his list of supplies to ensure we were fixed for the trip north, and Neo was getting ready to moor the boat.

I went down to my quarters and put on something pretty for our excursion. I had become complacent since it was just us on the boat, and we were sailing. It would do me good to put on some makeup and fix my hair. One last mirror check, and yes, I think I am ready now. I went back up on deck to wait for Alejandro.

"Perfect timing," I said as Alejandro was coming up the pier.

"You look amazing," he said with a twinkle in his eye.

"Thank you," I said. "I decided it was about time to dress up a little."

"The car will be here in about 20 minutes."

"Great, I can't wait to see Charleston again. It is such a beautiful city."

"Did you get caught up on your emails?" Alejandro asked.

"Yes, I checked in with everyone, and everyone is taken care of, so now it's just you and me!" I said.

"Awesome, that's how I like it," Alejandro grinned.

We walked down to the end of the dock to wait for the car. There were yachts from all over the world, and people scurrying around speaking languages of every nationality. It was busy for October. Then it hit me that this freedom to come and go as I pleased would soon end as people began to know my identity. I better enjoy it while I can.

The car rolled up, and we headed to the City Market.

"The City Market? Are we going to a grocery store?" Alejandro teased.

"No, silly, it's the center of downtown with shops, boutiques, and restaurants. I wanted you to feel the vibe of a major southern city," I said.

"Well, that sounds a little more promising," said Alejandro.

The driver dropped us off and told us to text him when we needed him. The market was alive with tourists and locals alike. I couldn't resist a handmade basket made of pine straw to add to my collection. I have a thing for handmade baskets. We moved on down the street and browsed some beautiful textiles. Out of the corner of my eye, I noticed a quaint jewelry stand with handmade sterling silver pieces.

I immediately went to the gemstone section and tried on a beautiful blue topaz ring. "Do you like that?" Alejandro asked.

"It reminds me of the water," I said, admiring it on my hand. It was beautiful, a heart similar to the one from the Titanic, but much smaller, of course. I handed it back to the cashier. "Thank you," I told her.

"Let me buy that for you, a gift to celebrate new beginnings," Alejandro said.

"It's too expensive," I said.

"Let me be the judge of that," he said and went back to the cashier.

In a flash, he was back with the ring nestled in a beautiful box with the maker's card and information about the stone. He had a massive smile on his face. He handed it to me and said, "Something to remember this trip by."

I took the box and slowly opened it. There was the beautiful blue topaz heart. I slipped it on my finger and gave Alejandro a big hug! "This is the most beautiful gift I ever received," I said.

He took my hand, and we walked on along the market. There were so many restaurants and food stands it was hard to choose one. "What looks good to you?" Alejandro asked.

"Everything," I replied.

"That's not much help."

"Well, we just ate about two hours ago. Let's shop some more and eat later."

"Never get between a woman and shopping," Alejandro said with a chuckle.

The line of boutiques led us to the downtown retail center of Charleston. Oh, my goodness, it looked like Rodeo Drive. High-end shop after shop after shop. "Wow, Charleston has become the shopping mecca of the South," I said.

"Yeah, looks like you can get just about anything here," Alejandro replied.

"Are you bored?" I asked.

"No, it is just getting late, the guys still have to shop, and I have to make dinner," Alejandro said.

"Okay, let's head on to the mall to pick up winter gear," I said.

After a quick call to the driver, he magically appeared in minutes. "I love this service," Alejandro said.

"I am finding that being rich has certain perks that are worthwhile," I replied.

Once inside the mall, we were surprised that winter gear was almost impossible to find. Finally, we found some jeans and a couple of sweaters at one store. Then we walked further down the mall and found a ski shop. Inside we found down coats, wool hats, and gloves. Soon we were well-outfitted and, on our way, back to the boat.

"Ma'am, Captain, it's good to have you back," Neo called out. "The dock superintendent came by with a quote on the repairs and needs to have it approved today so they can get us repaired and out of here by Monday."

"Okay, give me the quote, and I will take care of it," Alejandro told him.

"The car is waiting for you guys at the end of the pier, so have fun and call him when you need to go somewhere else. It's on me," I told Neo and Kosmos, and they happily went shopping.

"I will be back in a few minutes," Alejandro said. "I am going to see the harbormaster about the repair."

Chapter Thirty-Six

I was down in the living quarters when Alejandro returned.

"Do you have a few minutes? I want to talk to you about something," Alejandro said.

"Sure, that would be great," I replied. We took a seat on the couch.

"Stacey, these weeks have been amazing, and I never expected to have these feelings for anyone, let alone my boss," Alejandro began.

"Yes, they have been quite unexpected, and it has been an interesting journey," I answered.

"I could very easily fall in love with you, but I know you are not ready for a committed relationship. I think it would be better if I didn't go with you to Jackson Hole. Mountains aren't my scene, and you need time to fit into your new life."

"Alejandro, these days with you have been amazing, and I think I could easily fall deeply in love with you, too, but I know you're right. I don't even know who I am right now. I had a life, a good life. I just wasn't rich. All of this was overwhelming, Annie's death, this inheritance, the businesses, the boat, the houses, I hardly know where to start,"

"I completely understand, and I admire you for how well you have handled everything up to now, but when the guys and I return home, you will have to begin charting a path for your future, the reality of your life, and where it will take you," Alejandro said. "That won't be easy, and the last thing you need is a long-distance romance to complicate it."

"This is so hard, I know you are right, and I had prepared myself to give you the same speech, but I didn't expect to feel so heartbroken and lonely," I said.

"Well, that's a good thing. It means your feelings for me are genuine and all I am saying is let's just put them on the back burner while you navigate the land map to your life," Alejandro said with a smile.

"Reluctantly, I agree," I told him. He swept me up in his arms and kissed me, feeling like the first kiss. Then he turned and went back up on deck. I took a few minutes to compose myself. Oh my gosh, maybe I need to rethink this thing. No, for now, this is for the best. We had both agreed that neither of us was ready for a long-term relationship. How could I possibly be? I didn't know where my life was headed. I didn't even have a plan. So far, I had just been riding this beautiful dream, piecing together some things about business, but I was avoiding piecing together myself, my life, and my happiness.

I headed up on deck, though I dreaded seeing Alejandro. I knew this was the correct answer, but it would be so easy to give in to the emotions I was feeling now for a short-term pleasurable relationship. But that wouldn't be fair to either of us. I sat down on the lounge and soaked up the evening sky.

When Kosmos and Neo had returned, they looked better outfitted for the change in seasons.

"Ahoy, guys!" I called out to them.

"Ahoy, Ma'am, what a beautiful city Charleston is!" Neo said.

"Did you find everything you needed for now?" I asked.

"More than enough, Ma'am, thank you," Kosmos answered.

"I am going below and see if I can find a place to stow all this stuff," Neo said with a big laugh as Kosmos followed him down the stairs.

"Can I join you?" Alejandro asked me.

"Sure," I answered.

He sat down and leaned back. "This sky is magnificent, isn't it?" Alejandro asked.

"It is! I don't remember seeing it so clear and beautiful before," I told him.

"We are now officially in fall. The sky is crisp and clear in the fall and winter. It's my favorite season," Alejandro said.

"Mine too," I said.

We sat there enjoying the night, talking about anything and everything, and drinking wine until well past midnight. Finally, I was too sleepy to continue, and I fell asleep on his shoulder. He woke me up to tell me to go to bed and get some rest. We said our goodnights, and I went downstairs to bed. Sleep came easy, as I was exhausted.

I was up by eight a.m. and began to pack my things. I knew I had to go. It had been an exciting month at sea. We had gone through our first journey, a hurricane, being kidnapped, a potential pirate attack, incredible beauty, snorkeling, horseback riding, eating fantastic food, and romance. How would the ordinary world ever compare? I said a silent thank you to Annie for this opportunity and this amazing boat and went to the galley for breakfast.

"Good morning," I greeted the crew as I entered the galley.

"Good morning, Ma'am," Kosmos said, with a big smile.

"Are you okay?" Alejandro asked.

"I will be leaving the boat this morning," I told them. "I have to take care of some business that has come up, so I'll be flying out of Charleston in about two hours.

Alejandro, will you call for a car?"

"Of course," he answered.

"Anxious to get rid of me?" I asked.

"No. It is my last chance to take care of you," Alejandro answered with a disappointed look in his eyes.

"Alejandro, you can pilot the boat back to Key West. You will all be more comfortable closer to home," I said.

"Are you sure?" he asked.

"Yes, I may be a while, and this is best," I said.

Almost before I knew it, the car was at the end of the dock. The hardest thing I ever did was get off that boat and walk down that pier. I turned for one last look and saw Alejandro on the dock watching me leave. Tears started streaming down my cheeks, and I could not hold them back.

The driver greeted me with a smile until he saw my tears when he reached out to take my bags.

"Where to, Ma'am?" he asked.

"The airport," I told him.

At the airport, the driver checked my bags, and I went through security. Same old drill, no shoes on, and put your bag on the conveyor. But, this time, it seemed agonizingly painful and prolonged.

Finally, we boarded, and I was glad to be flying First Class. The last thing I needed was a nosy passenger beside me. I just wanted to be alone. My phone lit up with a sweet text from Alejandro with a sad face with a note "Miss you already." I answered with "Me too," and that was it. The plane took off, and almost before I knew it, I was landing in Boca. I had texted Jimmy, and there he was at the airport to pick me up, right on schedule.

"It's great to have you back, Stacy," he said with a smile and seemed to sense I needed a friend.

"Thanks," I said and quietly got in the car.

Chapter Thirty-Seven

The house in Boca was a welcome sight. Right now, it was home. Debbie was right on cue and greeted me at the door.

"Hey gorgeous," Debbie said with a smile but quickly saw a smile was not in order.

"Hi," I said as I gave her a quick hug. Jimmy brought my bag in, and Debbie took it from him.

"Ma'am, I'm here if you need me, just text me," Jimmy said with a concerned look in his eyes.

"Thanks, Jimmy," I replied.

Once inside I told Debbie I wanted a quick meeting with her about the magazine. On the way from the airport, I texted Scott and would be meeting with him at 1 p.m. tomorrow.

As I started up the stairs, I heard Debbie say, "Not so fast"

I stopped and turned to look at her. "You have some explaining to do. Why are you here?" Debbie asked.

"I was tired of sailing and anxious to get to the Hamptons to get the house set up," I told her.

"Not so fast," she said again. "The last time I talked to you, you were happy and basking in love. Now you're running as hard as you can in the other direction. What gives?"

"Let's take a walk on the beach, and I will tell you all the details," I said.

"Sure, go put your stuff away, and I will meet you down here in ten minutes," Debbie said.

I put my bag down, washed my face, and changed clothes. It is amazing how warm it is here in Boca, so for now, back to shorts, t-shirts, and flip-flops!

"Okay, let's go for a walk," Debbie said, and we headed up the beach.

"The air smells so clean here, fresh and salty," I said.

"Yeah, this is a beautiful place, no doubt about that," Debbie answered.

The gulls were squawking as they flew about the sky like they knew something was wrong. The city lights were starting to come on across the bay, and I thought how beautiful this place was. We had walked about half a mile when Debbie broke the silence. "So, I am assuming you and Alejandro decided to call it quits."

"Yes, we agreed that neither of us was truly ready for a long-term relationship," I told her.

"Sure, that is what your brain says, but what about your heart?" Debbie asked.

"My heart says throw caution to the wind, fall in love, float on the cloud, take a chance," I told her with a chuckle.

"Then what in the heck are you doing here?"

"Danny."

"I thought you were long over him."

"Not him, in particular, but I took that chance once and was all in, and look how that turned out. Right now, my life is so upside down I don't even have a home anymore," I answered and started to cry.

"Stacy, you overthink things way too much," Debbie said as she hugged me.

We sat down in the sand and talked about my dilemma. "When all is said and done, I know I made the right choice," I told Debbie.

"Yeah, I can see that," Debbie replied. "But what if you decide later that you were wrong?"

"I guess if that happens, I'll have to hope that Alejandro will feel the same way."

"Well, I guess we'll cross that bridge when we come to it," Debbie said.

"So, tell me, how are you doing?" I asked.

"Chip and I have come to the same conclusion," she answered. "I am attracted to him, and I have strong feelings for him, but, like you, my life is upside down, and so is his."

"I feel like I just need time to let it all settle down and figure out where I am going. With so much, so quick, it has been overwhelming and exciting all at the same time," I told her.

"Me too, so for now, I am throwing myself into my new career and giving myself some time to take it slow in the love department," Debbie said. "Now that we have those problems solved, let's go get a drink and have a little dinner."

"Let's," I answered.

As we walked back to the house, we discussed our plans for going forward with the magazine, and by the time we got to the house, we were both excited about the first issue!

We dressed in cute outfits and called Jimmy to take us out for some time on the town. He drove us to downtown Boca, and we got out to walk around. We both needed some retail therapy before dinner.

With shopping bags in town, we found a great little supper club and went in for a drink and to have dinner. The music was loud, which Debbie liked, and folks all around us were eating, laughing, drinking, and having fun. It felt good to be out on the town with that vibe all around us. After a few margaritas and dinner, we called Jimmy for a ride home.

"It's good to see you two ladies laughing and happy," Jimmy said as he stowed our bags in the trunk.

"It's good to be having some fun with my friend," I told him. I realized that I might be a little tipsier than I thought, and I chuckled to myself.

Soon we were home safely. "Thanks, Jimmy," I called out as I went inside.

Debbie came quickly behind me and stated, "The room is spinning a bit. I am going to bed."

"Me, too," I told her. "See you in the morning."

The alarm clock was going off, and my head was still banging a little. I got out of bed and decided today was a good day to do my morning ritual. I sat out on the deck looking at the ocean and thinking about where my life was, where I was going, and how I would get there. I thought about love, Alejandro, safety, and happiness. I said a prayer for guidance going forward. I listed all the things that I am grateful for today, and I silently thanked Annie for all the opportunities I had before me. I always felt much better after the ritual. I jumped in the shower and got dressed.

Chapter Thirty-Eight

Debbie was right on time for our meeting. "Good morning," she greeted me.

We went into the office and discussed her editorial calendar and possible articles. She had made beautiful notes, projections, and plans. I had chosen the right person.

"So, where are you off to next?" Debbie asked.

"I'm going to head up to the Hamptons estate. I had my things shipped after the sale of my house in New Bern. So, I am sort of anxious to get there and make it home," I told her.

"When do you fly out," Debbie asked.

"I have a meeting with Scott at 1 p.m. and go to the airport afterward," I answered. "It was great to have some downtime with you last night. Thank you for understanding and listening."

"What are friends for, if not to listen?" Debbie replied.

"Well, I better go get packed and dressed," I told her, and I went upstairs.

I texted Jimmy and as always, he was right on time. Debbie and I said our goodbyes, and I climbed into the car. Jimmy greeted me with a smile and loaded my bag. "How are you today, Ma'am?" he asked.

"I am doing well, making some firm plans for my future, and feeling confident about my life," I told him. I was looking forward to getting to the house in the Hamptons. It was going to be my new home, and I couldn't wait for some solitude and a chance to unpack.

As we rolled up to Scott's building, Jimmy said, "I'll just wait here in the parking lot for you."

"Okay, I won't be long," I replied.

Scott had a different receptionist today, and she greeted me very professionally, "Good Morning. Scott is in the conference room waiting for you."

I thanked her and walked down the hall.

Scott stood up to greet me. and we exchanged "Good mornings."

"I am glad you had a chance to come by," he began. "Mostly just routine stuff to sign today."

"Great, I have a 3 p.m. flight. I'm headed to the house in the Hamptons," I told him.

"I thought you were sailing up there," he commented.

"I had planned to, but I realized that things were not going to go as I thought, and it would be better to head on up. I sent the boat back to Key West for the winter," I told him.

"Good, it is beautiful in the Hamptons, and I know you will enjoy it," Scott said.

"Have you had time to review Chip's proposal for his restaurant?" I asked.

"Yes, and it looks like a pretty sound investment."

"Then we can move forward with it?" I asked.

"Of course, I think it's a sound decision, and I am already working on the paperwork."

"When should Chip expect to be funded?"

"I'll have it all done by the end of next week, and I'll give him a call."

"Wonderful, I think he is a great chef and a good businessman. I am glad to help him out."

"Me, too. I might even investigate putting some of my cash in as well."

"Awesome," I replied. Lunch came, and we chatted a little more before it was time to leave. "Thank you for lunch, Scott, it was good to see you," I told him. He hugged me, and I went out to meet Jimmy.

I was anxious to get to the airport and finally be "heading home," whatever that meant. It would be good to unpack, unwind, and relax with just me. I sent Jimmy a text on my way down in the elevator. He was waiting at the door.

"Where to Ma'am?" Jimmy asked.

"To the airport, I have a 3 p.m. flight.

"Yes, Ma'am," he replied.

As we drove through town and past the docks, I couldn't help but think about all that had happened since I came down here for the very first time to attend my cousin's funeral! So much, so fast, and all of it seems so unreal and impossible. I was anxious to get back to the Hamptons and step back away from it for a bit.

The security checkpoint was smooth. I made my way to the gate, boarded the plane, and took my seat. We were due to take off right on time. As I settled into my seat my phone started buzzing, and it was a message from Alejandro.

"Don't go," was all it said.

About the Author

Rose Cushing is a successful entrepreneur. Her love of writing came from her career as a newspaper reporter for various local newspapers. She has had hundreds of articles and photos published. From there she went on to publish a regional equestrian magazine for many years. She has been a television host and producer of Carolina Hoofbeats TV as well as several additional equestrian television shows. Rose also is an award-winning documentary filmmaker. She is the founder and host of the popular Today's Horsewoman podcast.

Chasing the Wind is Rose's first novel. In addition to writing, Rose hosts two literary podcasts: Carolina Writer's Speak and Speaking of Writing, and owns Cushing Publishing.

Follow Rose
Twitter: @RoseCushing6
Instagram: @RoseCushing6
Website: RoseCushing.com